Silverbirds

by Rocky Magaña

Rocky Magaña - Silverbirds - 2

*The young bowhunter dies an old man.*

## The Word of God

*In the beginning, there was nothing but God. He forged the Heavens and the Earth, and the Earth was void, a maelstrom of chaos. From that chaos, He shaped all living things. Surveying the work of His hands, God declared it good.*

*Among His creations was Iblis, the fallen one born of fire. Twisting the good, Iblis seduced them into darkness. From sky and sea, he corrupted the creatures, warping them into monstrous abominations and loosing them upon the earth.*

*The beasts of the sky are the most perilous, bound neither by land nor sea. They roam the world, unbridled, preying upon the flesh of the upright.*

*— Translated from The Holy Scriptures*

Poya's: Part I

—*Don't go out on a starry night or clear day, because that's when the silverbirds come out to play*—
Smoke slithers through the crags and charred precipices. When the foul ether sinks to earth, it blurs the line between what's burning and what's already ash. To know for sure, you must reach out, wave your hand through the haze of floating cinder—feel the heat prickling your skin. Only then can you grasp how much heavier smoke is than fog. It scalds the lungs, raking their walls like a cheese grater scraping bone.
This mountain is Kosha Poya's home. It's where he was born. God willing, it won't be where he dies.
A black river cuts through the valley floor. Long ago, when it ran blue, children played along its banks, splashing cold water with their dusty toes. They'd sprawl on their bellies in the grass, counting dandelions gone to seed—pillowed fireworks spreading themselves wide.
That river vanished before Kosha drew breath. All he's ever known is the black sludge,

lifeless and aimless, lurching forward like it forgot why it flows.
 Everyone else is gone now—driven away by the silverbirds. The nearest neighbor is fifteen kilometers distant. These mountains could crumble, swallowing Kosha's family whole, and no one would notice. It wasn't always like this.

The silverbirds came on June 18, 2001. It was the day bedtime stories turned into waking nightmares.
 Yellow and purple kites fluttered in the streets. Fathers toiled in the fields, wiping sweat from their necks with sun-bleached handkerchiefs. Mothers worked their fingers raw over basins of soapy water. Babies tugged at skirt hems, carefree under a sky as blue as the first day.
 The monsters came out of nowhere—fallen angels cloaked in fire, consuming everything indiscriminately: old, young, unborn. It didn't matter. Flesh is flesh.
 No other beast is so detached from the ruin it leaves behind. These are no dragons. They're worse—phantoms whose silence gnaws deeper than any roar. You don't see them until they're there. By then, it's too late. You're already gone.
 Their wings blot out the sun. Feathers glint like razor blades, slicing through the light. A single, red cyclops eye peers down, its gaze reporting all it sees to the master.
 They have one weakness. They can only fly on clear days. Rain blinds them, and clouds obscure their prey.

The night sky stretches flawless above, bursting with endless starlight. Drops of white gold shimmer in the ivory moonlight, glinting off the glassy eyes of the insubstantial figure below. Kosha stares upward, mouth agape. He's eight years old now. Last week, he was seven, but that feels like a lifetime ago. A lot can change in a week. People are always changing. No one goes to bed the same person they were that morning.

The mountains are far older than Kosha. Older than his father. Older even than his grandfather, who died before he was born. Before that? He has no sense of time. In his mind, anything predating his grandfather belongs to the days of the Garden of Eden. These mountains, this valley—it must've been Eden itself. He wonders if he's standing on the decayed carcass of paradise.

Kosha slings his bow over his shoulder. It was a birthday gift from his father two years ago. His mother hates it. When his father brought it home, she slammed her slice of cake on the table and said, "That thing will only bring trouble."

Motherhood, Kosha has learned, is a painfully beautiful thing. The labor, the blood, the tearing—every wail, every curse—all of it just a sign of things to come. He didn't understand her words then, but he knows she doesn't lie. If she says trouble's coming, it probably is. Still, he loves the bow because it came from his father, and nothing can come between a boy and a gift from his dad—not even the truth.

When your dad shows interest in something, it instantly becomes your favorite thing. His football team becomes your football team. If he plays chess, you play too—until adolescence comes and every word he's ever spoken feels like a ten-pound weight around your neck.

That's what happened with Isah. Kosha's not allowed to talk about his older brother. His father says Isah is probably dead, but nobody knows for sure. To find out, they'd have to ask Uncle Nader, and they're not allowed to talk about him either.

Kosha wears his brother's hand-me-downs: a merlot stocking cap and a gray wool sweater. If he were older, the pants might be called slacks. But you can't play in the mud in slacks, so Kosha just calls them pants.

There's a book of matches in his pocket. He found it when he tried on the pants for the first time. They must've belonged to Isah. He doesn't know why Isah needed matches, but something won't let him throw them away. They're relics of a lost world—a place that existed before the silverbirds were real.

Isah left before Kosha was born. Even though his name is forbidden, sometimes Kosha whispers it under his breath at night, pulling the covers over his head.

"Isah," he says, soft and tentative.

"Isah," he repeats, a little louder.

He dares himself to push further.

"Isah," he says again.

And again.

"Isah."

"Isah."

Each repetition grows bolder, the name a ghost twisting a knife between his shoulder blades. It's everything he has to be because Isah wasn't—or is—or was—or never will be.

On certain nights, like tonight, Kosha is brave. Brave enough to scream his brother's name at the top of his lungs.

"ISAH!"

His voice echoes, startling his mother awake in the next room. She lies beside his father, but it doesn't take much to wake her these days. Even awake, she drifts through a fog of memories: her firstborn son, her lost soulmate, his weight still imprinted on her body.

She's never told her husband she hears Kosha calling Isah's name. He'd be angry if he knew. But she lets it slide, because she needs to know her firstborn still exists in the collective memory of mankind. That he hasn't been forgotten like so many other lost boys.

As long as someone invokes the names of the dead, they're never truly gone. They live on—in you, in the love you carry for them.

His mother's name is Ara. She lies in bed, listening to the sound of her son's voice slipping through the walls, struggling to rise above the roar of her husband's snoring.

"Isah."

The walls seem to breathe with her, thick with memory. She inhales her eldest son's name, holding a bit of it in her lungs before exhaling the rest. She keeps more than she lets go—just enough to bear. Rolling over, she lets out a tearful sigh, grateful she's not the only one still trying to remember.

Her memories carry her back to sleep. She dreams of the day she became a mother for the first time.

She lay there, exhausted and bloodied, crying with the horror and joy of it all. Bringing new life into the world—it was the scariest, most beautiful moment of her life. In that instant, she knew no matter what he did or how much he hurt her, she'd forgive him for anything. She'd love him until her last breath. Even if he never sought her forgiveness, she'd give it freely. It was his birthright.

Everything Isah was, or is, or will be, came from her.

She had formed him from nothing. From egg to human. Human to boy. Boy to man. And whatever he had become now—whatever monstrosity or miracle—had grown from her first. They are one. His body is her body. His hands, her hands. His feet, her feet. Whatever evil he has done, she has done too. Wherever he goes, she goes with him.

She's heard the rumors—each more terrible than the last. And she knows, deep down, every one of them is true.

No matter how much she hates what he's become, she can't hate him. It's impossible.

"Isah," she hears Kosha say from the next room.

Kosha has never said his brother's name

loud enough to wake his father.

Nobody's that brave.

The sky opens at dusk, spitting drizzle from Dalmatian-spotted clouds. It hasn't rained in a week. The brief downpour feels like freedom to Kosha, a fleeting respite from captivity. The cold rain kisses his face, washing away the restless energy coiled inside him. And then it's gone—vanishing as quickly as it came.

The sun slides lazily behind the hills, extinguishing the rainbow of day and ushering in night. Stars pirouette into view, prancing across the resplendent heavens. Kosha isn't allowed to be outside anymore—not under a sky this clear. This is when the silverbirds come out to feed. But the infinite blue above, saturated with gold and white sparks, calls out to him, pulling him deeper into its shimmering depths.

Kosha's father's name is Kamal. There's a strange sadness in him that Kosha doesn't understand. His father carries it the way his mother does when she thinks about Isah, but for Kamal, it never goes away.

Once, Kosha asked him, "When you were a kid, what did you want to be when you grew up?"

"An astrophysicist," Kamal answered.

"What's that?"

"Someone who studies the universe and tries to solve its mysteries." Kamal cleared his throat, his voice thick with the effort of brushing the sadness away. "I used to be really interested in that sort of thing when I was a kid. But that was a long time ago."

"What's in outer space?"

"A whole lot of nothing—and a ton of everything."

"Are there silverbirds?"

"No," Kamal said, a faint smile tugging at his lips. "There aren't any silverbirds in outer space. At least not yet—or that we know of."

"I want to go there. What do you call someone who goes to outer space?"

"An astronaut."

"I want to be an astronaut."

It's a beautiful dream for a boy to have, one Kamal wants him to hold onto for as long as possible. Even if the odds of Kosha becoming an astronaut are as slim as Taylor Swift showing up at their door, begging Kamal to run away with her.

A lot of who you are—and who you can become—depends on where you were born and, more importantly, who you were born to. If they lived in the West, Kosha might have a chance. But here, in the Far East, in these mountains, it doesn't matter if you could detect a Higgs boson with the snap of your fingers. You'd still only ever be the son of a sheep farmer.

Still, just because a dream is impossible doesn't mean it has to be stillborn. Even the frailest dreams deserve a few breaths of cold air before they fade.

Kamal wrapped his arm around his son and kissed the top of his head. "I want you to be an astronaut too."

Ara stands in the doorway of their house, her gaze fixed on the black and blue sky. Her voice carries a nervous rattle. "Kosha, it's time to come inside."

"In a minute!" he calls back, reluctant. Just a little longer.

"No—now," she orders. "You know better than to be out here when the sky is this clear."

Kosha grumbles under his breath but obeys. He's not the kind of kid who enjoys defying his mother outright. He lives by the unspoken code of childhood: you can do whatever you want, as long as your parents haven't told you not to do it yet.

The Poyas' house teeters on the peak of the smallest mountain in the valley. It's not too high—close enough to reach the river and return in a single trip. Once, it offered a fine view of the sloping red poppy fields, tilting and swaying like the world's crooked grin. But that was before. Now, the valley is a scarred battlefield, blackened and barren.

The western treeline, where chinkara stags used to mate, looks no different from the eastern cliffs where Indian wolves still howl. The house itself is ordinary, as though it belongs right where it stands. It is what it needs to be, down to the last mud brick.

Kamal built it for Ara when they fled the city. With no money to buy a home, he fashioned a kiln, cooked each brick, and worked from dawn until well after dusk for six long months.

He was always tired back then, but it

didn't matter. He built it for love. Arranged marriages were the norm, but Kamal and Ara were lucky—both their fathers were dead, so they married for love.

    Ara studied literature in university. Her favorite book is *The Catcher in the Rye*. She keeps a tattered paperback copy hidden under her pillow. Its yellowed pages are dog-eared and torn from overuse, the back cover long gone. She tried taping it back once, but you can only tape something so many times before you let it fall apart at its natural pace.
    This might be the last copy of *Catcher* in the country. Books like it were banned by the culture police twenty years ago. The thought of getting caught pumps Ara full of a giddy, predatory thrill. She doesn't love the book anymore—she hasn't for years—but it's a relic from another life, a time when she was someone else. She hasn't cracked its brittle spine in ages. She doesn't need to. She knows all 73,404 words by heart.
    Kamal lies asleep beside her. She still loves him—for now. Ara reaches under her pillow, fingers gliding over the bold white font on the cover. It feels like she's committing adultery.
    Kamal knows about the book but gave up mentioning it long ago. Ara tells him everything else, so he lets her have this one secret. Sometimes, he hears her murmuring lines from it under her breath, like a prayer.
    She does it in the kitchen while cooking.

Behind the house as she does the laundry. In the bath when she's alone and naked: *"Don't ever tell anybody anything. If you do, you start missing everybody."*

Kamal pretends not to notice. If he made her choose, he already knows what her decision would be.

Ara can only bear the weight of loving two people—her husband and Kosha. If they're gone, she'll be gone too.

Kosha doesn't know much about his father. He knows Kamal wanted to be an astrophysicist. He knows about the scar stretching down the right side of his mouth, hidden beneath his beard. And he knows about the fake teeth, though he's too afraid to ask how his father got them.

Kamal speaks only when necessary. When he does, his words come through gritted teeth.

Kosha smashes these fragments of his father together in his heart, and it makes him feel both love and fear. That's how Kamal wants it.

Unlike Ara, Kamal has already lost everyone he could bear to lose. He's like a cracked teacup, trying to keep his family inside, but they're bleeding through the fissures. He wishes he were strong enough to mend himself with Kintsugi gold, to hold his family the way he wants to.

He loves them. He loves Ara. He loves Kosha. But when he kisses them, they taste bitter, as if they've steeped too long. Maybe it's better this way—better to let them leak out of him, little by little.

The dinner table is quiet. The stars stirred something in Kosha—something he can't quite understand but knows he needs to feel.

"Mama," he says through a mouthful of food.

Ara's voice is heavy, as though raising a syllable hurts. "Yes, my dear?"

"Where's the land of the silverbirds?"

The word hangs in the air, thick as lead and twice as poisonous.

Silverbirds.

She locks eyes with Kamal before answering, curt and agitated. "It's beyond the mountains."

"Where beyond the mountains?"

"Far. That's enough—now eat your food."

Sometimes, it's best to keep your head down at the dinner table. Kosha mashes a carrot with his fork, grinding it into mush. Kamal stabs his food in silence. The stars stirred something in him too.

He wishes it was wonder. But he's past that. He's longing for lost things—things he'll never have again. A time of possibility, when the future still hung in the balance.

He misses the feeling of discovery, of learning something new. He remembers jotting down facts and figures in his notebook, the thrill of traversing uncharted territory. It felt like his first kiss—how awkward and plump her wet mouth had been against his chapped lips. The way her skin trembled slightly, the way her hair caught the light. He remembers holding Ara's hand for the first time.

He'll never touch another woman for the first time again. Not that he wants to. It's just a fact, simple as the distance from the earth to the moon.

Nothing is fixed, but nothing changes very much either. Life drifts out of orbit, a centimeter or two at a time, until one day, you wake up and hardly recognize the person lying next to you.

That's the problem with loving something. Once you love it, you no longer have time for it. You spend all your energy trying not to lose it. And when you love more than one thing, you usually lose them all.

Kosha smears orange carrot paste across his plate. Kamal watches his son, jealous of how fresh life must feel to him.

"Stop playing with your food."

Kosha stares at the mess he's made, saying nothing.

Kamal hears the sternness in his own voice.

*Why can't you just let him be a kid? It's not his fault you're broken—he didn't choose this. He didn't choose you.*

Who would?

The questions echo unanswered in his mind. He sees his lost dreams in everything Kosha does.

*I had dreams too. Didn't they matter?*

He wants his son to have those dreams. But the words to say it are gone, chipped away a little more every day. One day, the things he's left unsaid will topple over, crushing him beneath their weight.

He wants to say something that will make his son smile. Instead, he says, "Take off your hat. You're at the dinner table."

Kosha knows better than to wear his hat at the table. But no one had told him not to yet, so he'd been testing the waters. Feigning contrition, he slides his hand to his head, removes the cap, and sets it in his lap.

"Don't be so gruff," Ara says. "He's just a boy."

"He won't be a boy forever," Kamal replies. "He needs to learn how to do things the right way."

Ara rarely disagrees with Kamal in front of Kosha, but the discontent in the room is already palpable. "You don't have to be so rough with him."

Kamal tightens his grip around his fork. It's been a long time since Ara cared enough to rebuke him. Why now? Why this?

"The world is a rough place," he says. "It's better he learns it from me than someone else."

To Kosha, their argument is the most entertaining thing that's happened in weeks. He pops an unmashed carrot into his mouth and says, "Mama covers her head all the time. Why does she get to wear something on her head?"

"That's different, Kosha," Ara says.

"Why?"

"You know why. Don't talk with your mouth full."

Kamal's patience snaps. He wipes his scarred mouth with his napkin and throws it on his plate. "It's time for bed."

Ara knows when to pick her battles. This isn't one of them. She smooths the sides of her *firaq* with her hands, steadying herself. "Come on, Kosha. Let's brush your teeth."

Kamal watches her go, knowing he's hurt her. Misery loves company, and clichés exist for a reason.

*I had dreams too. Impossible dreams. Dreams that would've taken us away from here. Didn't they matter? Don't they still? They weren't selfish. They weren't just about me. We would have been safe—all of us.*

Ara pulls Kosha's shirt over his head. The cold air hits his skin, and goosebumps ripple across his body. His light brown nipples perk in the chill as he wraps his arms around his bare torso for warmth.

"How long would it take to get to the land of the silverbirds?"

"It doesn't matter, because you're never going there." Her voice is sharp, final. "Give me your arms."

Kosha lifts his arms, his face momentarily caught in the neck hole of his nightshirt. Ara's movements are brisk but gentle, her thoughts heavy. Too many mothers have already put their children in the ground. Kosha is still naive. She wants him to stay that way—for as long as she can manage. He only needs to know they're dangerous. That's enough.

"Nobody comes back from there. Do you hear me? They'll burn you up with their fire until there's nothing left."

If it came to it, she would chain herself to his leg to keep him from going to that terrible place. Her love is strong enough—strong enough to keep him safe. She's already lost one son. She won't lose another.

*Why didn't you love Isah enough to chain yourself to him?*

*I did. God knows, I loved him enough.*

*Then why didn't you? Why didn't you die trying to stop him?*

*I don't know—if I could do it over, I would. I'd die now if it would bring him back.*

But you can't bring people back. You can only stop them from going in the first place.

She bends down and kisses Kosha goodnight. He places his small hands on her cheeks and squishes them together. She always likes when he does this—it's his way of apologizing, of saying all the things he doesn't know how to put into words.

Kosha gazes into her big, black-olive eyes. From this close, they're deep enough to swallow him whole. He understands, for the first time, why his father loves her. He leans forward and kisses the tip of her nose for good luck. It makes her smile, even when she's mad at him.

"OK, time for bed."

Kosha climbs beneath the covers. "Mama?"

"Yes?"

"I promise I'll never talk about silverbirds again."

"A promise is a big thing to make."

"I know, but I want to make it anyway."

His voice is small, but it carries sincerity. Ara knows it's a promise he won't keep, but it melts her anyway, the warmth spilling down her chest and spreading across her skin.
"Goodnight, my dear."

Kosha lies in bed, staring at the false phantoms on the walls.
*I promise I won't talk about silverbirds anymore.*
He doesn't know his mother can only bear the weight of losing two more people.
*I'm not going to make her sad anymore either.*
*A promise is a big thing to make.*

## The Story of The Silverbirds

This is the story my mother told me when I was young, and her mother before her, going all the way back to the beginning of time—when God first breathed life into the dead soil and shaped all living things from the blood of His beating heart.

Long ago, in those first days, there was an island in the middle of a crystal blue sea. On this island was a village, a peaceful place without war or poverty. The village had only one rule: do not harm others and take care of each other.

In this village lived a fisherman named Tajj. One day, while walking along the shoreline, he discovered a golden egg as large as a man's head. Holding it to the sun, he marveled at how it glistened in the light. It was heavy, as if something inside it was alive, whispering to him.

"There's something odd about this egg," he murmured.

Tajj knew the men in his village would grow jealous if they saw it. They would try to steal it.

"This is my egg," he decided.

He took it home, concealing it beneath his cloak. When he presented the golden orb to his wife, it began to pulse with a strobing light, as if a star was being born within its shell.

"You need to take it to the elders," she said, alarmed.

"Why? So they can divide it among themselves? I found it."

"Because that's what we do."

"No, I won't. It's hard to explain—I can feel its power reverberating through me."

"I don't like it," she said. "There's something wrong with that egg."

"Just think of all the good we could do with it."

"You don't even know what it is."

"There's something great inside—I can feel it. This egg is going to change everything."

For weeks, Tajj kept the golden egg in a basket by their bed. Every night, after his wife fell asleep, he took it outside, holding it up to the moonlight. He caressed it, kissed it, marveling at its glow.

"I won't let anything happen to you—I promise," he whispered.

The pulsating grew stronger, as though the egg were a part of him.

Night after night, this ritual continued. Until, at midnight one evening, the egg began to hatch. The first thing Tajj saw was a single red eye, made of fire, peering through a crack in the shell. Then came a wing, covered in razor-sharp feathers. Bit by bit, the shell flaked away, revealing a creature like nothing Tajj had ever seen. Not quite bird, not quite dragon—something far more terrible.

Cradling the fire-eyed beast in his arms, Tajj whispered, "You are mine, and I am yours."

When he returned home, his wife was awake, waiting by the door.

"What are you doing up?" His words were sharp, lunging from his mouth like hands reaching for her throat.

As soon as she saw the creature, she gasped. "My God, it's worse than I imagined. You have to take it to the elders."

"I won't let them have it."

"You don't even know what it is."

"It's mine."

Tajj placed the beast on the table and tried to feed it dried fish, but the creature turned away in disdain.

"It's not hungry," his wife said.

"Maybe it doesn't like fish."

As he spoke, a mangy rat scurried across the floor. In a blur of wings and fire, the beast pounced, tearing the rodent open with its razor-sharp beak. Tajj and his wife watched in horror as it devoured the rat, growing visibly larger with each bite of flesh.

"It craves fresh blood," his wife whispered. "You have to kill it now, before it's too late."

"It needs me."

"This thing will ruin you," she pleaded. "And me."

But Tajj refused. "I can't kill it. I'm its father."

"It's not even human."

Tajj stared into the creature's fiery eye. He felt its hold on him grow stronger, the blood in his veins boiling, his heartbeat syncing with the beast's pounding pulse until they thumped in unison. Only then did the maddening sound subside.

    The days passed, and the beast continued to grow, nearly too large to keep in the house. Tajj fed it their livestock and every rat within a three-mile radius. Still, it craved blood.

    Tajj and his wife grew emaciated and weak, having gone days without food. Yet Tajj loved the monster. When they had nothing left, he took all the money they had and prepared to buy a cow.

    "Don't do this, Tajj," his wife begged. "We'll starve. Let's leave the monster and start over somewhere far away."

    "Are you insane?" His tone dripped with contempt, as though she had insulted his god. "I can't just leave it. You can go if you want, but I'm staying. This is our home."

    Despite everything, she loved him. She couldn't bear the thought of a life without him, just as he couldn't bear the thought of losing the beast.

    Tajj set out on foot for the village, beginning the hour-long hike to buy the cow.

    That afternoon, Tajj returned home, leading a brand-new cow by a leash of fresh rope tied around its neck. As he approached, his heart sank. The front door was wide open. A thin trail of blood trickled down the threshold, pooling on the cobblestone below.

    Terror gripped him as he crept inside. What he saw froze him where he stood—a nightmare made flesh.

The creature hunched over his wife's twisted, mangled body. Its spiked beak plunged into her chest, cracking through her breastbone. With a single, savage motion, it tore out her heart and swallowed it whole.

Overcome with grief and rage, Tajj snatched a knife from the table and lunged at the beast. But before he could bury the blade into its back, the creature turned. It unleashed a torrent of hellfire, engulfing him and the house in flames.

Black smoke rose over the hills, a signal of destruction. The townspeople came running, but they fared no better. The beast slaughtered them as easily as it had Tajj and his wife. It went from house to house, feasting on the flesh of women and children, cutting down the men who dared to fight back.

By nightfall, nothing remained of the village but ashes. The beast had razed it all. The winds carried the soot down to the sea, staining the coastal waters black.

And so, the first silverbird came into the world.

Poya's: Part II

Kosha dreams of a black wood, with black trees. The ash-covered earth swirls in the wind, falling back down like snowflakes. The only light comes from towering flames, twenty feet high, encircling him and closing in slowly.

Carbon fills his lungs. It's too thick to breathe, too dense to see through.

He runs.

The canopy stretches its charred branches like skeletal fingers, clawing at the sky. The wind howls, the flames hiss. He can't see it, but he knows it's there. The beast flies above, hidden in the smoke.

Twigs and brush lash at his face, leaving red trails of blood. The heat of the flames tightens his skin, pulling it taut. His chest burns from the inside out, his vision blurring. The smoke grows heavier, weighing him down like stones tied to his feet.

*I could just lay down here and die.*

But he doesn't.

Kosha bursts through the tree line at last, gulping fresh air in the open valley. The steep slope ahead is uneven, the loose sodding crumbling beneath him. His footing fails, and he tumbles down the hill, landing in a shallow creek bed. Jagged rocks tear through his pants, slicing into his knee. Blood seeps through the shredded fabric.

Scrambling to his feet, he winces in pain but keeps moving, dragging his injured leg behind him. The icy creek water washes the dried blood from his face, rehydrating it. In his peripheral vision, he catches a glimpse of the silverbird—its silhouette glimmering in the distance.

*Run!*

His chest heaves.

*Run now!*

His good leg obeys. He limps through a field of crimson poppies, but the beast is closing in, its wings slicing through the air like blades.

At the edge of a bottomless cliff, Kosha skids to a stop. He peers over. Jagged stones jut out below like spikes, waiting to impale him.

The silverbird dives, blotting out the sun with its immense shadow. Its feathers are knives, its fangs dripping with the blood of the innocent. The beast opens its mouth, spewing a torrent of fire that sets the field ablaze.

Kosha tries to move, but the ground beneath him is like quicksand. The more he struggles, the faster he sinks into the black earth. The flames close in, licking at his legs.

Crawling on his belly, he pulls his torso over the chasm's edge, freeing one leg, then the other. The soles of his shoes melt from the heat.

He looks back at the beast, its fury reflected in its fire-lit eyes, and screams, "What do you want with me?"

The silverbird's throat rumbles, a guttural roar gathering in its lungs. Red-hot coals smolder deep inside, snapping and growling as gas breaks the air.

Kosha flings himself over the edge into the abyss just as the beast unleashes its wrath. Fire consumes him, a sea of flame swallowing him whole.

## Poya's: Part III

Kosha wakes up drenched in sweat, his chest heaving as though the devil himself had been sitting on it. His cheeks are hot and red from crying. He gasps for air, his lungs straining as if the flames from his dream still lingered.

Something warm and wet pools between his legs. Urine soaks through his pajamas and into his sheets. The monster's face is burned into his mind. It was too vivid to be a dream, too unreal to be real.

He needs to change before his mother finds out.

Sliding out of bed, he walks to his pale green dresser. The paint on the fake gold knobs began chipping long before he was born. Like everything else he owns, the dresser used to belong to Isah.

He opens the top drawer and grabs a clean pair of pants. Quickly, he pulls them on. He doesn't know what to do with the wet ones. His room reeks like a urinal. He doesn't dare hide them under the bed again—last time, his mother found them and spanked him for it.

Instead, he opens the bottom drawer, pushes his socks aside, and stuffs the wet pants in the back.

As Kosha crawls back into bed, a loud banging startles him. Someone is pounding on the front door, hard and frantic, as though trying to beat it off its hinges.

Commotion erupts in his parents' room. Kosha hears his father stumble and curse, tripping over something in the dark. Light floods the front room, yellow rays spilling under Kosha's door.

He tiptoes toward the door, trying to be silent, but as he cracks it open, the old thing betrays him, creaking loud enough to wake the dead.

His heart stops.

But his parents don't seem to notice, caught up in the chaos at the front door. Wincing, Kosha presses his ear to the opening.

Kamal hobbles to the door, still barefoot, his voice sharp with suspicion as he opens it halfway. "What are you doing here?"

Kamal's words hang heavy, weighed down by shock.

"Do you know what time it is?"

Kosha inches the door open just enough to peek out.

"I need your help," says a voice—gravelly, unfamiliar, and strained.

Kosha has never heard this man before.

It's a voice Kamal never wanted to hear again.

Ara emerges from the bedroom, still tying

her silk robe around her waist. "Who is it?"
Kamal hesitates. His reply lands like a punch to her chest. "My brother."
The words nearly knock her off her feet. She catches herself on the arm of a chair.
"That son of a bitch," she spits, her voice trembling with fury. "How dare he come back here after—"
"Quiet, Ara!" Kamal snaps.
Kosha's never heard his mother curse before.
"Don't you dare let him in," Ara hisses.
Kamal turns back to the man at the door. "She's right, Nader. You shouldn't have come here."
The man groans. His voice is pained. "I'm sorry. I didn't have anywhere else to go."
Kosha can't see him yet, but he knows something is wrong.
Kamal stands frozen, caught between a rock and a hard place. He knows why Nader is here. It's his fault Isah is gone. Kamal should shut the door, or better yet, shoot him on the spot. But a bullet would be too easy—and revenge isn't in him anymore.
Kamal stares at his bare feet, at the big toe he stubbed on the way to the door. He sighs, resentful and exhausted. "You're sure you weren't followed?"
"I swear I wasn't."
"I'm serious, Nader."
"I swear."
Kamal sticks his head outside, scanning the darkness for signs of movement. Satisfied, he

pulls the door open wider. "Okay. Get inside before someone sees you."

Ara can't believe her eyes as Nader steps into the dim light of the entryway. Her rage burns hotter with every step he takes into their home.

"How dare he come back here," she thinks. "How could Kamal let him in?"

But here he is, standing in their living room.

"You're a coward," she says through gritted teeth.

Kamal isn't sure which one of them she's talking to.

Neither is she.

Probably both.

Nader is taller than Kamal by a foot, and his beard is just as long. His combat boots are soaked in blood. He braces himself against the wall, one hand pressing against the bullet wound below his ribs.

Kamal catches Ara's glare as he helps his brother across the room. Her eyes cut into him like razors, slicing him to pieces. Over the years, those looks have shaved him down, one sliver at a time. Now, the blade takes bigger chunks, and she seems to care less about the damage it does.

He knows what she's thinking.

*He's done a lot of shitty things in our marriage, but nothing like this.*
*This is it. This is the moment I stop loving him. Then it'll just be Kosha.*

Composing herself, Ara motions for Kamal to join her in their bedroom. "A word, please."

Kamal bolts the front door and closes the curtains, blocking the outside world. "Not now, Ara."

"Yes. Now."

The moment they are in their bedroom, Ara lets into him with all of venom that's been saving up since Isah left, "You bastard, how could you?"

"He's my brother, what am I supposed to do?"

"Throw him out in the street to get eaten by dogs like he deserves."

"You know I can't do that."

"Why not? Why can't you do that?"

"Because then I'd be no better than he is."

"You're worse than he is! At least he has the guts to shoot someone when they deserve it!"

"That's below the belt and you know it."

"He took our son from us! There is no below the belt! How could you let him into our home?"

"He's dying!"

"Good! Let him die!"

"I can't do that— I wish I could but I can't— I'm sorry."

"You want to save him so bad, you didn't even try to save Isah!" She bursts into tears and begins pounding on his chest with her fists, "He was our son! Why didn't you try to save him?"

"That's enough!" he says grabbing her by the shoulders, shaking her, "Get a hold of yourself. My brother is staying and you will help me take care of him. Is that understood?"

Ara has no choice but to try and compose herself— she wipes the tears from her cheeks.
*This is the moment I stop loving you.*
She wishes it was true.

The fates and spirits of the past are passing through Nader, trying their damndest to take his soul into the afterlife. By the time Kamal walks back into the living room, Nader's holding onto the wall it like it's the only thing keeping him in this world. Red spit bubbles percolate out of out of his mouth and dribble down his chin. The blood seeps through his shirt and runs down his leg, gathering in a puddle around his boots.
"I'm sorry baby brother," he says collapsing into Kamal's arms, "I'm sorry about everything."
Kamal struggles beneath the weight of Nader's massive frame.
"Ara's right, you should just let me die."
Kamal tries to reallocate Nader's weight more evenly across his shoulders, "Shut up you big bastard before I take her advice."
From their bedroom door, Ara watches her husband struggle beneath the dead weight of his older brother.
*I used to love you.*
*I hate you.*
She's trying to mean it, but sometimes even when you hate someone, you can't help but love them.
*It doesn't make sense.*
*It never does.*
Grabbing Nader by the legs, she relents

and helps Kamal carry Nader into their rook, "Let's get him in the bed before he dies out here and ruins my rug any worse than he already has." Ara catches Kosha's half-moon face peering around the corner, "Get back in bed Kosha."
    Kosha eyes grow wide at being caught.
    "Now!" She snaps.

    Kosha chastises himself as he climbs back into bed, *I said I wasn't going to make her sad anymore. I'm not going to make her angry either.*
    He wants his mother to be happy.
    What good are moms if they're upset all the time?
    The moment they step into their bedroom, Ara unleashes the venom she's been storing since Isah left.
    "You bastard, how could you?"
    "He's my brother. What am I supposed to do?"
    "Throw him out in the street to be eaten by dogs like he deserves."
    "You know I can't do that."
    "Why not? Why can't you?"
    "Because then I'd be no better than he is."
    "You're worse than he is! At least he had the guts to shoot someone when they deserved it!"
    "That's below the belt, and you know it."
    "He took our son from us! There is no 'below the belt!' How could you let him into our home?"
    "He's dying!"
    "Good! Let him die!"

"I can't do that. I wish I could, but I can't—I'm sorry."

"You want to save him so bad, but you didn't even try to save Isah!"

Her voice cracks, and tears flood her cheeks. She pounds on Kamal's chest with her fists, her grief spilling out in raw, furious waves.

"He was our son! Why didn't you try to save him?"

"That's enough!" Kamal grabs her by the shoulders, shaking her. "Get a hold of yourself. My brother is staying, and you will help me take care of him. Is that understood?"

Ara has no choice but to compose herself. Wiping the tears from her cheeks, she swallows her rage.

This is the moment I stop loving you.

She wishes it were true.

In the living room, Nader clings to the wall as if it's the only thing tethering him to life. The fates and spirits of the past claw at him, trying to pull his soul into the afterlife.

By the time Kamal returns, red-tinged spit bubbles at the corners of Nader's mouth, dribbling down his chin. Blood seeps through his shirt, streaking down his leg and pooling around his boots.

"I'm sorry, baby brother," Nader wheezes, collapsing into Kamal's arms.

"I'm sorry about everything."

Kamal struggles beneath the weight of Nader's massive frame.

"Ara's right," Nader groans. "You should

just let me die."

"Shut up, you big bastard, before I take her advice," Kamal grunts, trying to shift Nader's weight across his shoulders.

From the doorway, Ara watches her husband struggle under his older brother's dead weight.

*I used to love you.*
*I hate you.*

She tries to mean it, but sometimes, even when you hate someone, you can't help but love them.

It doesn't make sense.

It never does.

Grabbing Nader by the legs, she relents. "Let's get him in the bed before he dies out here and ruins my rug any worse than he already has."

As they carry Nader toward the bedroom, Ara catches Kosha's half-moon face peeking around the corner.

"Get back in bed, Kosha."

Kosha's eyes widen at being caught.

"Now!" she snaps.

Kosha climbs back into bed, chastising himself.

I said I wasn't going to make her sad anymore. I'm not going to make her angry either.

He burrows under the covers, thinking: *What good are moms if they're upset all the time?*

## Hiding From The Hunt

Thick black skies,
Taking what they want.
Sunken red eyes—
The silverbirds hunt.

First there is nothing,
And then they're there,
And then—everything is gone.

Breathing devil's fire,
The rain blinds them,
Extinguishing their pyre,
Quenching the blaze within.

Do not wander on a starry night
Or beneath a clear day's light.
Venture out in shower or storm,
Snowfall and skies of gray—
Will shield you from becoming prey.

Heed these words, dear child,
Whether warrior or waif,
In city or in wild,

I pray thee—stay safe.

## Poya's: Part IV

The sun is so bright that it's one of those days where stepping inside feels like walking into a cave. Your eyes struggle to adjust, and little purple dots float in the air until they fade.

Ara stands in the doorway, talking with an older woman. The same doorway Nader passed through last night. Kosha lies on his back near the threshold, staring up at the visitor's wrinkled face. He doesn't know who she is, but she's much older and fatter than his mom.

*She's probably from the next village over.*

Lying next to the door is as close to the outside world as he can get on a day like this. It's not as good as playing outside, but beggars can't be choosers.

The old woman's hands are spotted with liver marks. Her wide, wobbly voice is low and conspiratorial. "They destroyed the hospital," she whispers.

"The hospital?" Ara gasps. "Why would they—"

"Why do they ever do anything?" the old woman snaps, cutting her off. "The devil's in them, that's why."

"Was anyone hurt?"

"Of course people were hurt. That hospital's been packed since the day they got here."

"How many died?"

"They're still trying to count. Last I heard, nineteen dead, thirty-four wounded, but they think the number will go up."

"Wasn't there a western doctor working there?"

"They had two—and six nurses."

"Are they okay?"

"One's dead. One of the doctors, I think. He was Polish or something. And one of the nurses lost part of her arm. I'm not sure about the rest."

"That's terrible."

The woman shrugs, indifferent. "They knew the risks when they came here. If they wanted to stay safe, they should've stayed in their own country, where hospitals don't get blown up for no reason."

"How can you say that? They're here to help us."

"A lot of good it's done. Do you know what I'd give to trade places with them?"

The silverbirds took the woman's oldest son three years ago and her daughter last summer.

"This place is cursed," she continues. "God either hates us or has forgotten us. What's the difference? Listen, I have to go. It's not safe here. I'm going to stay with my sister in Panjshir for a while. There's a truck waiting for me down the road. I just thought you'd want to know about the hospital."

"Thank you. Be careful."

"You too. The closest hospital is 120 kilometers away now."

The old woman stumbles down the path, trying not to lose her footing on the hill.

"Hey!" Ara calls after her.

The woman steadies herself, grabbing a birch sapling for balance. She turns back.

"I know we've all lost a lot," Ara says, her voice steady but soft. "But God hasn't forgotten us."

Tears well up in the deep creases of the woman's face. "That's a nice thought. If only it were true."

She turns and continues down the path, disappearing into the heat-hazed horizon.

Ara looks down at Kosha, her expression tense, like she's holding something back—something she doesn't want him to see. "Forget everything you just heard."

Kosha doesn't respond. He just watches her as she walks across the room and picks up a steel bowl filled with freshly bleached bandages.

She looks tired. No—not just tired. Weary.

There was a time when the sway of her hips could turn the head of every stag in town. On the right day, in the right light, you can still catch glimpses of that lost allure. Flashes of bygone youth. Remnants of splendor.

Once, she was pretty enough to make a boy put out his cigarette just to talk to her. Kamal

was handsome back then, too.
　　He used to be such a know-it-all, with that stupid little smile because he knew he was right.
　　He never smiles like that anymore.
　　By the time Ara snaps out of her daydream, she's already back in the bedroom, standing over Nader as he bleeds into her sheets. Dried blood and pus glue the filthy, amber-stained bandages to his torso. She peels them off one by one, taking the scabs with them. Nader grabs a fistful of sheets and groans in pain. He reeks of rotten flesh. Blood trickles from the torn stitches in his side.
　　Using the heel of her palm, she presses a fresh rag into the wound, eliciting another groan. She pushes harder—harder than she needs to.
　　*You son of a bitch.*
　　She pushes with all her strength.
　　The stitches begin to tear. She smiles. She'll have to sew him back up before Kamal gets home.
　　"Don't worry," she says, voice cold. "I'm not going to let you die."
　　Nobody is more savage than a heartbroken mother.

　　Kosha stares out the front door.
　　*I could sneak out right now, and nobody would know.*
　　When you're eight years old, thirty minutes is a lifetime. If he runs as fast as he can, he could make it to the river and back. He could climb a tree all the way to the top. Maybe even catch a nightjar and tie a string around its foot to

swing it over his head.

He won't do that last one, though. He tried it once, and his mom wasn't happy.

"You shouldn't tie strings on things with wings," she'd said. "They're meant to be up there in the sky, not down here with us."

Kosha made a mental note.

*Never tie strings on nightjars. Always let them fly.*

Then he remembers the promise he made himself last night:

*She'll be mad if I sneak out. I promised not to make her mad anymore.*

Suddenly, Kamal appears in the doorway, out of breath, sweat dripping down his temple. He wipes his forehead with his sleeve.

"Where's your mother?"

"She's in the room with Uncle Nader."

Without another word, Kamal strides into the bedroom and shuts the door. Even after he's gone, Kosha can still feel the chill of his father's shadow.

Moments later, Ara emerges, carrying a steel bowl of bloody rags. Kosha's too young to understand the look on her face—quiet, restrained.

"How's Uncle Nader?"

She doesn't respond. Stepping over the remnants of Kamal's shadow, she walks outside without looking back.

Kneeling by the washing basin, Ara dumps the soiled bandages into the murky, blood-brown water. She swirls her hand in the basin, frothing the soapy foam back to life, then scrubs the cotton fibers together with force.

Friction cleans things. It rubs away the old filth. That's what she's trying to do—just feel clean again.

The soap bubbles spill over the edges of the clay basin. Standing up, she leaves the bandages to soak and walks to the clothesline, where sheets billow in the wind. Removing the clothespins, she folds each sheet and tosses them into a wicker basket.

When she walks back inside, Kosha wants to say something, but he doesn't know what. Before he can figure it out, she disappears into the bedroom.

Ara stares at Nader.
*I'll never get the bloodstains out of that mattress.*
*I wouldn't sleep on it again anyway—not after he's been on it.*

She's going to have to burn it all—the mattress, the frame, everything. In one night, Nader managed to ruin a place where love had managed to survive.

Kosha doesn't know what's going on, but everything feels strange.

Against his better judgment, he creeps to the cheap compressed-wood door of his parents' room and presses his ear against it. The door is thin, but it's still hard to hear.

Ara throttles the clean sheet in her hands, silently warning Nader.

*He better not rat me out for what I did. Say one word, and I'll kill you.*

Nader meets her eyes. He knows the score, but she nods anyway, reminding him what happens to snitches.

Kamal sits at his brother's bedside, gently brushing the hair back from his face.

"I never wanted to see you again," he says.

"I never thought you would," Nader replies, his cough wet and full of liquid.

"What happened?"

"We were ambushed in the western valley. We had the high ground, but for the life of me, I don't know how they got the drop on us."

"What about Isah?"

Nader grimaces. "I don't know."

"What do you mean, you don't know? You were supposed to look after him!"

Nader had promised to keep Isah safe. He knew it was an impossible promise when he made it.

*A promise is a big thing to make.*

"I made the impossible possible for so long," Nader says. "While others were choking on mud and dying, I kept the jaws of death away from your son."

His voice shakes.

"You don't know what it's like out there. It's a slaughterhouse. Mangled limbs, torsos twisted into impossible angles. The smell of burning fat cooling in the breeze, fusing the dead together. Grown men screaming at night, crying for someone to save them. No one is safe on the front lines. But how can I make you understand that?

"You just want someone to blame. Fine. Blame me. But I don't know what to tell you—I lost sight of him when the fighting got bad. I called his name, but then there was an explosion, and...he was gone."

"So you left him there?"

"We were surrounded. I didn't have a choice."

The walls feel like they're closing in. Both men know what Kamal wants to say.

Nader breaks the silence. "I wish I was the one who died."

There's a bond forged between men who kill together. It's not father and son, not brotherhood. It's blood guilt. Birds of a feather trying to keep each other in the air so they don't have to fly alone.

"If I could change things—if I could take his place—" Nader trails off, realizing how empty hypotheticals are.

The last time Kamal spoke to Isah, he said things he wishes he could take back. If Isah had knocked on that door last night, Kamal would have welcomed him home with open arms.

It's not Nader's fault that Isah is gone.

Kamal was the one who said, "If you leave, I never want to see you again."

If there's blood, it's on Kamal's hands.

"So he's dead, then," Kamal says quietly.

"I don't know."

And then, silence.

"I'm sorry," Nader whispers.

Kosha knows he should back away from the door, but something keeps him there. He's never met his brother, so he's not sure how to feel about the news that Isah is probably dead. It feels like he should be sad.

Older brothers are oxymorons. You look up to them and fear them at the same time. You want to be just like them, even though you resent them. He's supposed to feel for Isah what his father feels for Nader. But he's never had an older brother—just a brother he's not allowed to talk about.

He knows how he feels and how he's supposed to feel, and they're not the same thing.

Isah's never even socked him before.

*A fella isn't really your brother until he kicks the shit out of you. It's just how it is.*

He doesn't want to eavesdrop anymore. It's making him sad.

Kosha lays down in front of the front door and pulls his wine-colored stocking cap down over his ears. The sun creeps across the cement floor, swallowing the shadows. He stretches his hand into the yellow light, warm against his skin.

Reaching into his pocket, he pulls out a red racquetball. He doesn't remember where he got it. He probably found it, or maybe it was a gift from his father. Who knows.

He throws it against the wall and catches it.

Throw. Bounce. Catch.
Throw. Bounce. Catch.

The rhythm is hypnotic, a kind of juvenile catharsis. He tries not to think about whether

Isah is dead or not.
    Throw. Bounce. Catch.
    He still doesn't know why his father was out of breath when he came home.
    Throw. Bounce. Catch.
    Where was he coming from?
    Throw. Bounce. Catch.
    If Isah is a soldier now, does that mean he's killed people?
    Throw. Bounce. Catch.
    What is it like to kill someone?
    Throw. Bounce. Catch.
    What is it like to die?
    Throw. Bounce. Catch.
    One second, everything is inside your head like it always is, and then suddenly it's gone.
    Throw. Bounce. Catch.
    Are you still awake after you're dead? Do you know you're dead? Does paradise really exist like everyone says? How can anyone be sure?
    Throw. Bounce. Catch.
    It's impossible to know because nobody comes back from there.
    Why would they, if it's paradise?
    Throw. Bounce. Catch.
    You know because God says it's real.
    Throw. Bounce. Catch.
    But how do you know it's God?
    Throw. Bounce. Catch.
    Mama says God speaks to you.
    Throw. Bounce. Catch.
    He's never spoken to me.
    Throw. Bounce. Catch.
    Does that mean I'm not saved?

Throw. Bounce. Catch.
Maybe I'm going to hell.
Throw. Bounce. Catch.
Maybe God never speaks out loud.
Throw. Bounce. Catch.
Maybe it's all on the inside.
Throw. Bounce. Catch.
But if it's all on the inside, how does anyone know it's really Him?
Throw. Bounce. Catch.
What if you're just talking to yourself?
Throw. Bounce. Catch.
If I were God, I'd always speak out loud so people would know it was me.
Throw. Bounce. Catch.
I wonder where Isah is now.
Throw. Bounce. Catch.
If he killed people, does that mean he's going to hell?
Throw. Bounce. Catch.
But what if he killed them for God?
Throw. Bounce. Catch.
Don't you still get to go to paradise if it's for God?
Throw. Bounce. Catch.
But how do you know you're really doing it for God?
Throw. Bounce. Catch.
What if you never hear Him?
Throw. Bounce. Catch.
How do you even know He's real?
Throw. Bounce. Catch.
What if there's just…nothing?
Kosha stops thinking about it. It scares him

too much. He can handle the idea that good people go to heaven and bad people go to hell, but he can't wrap his head around the prospect that none of it matters. That you cease to exist.

Throw. Bounce. Catch.

He wants to see how many times he can bounce the ball without dropping it. His personal best is forty-two. He's at twenty-eight now, but he's sure he can beat it. If he really tries, maybe he can hit a hundred.

The sun's edge rests atop his head like a halo.

His mother walks into the room, tears still in her eyes. She turns on the faucet and takes a drink of water, her hands trembling so badly she can barely hold the glass.

Kosha watches as she wipes the sticky, sweaty hair from her face. He wants to help her, but he's just a kid. She's swimming in the deep end.

Letting out a deep sigh, she fixes her hair and disappears back into the bedroom.

Throw. Bounce. Catch.
Throw. Bounce. Catch.
Throw. Bounce. Catch.
Throw, bounce—

The ball hits the wall at a funny angle, ricocheting sideways. It skips off the leg of the table and shoots out the open front door.

Kosha scrambles after it, but it's too late. The ball is already rolling down the side of the mountain.

He knows what he should say.

*Whelp, it's gone. Better go find something*

*else to do.*
　But it's a red racquetball.
　*Where am I going to find another one? I don't even know where I got this one.*
　He has other toys, but he doesn't want to play with them. Besides, everything worth doing is outside.
　He looks over his shoulder, listening for any sign of his parents. They could be in the bedroom for an hour, or they could come out any second. There's no way to know.
　He promised his mom he wouldn't make her mad anymore.
　But he needs his ball back.
　These are the kinds of moral conundrums that keep a boy up at night.
　He checks one last time. The coast is clear.
　He sticks his toe out the front door, testing the waters. Nothing happens. No silverbirds burning him to bits. No mothers slapping or spanking him.
　He steps out a little further. Still nothing.
　The sun's heat radiates through the toe of his shoe.
　He takes another step, then another. He's fully outside now.
　Looking back, he's already ten feet from the door.
　There's no turning back.
　He squints against the sunlight, God how he's missed this clear blue sky. He hasn't run in a week. The fresh air is magic in his lungs.
　The crisp wind chaps his cheeks. His nose turns pink and begins to drip. He sniffles and

smiles.
    Running down the hill, loose gravel skids beneath his feet.
    He knows he shouldn't be out here, but the earth is begging him to come deeper into her.
    He can feel God out here.
    How could this be wrong?

    Kosha looks for his racquetball at the bottom of the hill, scanning the ground beneath the mulberry tree where he sometimes practices archery. He runs his fingers over a spot on the trunk where an arrow once lodged so deep it snapped off when he tried to pull it out.
    Peeling back a section of cracked bark with his fingernail, he exposes the sinewy green wood beneath. The dull metal of the arrowhead comes into view. Picking up a rock, he hacks at the tree, trying to dig it out, but it's no use—it's in too deep.
    Years from now, someone will cut this tree down and find it there, wondering where it came from.
    Kosha wipes his sap-covered fingers on his pants. Dropping onto all fours, he crawls into the bushes next to the tree. His racquetball lies ahead of him in the bramble. A fire ant crawls up his hand and bites him. He brushes it off, wincing as a small inflamed pimple rises on his knuckle.
    Grabbing the ball, he scrambles back out and turns to head up the hill.

    Without warning, a meteoric shadow flashes overhead.

Then, a deafening explosion.

The mountain shakes like a house of cards, cracking and crumbling. Slabs of granite and limestone tumble down the hillside.

Dodging back and forth like a cat in traffic, Kosha avoids the falling boulders, clawing his way back up the faltering mesa.

He has to get home.

*She's going to be so mad.*

*You can't make her mad again. You promised.*

Black smoke billows from the mountaintop. More rocks fall. He climbs and ducks. Flickers of orange, red, and yellow pierce the air, flames licking at the sky.

The earth trembles beneath him, and he trembles with it.

The flames are no longer flickers—they are nightmares made real.

His house is engulfed in fire.

Kosha blinks twice, desperate to convince himself it isn't true. But it is.

The roof and two outer walls have been blown apart, trapping everyone inside under the rubble. Fire shatters the windows, shooting through them in tongues of heat.

Embers rise into the air, floating upward until they disappear.

Embers are just pieces of things that no longer exist. Important things—wedding photos, baby shoes, urine-stained pajamas, kitchen tables.

Embers are memories—pieces of life dissolving into nothingness.

Inside the house, the latex paint bubbles and drips off the walls. The flames slither upward, ravenous. Smoke thickens, turning the inferno into a vague, blurred nightmare of red, orange, and black. The more he focuses on it, the more it burns his eyes.

Kosha screams.

"Mama! Papa!"

The sweltering air bakes his skin. Soot stains his face.

They're in there.

He's out here.

Looking down, he sees the red racquetball still clutched in his hand. Only moments ago, it seemed like the most important thing in the world.

He's not supposed to be out here. He's supposed to be in there with them.

Taking a step closer to the fire, he pulls his shirt up over his mouth to breathe and shields his eyes with his forearm.

His mother only had it in her to love two people. He's one of them, and that means something.

The skin on his cheeks and nose feels like it's about to peel off.

"Mama!"

The heat is so intense that his tears evaporate before they can fall.

"Papa!"

On the far side of the wreckage, he spots the metal bowl his mother had used to hold the bandages.

Shielding his face, he pushes forward

through the flames.
*I promised I wouldn't make her mad anymore.*
*I wish she'd made me the same promise.*
The heat presses down on him, crushing him like a weight on the side of his head. He bends down and grabs the first glowing stone from the rubble.
The oil and fat in his fingers sizzle and burn. He jumps back, coughing the smoke from his lungs.
He needs gloves.
Thinking quickly, he pulls off his shoes and slides his wool socks over his hands like mittens.
The last time he did this, he was helping his mom bake cookies. She'd scolded him, saying, "Using your socks as oven mitts is dirty."
He made a mental note: *Don't use socks as oven mitts.*
But everything is dirty in a fire. She can yell at him later.
He digs with everything he has, pulling back one steaming stone after another.
*You can yell at me.*
The rocks cool and turn black in the sunlight.
*Please yell at me.*
The flames burn through his socks, scorching his hands.
*Just yell at me.*
His hands throb and shake under the weight of each stone. He's terrified. Tired. Hurting.
Still, he digs.

The sock on his right hand ignites. Panicking, he yanks it off and throws it aside.

Suddenly, a skinless black hand reaches up from beneath the rubble.

Kosha grabs it.

It's too small to be his father's, but it doesn't feel like his mother's either. The flesh drips from the bones like liquid.

*Mama's supposed to have soft skin.*

This isn't her touch.

"Mama!" he shrieks, shoving his arm through the burning stones to get a better grip.

Hearing her name, Ara's hand tightens around Kosha's.

It's her last act of love—a lifetime of love compressed into one fleeting squeeze.

"Mama!"

And then, her hand goes limp.

"Mama!"

Kosha clings to her, shaking her hand, begging it to squeeze back.

"Mama!"

But she won't.

She can't.

She's gone.

Ara: Part I

Ara's mother died when she was two years old. She couldn't remember her mother's face, but everyone said she looked just like her. It felt like staring at a ghost every time she looked in the mirror. The older she got, the more noticeable the spirit became.
*I won't outlive the face of the dead until I'm old.*
When her mother died, Ara's father didn't know what to do with a little girl. So, he sent her to live with his older sister, Rahil.
Rahil couldn't have children of her own, so it made sense for her to take Ara in. Not long after, Ara's father took a job in Saudi Arabia as a refinery technician. Five years later, he married a beautiful Saudi woman and had a son.
When his second child was born, he was so overwhelmed with joy he nearly cried. "God has blessed me with everything a man could hope for."
His new wife gave him two more sons, and he lived a long and happy life. Ara never heard from him again.

She was a painful memory he wanted to forget.

He was a ghost she couldn't remember but thought about all the time.

None of this meant Ara lacked love as a child. Quite the opposite.

Ara was the child Rahil had longed for. Rahil had spent sleepless nights, pining in prayer, begging God to bless her with a child. Ara was the answer to those prayers.

Rahil loved her as if she'd carried her in her own womb, as if she'd labored to bring her into the world.

The fact that a woman can endure the agony of childbirth and survive is proof of how sacred and difficult life is. It's in those precious hours of labor, when a mother is dripping with sweat and screaming, that all the love in the world is proven to exist.

It isn't contractions or reflexes that bring a child into the world—it's love. You don't slide out. Your mother pushes you. She breaks and tears herself open so that you might live.

And once you're here, she drains herself for you—physically and spiritually—milk from her breast, prayers from her lips.

Mothers are the emptiest people in the world.

Rahil envied Ara's biological mother. She got to labor sixteen hours to prove her love for her child. She got to sacrifice.

Ara, for her part, was an unruly monster of a child. Even as a toddler, she could sense her father's abandonment. She spilled milk and broke things just to see them lay on the ground in pieces.

Rahil never lost patience with her. She would just wipe up the mess and say, "I see we're not thirsty today."

As Ara grew, her rebelliousness evolved from overt disobedience into subversive independence. She read ravenously. Most girls in her village weren't even literate. By the time she was in seventh grade, she'd already read everything by Charles Dickens. She didn't even like Dickens.

Slamming *The Old Curiosity Shop* onto her bed, she fumed. "He takes two paragraphs to say what he already said in the first three words. *She was dead.* We get it. We don't need the rest."

She hated fluff.

She wanted words that cut like razors. She preferred the freewheeling writers of the 20th century, whose words carried the sharp edge of intoxicated anxiety.

*Cut me to pieces,* she thought, cracking open *Fahrenheit 451* for the third time. *I'm ready.*

Ara knew, with absolute certainty, that she wanted to be a writer. To create something that evoked wonder and passion in others. To make them feel as riled up and unsatisfied as she did.

She also knew, just as certainly, that she never wanted to be a mother.

Every woman was supposed to cherish the idea of motherhood, but Ara hated expectations. She refused to live up to anyone else's idea of life.

"Mothers always look exhausted," she said once. "They spend all their energy on their kids. There's nothing left for themselves. I don't want that—I'd rather be pretty."

Rahil just shook her head. "There are more important things in life than being pretty."

Not really. I mean, not for me—I'm already smart. Staying pretty takes work."

"I'd rather have you than be pretty any day."

"That's because you're a mother. I'm your entire identity. I don't want that. I'd rather be myself."

"You think I'm not myself?"

Ara looked at the deep wrinkles ingrained in Rahil's face. She knew she was the cause of every one of them.

"I think I made you who you are."

It was true.

It was also true that the carefree young woman Rahil used to be was still buried somewhere deep inside her. But trying to unearth her would be like unrolling the Dead Sea Scrolls—if you ever managed it, she'd crumble into dust in your hands.

Rahil's husband, Abdul, was a hard man with short, fat fingers. He couldn't sneak up on anyone because of the cheap patchouli he bathed in. Ara didn't like him, and he didn't like her much either. Fortunately, he traveled for work and was hardly ever home.

Ara lay in bed, staring at two large stains on the ceiling. One was from a leak in the roof. The other was from when she got mad and threw a bottle of Coca-Cola at the wall last year. The glass had exploded into a billion tiny shards, and she was still getting little pieces of it stuck in her foot.

The pieces were so small you couldn't grab them with tweezers. You just had to wait for your body to push them out.

That's how Ara felt about all the pain inside her—waiting for the day her body would finally push it all out.

She was sick and tired of Rahil getting onto her about everything: her temper, her bitten fingernails, her habit of wearing the same clothes for three days straight.

Rolling onto her stomach, she stared at the dirt beneath her mangled nail beds. Chewing on her cuticles, she thought about the fight they'd had earlier in the day.

"Nobody wants to marry a girl with filthy hands," Rahil had said.

"That's good, because I'm not getting married."

It was blasphemy in their house.

"First no kids and now no husband? I swear, I don't know why God made you a woman."

"I don't know why people care so much."

"Because a woman's primary duty is to look after her children and be a dutiful wife."

"Is that straight from a sermon, or do you

have any opinions of your own?"

"That is my opinion."

"Okay, well, my opinion is that it's bullshit."

"Watch your mouth!"

"Maybe it was a mistake. Maybe I wasn't supposed to be a girl at all."

"God doesn't make mistakes."

"Well, He made men insecure, cruel, and controlling, and He made them in His image, so what does that say about God?"

"Don't ever talk like that," Rahil snapped. Her voice turned deadly serious. This wasn't just about a rebellious teenager anymore. "They'll kill you if they hear you saying things like that."

"I don't care what they do to me," Ara lied, folding her arms over her chest. "I don't want a husband. I want to go to the university."

"There's no point in wasting money on an education you'll never use."

"I want to be a writer."

"You've had your nose in too many books."

"You're just saying that because you don't know how to read."

It was a gut punch.

Rahil tried to take the high road. "I know all too well what is and isn't possible for a woman in this world."

But Ara dragged her back down. "It's only impossible because you believed it when they told you."

"Your Uncle Abdul would slap you if he heard you talking like this."

"Well, it's a good thing he won't be home for a week."

Rahil set the dirty dishes in the sink, drying her hands on a towel. She was content to let the argument die.

But Ara wouldn't let it go. She was mad, and she smelled blood in the water. Her wide, red eyes welled with tears.

"What about you?" Ara demanded.

"What about me?"

"You couldn't even give Uncle Abdul a son. You couldn't give him anything."

The words came out before Ara could stop them.

She'd wanted to draw blood. Instead, she'd slit her mother's throat.

Rahil clenched the towel so hard that the veins in her hands bulged. She didn't say anything. She didn't have to. Words don't disappear the moment you say them.

They both felt small.

Ara wanted to pull the emotional dagger out of Rahil's heart, but she didn't know how. The silence between them stretched unbearably long. Finally, Rahil released the towel, exhaling as if to let the pain out with her breath.

"You're my daughter, and I love you."

It was time for Ara to let go. To unwrap her dirty fingernails from the metaphorical knife. She wanted to, but she couldn't.

It was stuck there.

Why?

Was it anger?

No, it wasn't anger.

Was it embarrassment?

No, it wasn't even that.

It was envy.

Ara envied Rahil's complacency.

She wanted to be content like her mother, but she didn't know how. Ara was unsatisfied to her core.

She tried to stop herself, but it was too late.

Instead of pulling the knife out, she twisted it deeper.

"But I'm not."

"Not what?"

"I'm not your daughter—not really."

"How could you say that?"

The deeper she went, the more it hurt her too.

*Just let it be.*

*I can't.*

*Why?*

*Because I can't.*

*Why?*

*Because.*

Instead of stopping, Ara opened her mouth and let more poison spill out.

"Because it's true. You're just my aunt."

"I think you should go to your room before you say anything else you'll regret."

Ara wanted to get out of there more than anything. But she was already up to her neck in it, and now she was crying on top of it all.

She hated crying in front of people more than anything.

She didn't know why she couldn't stop her

tears. She didn't know why she screamed what she screamed next. She just wanted it to stop.
"Your whole life is a facade!"
Rahil didn't know what facade meant. That's why Ara said it. She wanted to make Rahil feel stupid—a cruel, emotional retaliation from a very real daughter to an endlessly devoted mother.
"Go to your room. Please."
But Ara didn't budge.
"I wish you were the one who died."

## Ara: Part II

Ara sat on the floor watching TV on their black-and-white twenty-one-inch Zenith, complete with coat hanger rabbit ears and three knobs, two of which you could turn for half an hour without them doing a damn thing. Nobody remembered where the TV came from. It had just always been there.

The state-run news agency flickered on the screen—protests in the capital. Through the static snowfall, footage showed men with Molotov cocktails, cars engulfed in flames.

Uncle Abdul sat in his chair on the other side of the living room, smoking a cigarette. Nobody else was allowed to sit in that chair, which was fine because it reeked of cigarette smoke and cheap cologne.

Ara was getting older. Her once frizzy, unmanageable hair had loosened into lovely auburn ringlets that tumbled past her shoulders. Her body was changing too, the soft beauty of adolescence replacing the ruddiness of childhood.

Abdul had noticed.

Over the past few months, he'd started looking at her in a way that made her skin crawl, as if he wanted to devour her.

"Come here," he said, gesturing with his limp hand-rolled cigarette.

He wasn't her father. He wasn't even close to being a father figure. She didn't even like calling him "uncle." He was just a man who lived in the house, a man she tried to avoid. But that was getting harder. His eyes followed her wherever she went, stripping her bare no matter how much she tried to hide.

She rolled onto her side, pulling her hair over her chest to shield her budding breasts. She knew what he wanted and didn't want to give him a single thing. His eyes followed her hands as if seeing straight through her hair.

Just the thought of him made her want to wretch.

"Come here," he repeated, smoke curling from his mouth as he scratched the back of his hairy neck.

He had always looked at her, but he'd never touched her.

Until now.

Her mother was at the market. They were alone.

*Why did she leave me alone with him?*
*She had to know.*
"It's better to just go along with it."
*Fuck that bullshit. Fight him!*
"I don't have a choice."
*Who knows what he's capable of?*
"I'm scared."

Before she even realized it, her body betrayed her. She was walking toward him.

*This isn't happening.*

It was an out-of-body experience. She wasn't there.

*This can't actually be happening.*

*This is happening.*

"What do you want?" she asked, her voice cold and lifeless.

Abdul took one last drag of his cigarette. The long gray ash fell onto his pant leg. He stubbed the butt out in a half-empty glass of water, brushed the ash from his slacks, and patted his thigh.

"Sit on my lap for a second. I want to talk to you."

Her heart pounded.

*Hold your ground.*

*Maybe Mom will come home.*

"What do you want to talk about?"

He grabbed her wrist—gentle but firm, the kind of grip that said, *Don't fight this. This can be nice. This can be gentle.*

"A lot of things," he said.

She tried to pull away. His grip tightened.

"You don't want to do that."

"Where's Mom?"

"She's at the market," he said, his voice indifferent.

Ara stared at the door, praying it would open and Rahil would walk in to stop this.

*Why did she leave me? She had to know.*

*Is this my punishment?*

"I don't know what you're looking for,"

Abdul said, loosening his grip and pulling her down onto his lap. "She'll be gone for a while."
*Just go along with it.*
*No. Fuck that.*
His large belly pressed against her side. She felt his erection through his pants as he wrapped his arms around her.
"You're a woman now," he said, sliding his hand up her thigh. "Soon, you'll get married and make some man very happy. It's important you remain pure for him. A woman's purity is the greatest gift she can give her husband."
Her legs tensed. Her entire body was rigid.
*Where is she?*
*Come home—please come home.*
*I'm sorry.*
She placed a pleading hand on his wrist, silently begging him to stop.
But Abdul was after her fear as much as her body.
"Are you still pure?" he asked.
She was already screaming on the inside.
*Please come home.*
*Just go along with it so he doesn't hurt you.*
His hand wandered higher. Tears welled in her eyes. He pushed her knees apart.
"What's wrong?" he asked, his voice thick with mock concern.
*Just go along with it.*
If she'd had a knife, she would have stabbed him in the heart.
*Please come home.*
*Is this my punishment?*

"I want you to tell me how much you like it."

*Just go along with it.*

"I like it," she said, her voice trembling.

"Tell me it feels good."

"It feels really good."

*I'm sorry.*

"Do I make you wet?"

She didn't even know what that meant.

"Yes," she said, just to make it stop.

Choking on the patchouli fog of his cologne, she turned her head away. She couldn't look at him. She couldn't look at what he was doing.

Her eyes landed on the TV.

The new president was on the screen, standing among men with long beards. He looked serious, but he was smiling.

She focused on his yellow smile, forcing herself to get lost in it.

*Let it take you away from here.*

Abdul's moans faded into the background.

Then the front door opened.

Ara was flung onto the floor, hitting her head as she landed. She sat up on all fours, staring at the golden fleur-de-lis on the red rug beneath her. Blood dripped from her nose onto her filthy fingernail.

The hem of Rahil's firaq came into view.

"What happened?"

Abdul sat in his chair, breathing heavily, refusing to make eye contact.

Ara wiped the blood from her nose. The president was gone from the screen.

Visibly upset, Rahil glared at Abdul. "Well? What happened?"

"I don't know," Abdul said. "I told her to get me some tea, and she must have tripped and fell or something."

Rahil wasn't buying it. "Is that true?"

Ara stayed silent.

*Just go with it.*

*Where were you?*

"I asked you a question," Rahil said again.

Ara stared at the rug as another drop of blood fell, blending into the red pattern.

"It's like he said. I fell."

"There's nothing else you want to tell me?"

Ara's shirt was untucked. Her hair reeked of smoke and patchouli. The back of her neck was damp from his sloppy kisses. She could still feel where his hands had been.

She wiped his spit from her skin.

*Where were you?*

"No," she said. "That's it. I fell."

## Ara: Part III

Ara stood over the sink. Rahil washed the blood from her face with a damp cloth, but the shame remained, a stain that water couldn't touch.
    Ara couldn't bring herself to say what Abdul had done to her. Some truths are self-evident.
    Rahil set the cloth down with a sigh as heavy as the pain in her heart. At last, she spoke.
    "You can't stay here anymore. I don't know where you'll go, but I'll figure something out. Listen to me carefully: go pack your bag—only the absolute necessities. That means no books. You're leaving tonight."
    Ara froze. She didn't want to leave. Her skin crawled as the memories clawed at her mind.
    This was her home.
    Fuck him—she never wanted to see him again.
    But she didn't want to leave either.
    She just wanted to crawl beneath her covers and forget everything.
    But she would never forget.

She wanted her mother to hold her, to tell her everything would be okay. But Rahil's arms felt as unreachable as a place where things like this didn't happen.

She could still feel his eyes devouring her. His hands.

This was her home.

She hated being here.

She didn't want to leave.

She was caught between two impossible truths, each one pulling her apart.

"Why do I have to leave?" she whispered, though she already knew the answer. She didn't want to hear it.

"What—no—I don't want to leave!"

"Shhh!" Rahil's voice cracked. "He'll hear you."

Rahil kissed Ara's forehead, tears welling in her eyes. "It's not safe for you here."

It's a mother's job to protect her child at all costs—even if that means letting them go.

Rahil wanted to say she was sorry. Sorry for letting this happen. Sorry for not seeing it sooner. She wouldn't let it happen again. She'd kill Abdul first. She should have killed him a long time ago.

She wanted to say she knew what he'd done, that none of it was Ara's fault. But to speak such unspeakable things aloud would give them even more power—and that just wasn't done.

Not here.

Not anywhere.

Ara cried within herself: *Where were you?*

Rahil wept within herself: *I'm sorry. You were supposed to protect me. I was supposed to protect you.*

"I don't want to leave," Ara whispered.

Rahil swallowed her pain. "Go and do it now. We don't have much time."

For once, Ara obeyed her mother.

## Her Name Was Shabana

Why didn't you drown that beast in the sea?
O' Tajj, you coward, why didn't you listen to me?
I was the love of your youth,
The one who opened herself to you—
My flesh, my blood, my grinding tooth,
And ashes and tears and misery's brew.
I peeled away like the petals of a rose,
I gave you the sweetest days of my life,
And I reaped everything that I sowed.
You kissed me and made me your wife.
It was no figment, no mirage.
I was half of you, and you of me.
I was your wife, Tajj!
And now I'm blown into the sea.
Because you brought the devil through our door,
And through the door of every nation.
And through even more—
Haunting all of creation.
This was you, when it was supposed to be

us.
Can you hear my heart breaking?
Of course not.
It's in the belly of the beast.
This was you, loving the silverbird more than me.
This is me, filling the sea with my tears.
And now I'm gone—my name not even recorded.
Known only as the wife of Tajj the coward,
The bride of Tajj the fool.
The selfish, the wicked, the vile.
The sweet, the tender, the man I gave my heart to.
O' damn you, Tajj, why do I still love you?
I pray you burn in hell.
I pray you receive God's sweet mercy.
I pray you get the rest I'll never have.
For I will forever haunt this place,
Where our bed of love once stood.
Where a sweet and simple boy entered into me,
And made me a part of him,
Giving me my name.
The wife of Tajj the fisherman.

## Ara: Part IV

    Our possessions serve as a timeline of our history. They prove who we are and what we love. How do you encapsulate all of that into one bag? How do you not leave a huge part of yourself behind? How do you discard it all and forget who you are, and instead focus on who you will become?
    Her mother said no books, but surely she didn't mean it as an absolute prohibition. Ara didn't know where she was going, but in a country where only 38% of the population could read, the odds of there being a library seemed slim.
    *Only the necessities.*
    She picked up her tattered copy of *Emma*. It was one of her favorites, but at 474 pages, there was no way it was making the cut.
    The only book she owned that she hadn't read yet was a water-stained copy of *As I Lay Dying*. Its yellow, warped pages puffed out, making it look thicker than it was. Sliding it into the side pocket of her green duffel bag felt good—like a thief hiding a knife in her boot.
    Everything felt out of control, but that

small act made her feel like she had a say in it all.

She added *The Prophet*, followed by *Siddhartha* and *The Red Badge of Courage*. By the time she crammed *Where the Red Fern Grows* inside, she had smuggled her little anorexic library into whatever life lay ahead.

She stood back and looked at her bag. Fourteen years of life crammed into three feet of polyester-blended fabric. It was bursting at the seams, trying to get out.

Then the energy in the room shifted. She felt it before she saw him. The temperature dropped four degrees.

He was in the doorway.

Abdul's voice slithered across the room and up her spine.

"Going somewhere?"

Startled, Ara pulled her blanket over the bag like a child hiding a stolen treat.

*Why did I do that?*
*He already saw it.*

If the bag hadn't made him suspicious, her reaction certainly did.

God, she could smell him from here. That awful cologne. Everything he had done.

"No," she stuttered. "Just putting some stuff in storage."

His eyes narrowed, dissecting her, scratching his scruffy cheek.

"What did you tell your aunt?"

Her stomach dropped. She wanted to puke. To run away. To cry. To kill him.

*Fuck him.*

She was losing everything because of him. He took it all.

"Well?" he pressed.

Ara realized she'd just been staring at him.

"Nothing," she muttered. "I didn't say anything."

"You wouldn't lie to me, would you?"

*Motherfucker.*

"No. I wouldn't lie to you."

"That's good," Abdul said, his voice low. "Because your mother would be very upset if she found out what you did."

*What I did?*

It took everything Ara had to stay composed. Girls got stoned for this. Was he going to kill her to cover up his shame?

*Oh, Cain, Cain, why does your brother's blood call out from the soil? You're not a believer at the time of stealing. What about this? He stole everything from me.*

Her stomach acid rose into her mouth. "I know."

"Your beauty has great power. You need to be careful not to tempt men with it."

He looked over his shoulder, ensuring they were alone, before stepping into the room.

"See—there you go again, tempting me."

"I didn't do anything."

"That's a lie. You did plenty," he said, walking toward her. "I haven't been able to stop thinking about you all day. I need to feel your soft skin pressed against me just one more time."

"I don't lie," she said, cutting him off and stepping backward.

"You lied earlier."
She stepped back again, cornered now.
"No. I just didn't tell the truth."
"It's the same thing."
He was sweating. The humidity radiated off his body, gathering like mist on her skin.
*Motherfucker.*
*Don't go along with it.*
"Either way," Ara said firmly, "I'm not going to lie for you anymore."
He reached out, running his fingers through her hair. The floral aroma made her stomach churn.
Her skin crawled.
*Don't go along with it.*
Where was her mother?
*It doesn't matter. This is up to you.*
"The truth is, you want this as much as I do," he said, sliding his hand around her throat, his fat fingers tightening as a warning.
"Tell me you want this."
*Don't go along with it.*
She was like a sparrow's egg in his palm.
*Fight. Scream. Do something.*
"I'll scream."
"No, you won't." He leaned in to taste her.
Just when Ara thought her mother had forsaken her again, she saw Rahil standing in the doorway, her eyes brimming with rage.
Rahil already knew her worst fears were true. But seeing it was different than knowing it.
"Mama," Ara whispered.
Abdul's head snapped around, like a child caught stealing from a cookie jar.

"What are you doing?" Rahil demanded.

"Nothing," Abdul said quickly. "She was asking me a question about her homework."

It took everything Rahil had not to lose control right then and there. But she had to keep the plan intact.

"It's time for dinner," Rahil said.

"Good. I'm starving," Abdul muttered, stepping toward the door.

He tossed a questioning glance toward the bag.

"Storage, huh?"

Ara nodded.

"You want me to put it away for you?"

*I can't let him touch that bag,* thought Rahil. *I won't let him.*

Terrified, Ara shook her head no.

Abdul reached down and picked it up.

"It's heavy," he said, then set it back down on the bed.

He studied them both, suspicion creeping across his face.

He could feel the fear in the room.

"What's for supper?"

Nobody said a word at dinner. When the meal was over, Ara cleared the plates in silence. At the sink, she washed them quietly. Rahil joined her, placing a gentle hand on the small of her back. It wasn't enough to say everything that needed to be said, but it was something. A reminder: *I'm here.*

Once the dishes were done, Ara made an excuse about having a headache and went straight to bed, which was true. There's only so much a mind can take before it shuts down to protect itself.

She wanted to spend her last few hours in her mother's arms, telling her how much she loved her, thanking her for everything—for all the school lunches, the mended clothes, the times she held her after a skinned knee. For all of it and more.

She needed to tell her it wasn't her fault.

But instead, she lay in bed awake, already dressed in the clothes she would run away in.

She looked around her room, taking inventory of everything she was leaving behind.

*Goodbye, ribbons I won at school.*

*Goodbye, picture of a horse on my wall.*

*Goodbye, big thick books with all your words that are too heavy to carry.*

*Goodbye, colorful scarves.*

*Goodbye, dresser—thanks for holding all my socks and secrets.*

*Goodbye, lamp that gave me light to read by.*

*Goodbye, four walls that protected me as best as you could.*

*Goodbye, roof for doing the same.*

*Goodbye, pillow, thanks for giving me a place to lay my head.*

*Goodbye, blanket, you made me feel safe even when I wasn't.*

*Goodbye, old toys that I haven't touched in years.*

*Goodbye, everything.*

It was late when Rahil came into her room. Her voice was a hurried whisper.

"Are you ready?"

The house was silent, except for Abdul's loud snoring, audible from two rooms away.

"No—I mean, yes—my bag is right here."

Rahil picked up the bag from the end of the bed and took Ara's hand. "Come on, we have to go before he wakes up."

The sky outside looked like a bruise, stars scattered across its surface. Pale purple moonlight barely lit the way, leaving them unable to see more than a few feet ahead.

They couldn't risk using a flashlight. If Abdul woke up, he would come after them.

Heading west, they stumbled over uneven terrain. The hemlines of their *partugs* and *firaqs* snagged on bushes and bramble at every turn, filling their clothes with stickers and thorns.

In the distance, the headlights of a truck crested a hill.

"Come on," Rahil urged. "They're waiting for us."

"Who are they?"

Reaching into her pocket, Rahil pulled out a thick wad of money. "They're friends of my cousin. Here, take this."

Ara stared at the cash in disbelief. She had never seen so much money in her life.

"What's this for?"

"I've been saving to send you to university," Rahil said, thrusting the money into Ara's hand. "But now we need it for something

else. Put it in your pocket and don't let anyone know you have it."
"Where am I going?"
Rahil ignored the question and pointed toward the truck.
"Don't show it to anyone, especially those men. Give them half of it once you get there—no more. The rest is for you. You'll need it to buy what you need."
"But where am I going?"
"Away from here."
"But where?"
"Somewhere safe. It's better if I don't know. I don't want him to come looking for you, and God knows he'll do whatever it takes to get it out of me."

They fought through the dense undergrowth until they emerged into the bright white light of the headlights.
The man in the driver's seat got out without turning off the engine.
Rahil embraced Ara tightly.
"Don't talk to these men unless you have to," she said.
"Are they like Abdul?"
"No," Rahil replied. "But that doesn't mean you can trust them. Do you understand what I'm saying?"
Ara nodded, fighting back tears.
"I think so."
"You have to leave now. You will always be my daughter. You will always have my heart."
Rahil kissed Ara one last time.

Unable to hold back her tears, Ara cried, "Mama, I don't want to leave you!"

"You have to," Rahil said, her own tears flowing freely now. "Go—now—I love you."

"No, I don't want to leave! It's okay—I'll let him do whatever he wants to me—just let me stay with you!"

Her daughter's desperate pleas were worse than anything Abdul could have done.

"I'm sorry, baby. I'm so, so sorry. I love you," Rahil said, her voice breaking. Then she turned to the men.

"Take her. Take her, before I change my mind."

And with that, she entrusted her only child—her reason to live—into the hands of men who couldn't be trusted.

"Take care of her. Take care of my baby."

The men led Ara to the back of the truck. She screamed, "Mama, no! Mama, please! I want to stay with you!"

"Don't ever forget that I love you!"

"Mama, please!"

"It's going to be okay!"

"Mama!"

"I love you!"

"Mama!"

"I love you!"

They laid Ara in the bed of the truck and draped a dirty, oil-stained tarp over her. It smelled of sawdust and paint fumes.

She couldn't see anything except for a single star shining through a small hole in the canvas. The metal bed vibrated as the truck started moving.

The sky passed so slowly overhead, it seemed to stand still.

*This is it.*

*This is what saying goodbye feels like.*

Rahil watched the truck disappear into the night, growing smaller until, at last, her entire world was gone.

She collapsed in the dead grass, weeping in the darkness, becoming formless herself.

Ara was right. She was a mother.

There is nothing more unbearable than being a childless mother.

Ara was all she had.

And now she was gone.

Rahil was nothing.

Broken, she stood and stumbled back toward the house, wading through the wake of her heartache.

# Rahil

The house was a mausoleum without her. Dark and absent of life.

Rahil slipped in through the front door, her steps light and deliberate. She went to Ara's room, longing to wrap herself in her daughter's blanket, to hold onto the faint scent of her.

But when she got there, she found Abdul waiting for her, hell burning in his eyes.

"Where is she?"

"Far away from here."

"How dare you defy me, woman!" he roared, slamming his fist on Ara's dresser, nearly breaking it to pieces.

"How dare *I* defy *you*?" Rahil screamed back, the rage erupting from deep within her. She slapped him across the face with all the strength she could muster.

"You defy nature! You defy God! You defy me! You took my daughter! I lost her because of you!"

She had never raised her voice to her husband before, let alone struck him. In this region, such defiance was enough to get a woman set on fire.

Furious at her audacity, Abdul backhanded her across the face.

But Rahil didn't fall. She didn't even reel back.

She took it on the chin like a prizefighter.

A thin trickle of blood ran from her split lip as she straightened herself. "You bastard. How could you? She was our daughter. Kill me if you want—it doesn't matter anymore. I'm already dead. But you'll never lay a finger on her again. She's safe. I've made sure of it."

She wiped the blood from her lip, her eyes blazing. She may have lost everything, but she had crowns in her eyes. Before the night was through, he would know who the motherfucking queen of this castle was.

Abdul was a man who believed in ownership—of things, of people. But Rahil was done being his. She had gone into Ara's room to find solace in her daughter's bed, but now the space reeked of his putrid odor.

"You think you own the world," she spat, her voice sharp and cutting. "But you don't own me anymore. And Ara was never yours in the first place. You're just a little man with nothing. And the worst part is, you haven't even realized it yet."

Abdul's face twisted with fury. "What's that supposed to mean?"

"It means you're going to have a hard time explaining this to our neighbors in the morning."

As dawn broke over the sky in liquid

watercolor, Rahil moved silently out the back of the house while Abdul slept.

She carried a rope in her hands.

Behind the house, she found the nearest tree and tossed the rope over a low-hanging branch.

The last thing she saw before she left this earth was the sky, purple and orange waltzing over the horizon. It was beautiful. The air smelled like citrus.

*This is my life.*
*It will end on my terms.*

She had given him everything. And still, he wanted more.

*Oh, Abdul, Abdul, why does your wife's blood call out to me from the soil?*

When they went to cut her down, they didn't find a person swinging from the branches.

It was just a body.

Just a mother.

## Poya's: Part V

It's mid-afternoon by the time the flames burn out.

Kosha sits crisscross applesauce with three charred bodies lined up in front of him, arranged in order of importance. He's stained black from head to toe. If he didn't still have his skin, he'd look just like them.

His mother is first in line—her fragile, scorched hand still reaching into the air, trying to grab him.

His father is next, and then Nader.

You look a lot thinner with all the fat and muscle rendered off your bones. If they weren't different heights, he wouldn't have been able to tell them apart.

Nader lost his arm in the blast. Kosha tried to find it, but there was nothing left to find.

Last year, Kosha went to a funeral with his mom for an old lady named Omira. He had no idea how they knew her.

"She's an old friend," his mom said. "When I was young, she was like an aunt to me.

You know the rug in our living room?"

"Yeah."

"Well, she's the one who gave it to us."

"I like that rug a lot."

"Me too—I liked her a lot."

"Would I have liked her?"

"Yeah, I think you would have."

His mom cried a lot at that funeral. That's when Kosha learned you're supposed to cover people with linen when they die.

But Kosha doesn't have any linen.

He doesn't have anything.

He also knows you're supposed to bury the dead as soon as possible so they can go to heaven. But you have to do it the right way, or else they'll be defiled.

Kosha is too small to dig three graves. He's only got it in him to dig one.

He'll dig his mother's.

His father will just have to forgive him. If heaven is real, Kosha hopes God lets him in, even if he's not in the ground.

He doesn't care if Nader gets into heaven. He doesn't even know him.

Kosha digs through the wreckage until he finds a shovel head with the shaft burnt off. Wiping the soot from the steel blade, he inspects it.

It's going to be hard to dig a grave with this thing, but it'll have to do.

His mother had a garden at the rear of the house. If she could be buried anywhere, it would be there. The earth is already tilled.

It feels strange thinking of her in the past tense.
In his head, she still *is* his mother.
He's not ready for her to be a *was*.

The hours pass slowly. The sun sets behind him, and he digs into the moonlight. His parents look like ghastly apparitions, scaring him a little.
*It's just Mom and Dad.*
*They don't look like Mom and Dad.*
*You can't be scared of your own parents.*
*But I am.*
*You can't be.*
He needs to get his mom into the grave before she springs up and grabs him.
His back aches. He hopes he's digging deep enough; he doesn't know how far you're supposed to go. Six feet is a long way down when you're four foot two.

The hole is as deep as it's going to get.
Kosha climbs out and drags his mother to her final resting place.
Even with the fat rendered off and everything burned to a crisp, she's still heavy. Bones are dense, but guilt is worse.
He's not looking for anyone to pardon him, but he still has to stop and catch his breath a few times.
Rolling her onto her side, he lets her plop down into the hole. Some dirt from the edge gives way, falling onto her face.
Panic shoots through him—he's not ready to cover her face yet. He wants to look at it a

little longer, but he's not about to crawl down there to brush it off either.

The karmic gods might bury him with her for all he knows.

Maybe he should just jump in and kick the walls until they collapse on top of him. At least then he'd get what he deserves.

At least he wouldn't be alone.

Kosha picks a single wild iris and sniffs it. It smells like an old woman's perfume on a hot day. He sets it atop the loose dirt on his mother's grave.

Whenever he brought her flowers, she'd always tell him how pretty they were.

This is what you're supposed to do at a funeral: put flowers on the grave and say something nice about the person.

But Kosha doesn't want to say anything.

Saying something also means saying goodbye.

And he's not ready to let go yet.

Maybe Nader.

But not his mother. Not his father. Not even Isah.

The red racquetball bulges in his pocket.

He takes it out, staring at it for a moment.

A few hours ago, it seemed irreplaceable.

Now it's just a worthless, meaningless object that doesn't matter anymore.

The ball never loved him.

It didn't teach him to read, make him dinner, or sew his clothes.

It didn't do anything except bounce off the wall at a funny angle and shoot out the door at the worst possible time.

He should've let it bounce out of sight.

He wishes his father—or whoever—had never brought it home.

It doesn't matter.

His father mattered.

Kosha hates the ball.

He squeezes it as hard as he can, trying to crush it, but it just bounces back perfectly into place, unaffected by his rage.

Screaming, he throws it as far as he can.

The red ball sails into the sky and disappears into the purple haze of night.

Kosha looks down at the broken blisters on his hands. The raw, wet skin stings in the crisp air.

His whole body feels like a popped blister. A wet, exposed wound.

The moon sets behind the mountaintops. Kosha is exhausted, but his father deserves to be near his mother.

He drags Kamal's corpse to the garden and lays him next to Ara's grave.

Kamal is heavier than Ara. It takes nearly an hour. Sweat runs down the side of Kosha's face, stinging the raw blisters on his hands. He wipes it off with the back of his hand, but the moisture makes his grip slip.

His father's pitch-black skin peels away, crumbling in his hands, staining them.

Kosha doesn't flinch.

Nader can stay where he is.

Once Kamal is beside Ara's grave, Kosha lays down next to his father's corpse, resting his head on the brittle remains of his chest. The blackened flesh flakes away, speckling Kosha's cheek. He doesn't care.

Reaching across Kamal's torso, he pulls his father's crumbling arms around him one last time.

Nuzzling deeper into the hollow of Kamal's chest, he tries to remember what his mom said at Omira's funeral:

It's important to remember what the person looked like—the way they smiled, the way they laughed, and all of that. The whole day is about remembering them.

Kosha closes his eyes and pictures his mother's smile. He tries to hold onto the image, but it keeps slipping away.

He thinks about his father.

He tries to remember the way Kamal looked out in the fields, the quiet pride in his movements.

He thinks about the countless times he saw his parents kiss, how he would squeeze himself between them in bed after a nightmare, his small body nestled in their warmth.

He remembers how safe it felt.

Kosha makes a mental note of it all.

And then, he cries himself to sleep.

## Kosha: Part I

Dull orange beams of morning light shine through Kosha's eyelids, waking him.
For one brief, happy moment, he's forgotten what happened yesterday.
Smiling, he opens his eyes—and everything comes rushing back.
His father's corpse is still lying next to him.
Streaks of ash coat Kosha's arms from hugging his father through the night. It's on his clothes, his face, in his nostrils.
He spits into his palms and rubs them together, trying to wash the ash off.
Then he realizes—he just spit on his father's remains.
He starts crying again.

*What do you do when your world is gone?*
*What's the use of waking up when you're the only one left?*
There's more to living than breathing, but it doesn't take much to die. He could just lay back down on his mother's grave, close his eyes, and never wake up again.

It doesn't feel right that he didn't dream about her last night.
*If you really love someone, you dream about them.*
*You should have woken up crying.*
He doesn't know who he's trying to justify himself to.
God?
His parents?
Himself?
Everyone?
It doesn't matter.
Dreaming about something doesn't make it real.
His family is dead. That's real.

*It's important to try and remember what they looked like.*
*A promise is still a promise, even when the person you made it to is dead.*
Kosha stares at his father, trying to picture his face—superimposing a rare smile over the blackened remains of his gumless mouth.
It doesn't fit.
He doesn't want to look anymore, but he forces himself to. His mother was right—
*The silverbirds will burn you up until there's nothing left.*
He doesn't need to dig her up to remember her smile.
It was always a little crooked.
She got it from Holden, but Kosha never knew that side of her.
*Maybe if I put their faces back together*

*just right, they'll come back.*

But the rest of her face is harder to reconstruct.

He focuses as hard as he can. Beads of sweat gather on his fire-burned skin and trickle down the cracks.

He wants to see her eyes. Her fat cheeks. Her thick, lovely eyebrows. The beauty mark next to her nose.

It's no use.

The harder he tries, the faster she slips away.

He tries to think about her, but that doesn't work either.

He tries to think about not thinking about her, but she's already gone.

He can't even see her Holden Caulfield smile anymore.

*If I could just see her one more time, I promise I could get it right.*

*I should have been in there with her.*

*You're a rotten son. She told you not to go outside, and you did it anyway. You disobeyed her, and now you're not dead like you're supposed to be.*

*I wonder if she noticed I was gone before she died.*

*Of course she did.*

*What was the last thing she thought?*

*I bet it was, 'I told him not to go outside.'*

*Was she mad at me?*

*I broke my promise.*

*I'm sorry.*

Sorry doesn't mean anything when the person you're apologizing to is dead.

*It's your fault.*
But it's also the silverbirds' fault.
Sometimes the only way to make amends is to blame someone else. Deflection is easy. Kids always choose the path of least resistance.
The silverbirds put his family in the ground. That's a fact.
There's no room for gray areas in the black-and-white world of a child's heart.
Revenge froths in Kosha's gut like a virus.
He clenches his fists around his heart, hardening it, making it ready for what must come next.
He might only be a kid, but there's man-sized hate inside of him.
He tightens his jaw and grits his teeth. His cavities press against one another, little rotten holes connected to the gaping black hole in his core.
His body is still covered in the ashes of his father's flesh.
Tears and snot streak down his face.
There's no one left to see him cry.

*The silverbirds.*
*It's their fault.*
*It has to be.*
*It can't be me.*
The guilt is too heavy. It's crushing him, choking him.
He has to shift the blame.

He coughs and spits, wiping the tears away.

His father's ashes streak down his cheeks like reverse mascara.

*It's their fault.*
*It has to be.*

Digging through the wreckage, Kosha uncovers a mangled wad of wrought iron that used to be his bed frame.

His mattress has a huge hole burned straight through the center. Smoke still smolders at the edges.

Getting down on all fours, he looks under the bed. His bow is right where he left it.

Other than a slightly singed bowstring, it seems to have survived the inferno.

He doesn't know what bows are made of, but he wishes humans were made of the same thing.

He draws the string back a few times to make sure it's okay. It snaps forward with a hollow twang.

Only three of his arrows survived the fire.

But it only takes one to kill a monster.

Kosha stops one last time at his mother's grave to say goodbye.

He wants to tell her that he'll avenge her death, that he'll kill the silverbird responsible for taking her away.

But he can't.

He promised her he wouldn't go there.

It doesn't matter if she's dead or not—

*A promise is a promise.*
*A promise is a big thing to make.*
He doesn't want to lie to her either, because lying is worse than breaking a promise.
So instead, he kneels down and kisses the fresh soil.
"I'm sorry—I love you."

Kamal used to say, "It doesn't matter if you're strong or not ninety-nine percent of the time. You just have to be brave when it matters."
"Help me be brave," Kosha whispers.
He doesn't even know what that means.
"Is it dark where you're at?"
"I hope it's a nice place."
"I don't want it to be dark there."
"But if it has to be dark, I hope you at least have a nightlight."
*Do they pass out nightlights in hell?*
Wherever Kamal is, if he can hear him, he already knows where Kosha is going.
He might just be a kid, but he's also a Poya, and Poyas never run.

Kosha doesn't know how to get to the Land of the Silverbirds, but he knows what his mother told him:
*It's beyond the mountains.*
Did she really say that only two days ago?
It feels like a million years. Another life. Another time. A whole other universe where nightmares never come true.
*Nobody comes back from the Land of the Silverbirds.*

*They'll burn you up with their fire until there's nothing left.*
Kosha adjusts the bow around his neck and sets off down the pathway.

Kids aren't naturally ruthless, but shit flows downhill—and so does blood.
The only way to be safe is to make sure you're at the top of the food chain.
He has to turn himself into the scarier monster.

The road winds through the poppy fields, along cliffsides too rugged to farm. Everything beyond that is wilderness.
Even the ruddiest outdoorsmen find these mountains unforgiving.
But when you're blinded by hate, the size of things doesn't matter.
The best thing Kosha has going for him is that he was born here. This is his home. The only place he's ever known.
The remains of his house have already disappeared behind the hilltops in his rearview.
He's glad it's finally out of sight.
When you're leaving home, it's easier if you don't look back. But it's even better if you can't see it at all.
The only thing worse than losing everything is staring at the hole where it used to be.
Kosha knows he'll never set foot in that place again.
And if he does, his father's body will be

long gone. Something will have come by and eaten him.
Nature doesn't let things sit still for long.
It's quick to pull the sheet over the violence of man.
In the end, we're all just fertilizer.
It's a beautiful joke—
The faster we kill each other, the quicker the cover-up.

The pale blue sky stretches on forever. He's exposed. A flock of brown birds flies overhead. Under different circumstances this would be a beautiful day, but beauty is in the eye of the beholder. In the distance he sees an old man riding atop a wooden cart. The donkey that is pulling the cart looks twice as old as the man it's carrying. The cart is gray brown and splintered from a thousand storms and fifty winters. The spokes of the wheel bitch like a tired washwoman. The old man teeters up and down with the ruts in the road. The hobbled cart limps by, he doesn't even look up to acknowledge Kosha's presence. Long ago this old man loved a girl. Maybe he had a house and something to call his own, but that's all behind him now— swept up in the dust of time— plumes in his own rearview. His sunken eyes follow the slow bend in the road. It's the only thing this man has left to look forward to.

Kosha ascends the top of the next hill. Down in the sloping valley is where his father's man Wali has their herd grazing. The dirty white sheep speckle the rocky bevel below, as a lackadaisical creek winds through the lowland floor. The water isn't fast, but it's deep enough to swallow a lamb if it gets sucked in. Wali has worked for their family since Isah was a toddler. Tales of Wali are were the stuff of legend in their home. When Kosha is was lucky, Kamal will would come to his room at bedtime and tell him a story about something amazing that Wali did that day. Kosha can still recount all of his favorites exploits of the brave and fearless Wali—

There was the time that Wali took on a pack of hungry wolves, armed with nothing but a knife, and fended off every one of them without losing a single sheep. Or when he saved a snake-bitten lamb who fell into a ravine, by climbing down into the black crag and sucking the venom out with his own mouth. Wali is an enigma to everyone who knows him— a man who can do everything, but who you know nothing about. Wali isn't even his real name. Only his father knows knew his real name—

"It's what he left behind that makes him the man he is now," Kamal once told Kosha, "Just because you've done things you're not proud of doesn't mean there's isn't still good in you."

"Even people who do really bad things?"

Kosha thought about Isah. He wondered if Kamal was thinking about Isah too. He was, but he was also thinking about Nader, and Wali, and all the other men in his country who had fallen

victim to the lies of fascists and warlords. A whole generation of men lost to anger and hatred.
"Sometimes good people do bad things."

    There's no way that Wali knows what happened to his parents. If he sees Kosha, he's going to ask him where his father is. Kosha doesn't want to be the bearer of bad news, but even more so, he doesn't want to have to talk about it all. He wants to leave it in his rearview— in the plumes of dust on the road. He's knows you're supposed to talk about what's bothering you, but he needs to keep it inside of him for now. He'll tell somebody about it someday, just not today.
    Kosha studies the lay of the land. If he passes along the high ridgeline, there's a chance he might be able to sneak past Wali undetected— it's a long shot but it's all he's got. Climbing between two giant egg-shaped boulders, Kosha scales atop the steep slate precipice. The ridgeling is only a couple feet wide and riddled with weak spots— if the soil gives way, he's going to meet a ninety-degree stone slope that dumps off the edge of a twenty-foot cliff real fast. He can hear the herd of sheep bleating below. Kosha gingerly navigates the ridge— dark soil and yellow green roots of baby grass upending with each step— he steps in the wrong place, causing a few of the rocks on the ridge to lose their grip and clack down the stone pitch loud enough to wake the dead. Hearing the echo of the falling stones, Wali looks up and sees Kosha standing frozen atop the bluff.

He's never seen Kosha out here without Kamal before. He calls out to the boy, "Kosha, is that you? Where's your dad?"

Kosha doesn't say anything, he just stands there. If Wali were closer, he'd see that there are tears in Kosha's eyes. Kosha's glad he's not closer. Even at this distance though, he can tell that something's not right, "Kosha, what's wrong?"

If Kosha has to stand here one more second he just might jump off the cliff and kill himself. Wiping the tears from his eyes, Kosha takes off running across the shaky terrain, letting the rocks and soil give way into the depths below without giving a damn.

"Where are you going? Hey, be careful, it's not safe up there!"

But Kosha's already around the bend and out of sight, hiding behind an outcropping of rocks. One of the sheep loses its footing and nearly falls in the creek. Wali lovingly runs his fingers through the creature's soft ringlets of wool, "You be careful too— something's not right."

Kosha's bow string feels tight around his neck. He rips it off and slams it on the ground in frustration. He can still hear the cries of his father's sheep in the distance, and Wali's voice calling after him. He can still turn back if he wants. He can live here in the valley Wali. But living with Wali would also mean living with the knowledge that he let the monster who murdered his family get away. The bleats of his father's sheep ring in his ears. They're deafening.

Looking ahead he can already see the burnt tips of the black mountains before him.
    You can't chicken out.
    Even if you want to turn back, you can't.
    It doesn't matter if you're strong or not ninety nine percent of the time, you just have to be brave when it matters.
    You have to be brave now.
    Poyas never run.

    Staring at the snow-capped peaks of the black mountains, Wali smiles.
    He's always liked the sight of snow.
    It's a symbol of renewal. Of redemption.
    He's just waiting for the seasons to change.
    *Things will get better once spring arrives.*
    His gaze lingers on the mountains, imploring their icy crowns to melt and bring healing water to this desolate land.
    The creek his sheep drink from is but a trickle of what's to come.
    *Come, O floods of change.*
    *Come renewal.*
    *Come respite from our present turmoil.*
    But seasons are as stubborn as sheep. They don't budge until they're ready.

    *Why is Kosha out here all alone?*
    *Where is Kamal?*
    Something's not right.
    Wali couldn't see the red in the boy's eyes. He had no idea that the soot on his face was his father's incinerated flesh.
    But somewhere in his gut, he knows things

aren't right.
    If he's honest with himself, he has an inkling of what happened.
    *I should go after him.*
    But his feet don't move.
    The only thing harder than building a legacy is living up to it.
    There comes a time in everyone's life when they stop trying to be the person they always wanted to be and settle for the person they are.
    The older you get, the closer you come to death—the more fearful you become.

    Kosha pushes his pain down as far as he can.
    It's all he has left of his parents.
    If he lets it out, they'll be gone.
    And he's not ready to be alone yet.

    *Remember how she laughed.*
    *The way she smiled.*
    *Cry harder.*
    *She deserves it.*
    *Be strong.*

    The pain makes him run faster.
    Smoke inhalation is a special kind of pain. It feels hollow and barbed in the center of your chest—sharp at first, but lingering.
    It grates your membranes and thorax like sandpaper, slowly scraping you raw.
    Kosha's lungs burn.
    But he doesn't care.
    He runs anyway.

Rocky Magaña - Silverbirds - 110

## Kamal: Part I

Kamal Bashir Poya was the second-born son, and that's pretty much how he felt every day of his childhood.

He was a foot shorter than Nader, but in their father's eyes, it might as well have been ten feet.

Kamal's shoulders never quite filled out like a real man's, whereas Nader seemed to come out of the womb with a fistful of whiskers.

Kamal was smart, though—he might have even been a genius. But no one would dare say that to his face. Such lavish veneration was reserved solely for Nader.

It makes sense in a way—when you're tall and handsome, people expect you to be successful. But when you're a know-it-all piss ant, they'll do anything to shut you up.

It's not natural for a kid to know more than an adult.

That's what they don't tell you about when Jesus was teaching in the temple as a child—it was all downhill after that. The Rabbis hated his guts. They were jealous of him. From that moment on, they were looking for a reason to kill

him.
When you're a kid, it doesn't matter if you're right or not—you're automatically wrong.
And a smartass.
Especially when you're right.
Back then, there were only two people who could tolerate Kamal—Nader and his mother. And they loved him deeply, even if they didn't understand half the stuff that came out of his mouth.

One night, after his father slapped him across the face for running his mouth, his mother reached into her purse and pulled out a simple black spiral-bound notebook. She handed it to him.
"So you can keep track of your thoughts," she said. "This way, you won't have to say them out loud all the time."
It was her loving way of saying, *People will like you better if you shut your mouth.*
It didn't work, of course. Everyone still hated him. But from that day on, he didn't go anywhere without a notebook in his hand.

One night, while looking through his telescope, Kamal spotted a star he had never seen before.
Excited, he scribbled its location in his notebook, grabbed his copy of *Norton's Star Atlas*, and flipped through the directory of celestial bodies.
The star wasn't listed anywhere.
*Did I just discover a new star?*

When it comes to billion-year-old cosmos, *new* is a relative term.
*Nothing is new in the universe.*
*It could be so old and far away that its light is just now reaching us.*
He closed the book and looked back through the lens.
*You don't have the right to name something that's a billion years old.*
Very few things have permanent names anyway.
Mom's last name used to be Nawabi before she married Dad.
Muhammad Ali used to be Cassius Clay.
Caligula's real name was Gaius.
He stared at the pale, distant fluttering light.
*History is full of places and things that have changed their names over time.*
*Turkey used to be called the Ottoman Empire.*
*You're older than any of them.*

The interesting thing about stars is that the smaller they are, the longer they last.
*You can be called whatever you want.*
*Do stars even want a name?*
*Everything wants to be called something.*
*Well, then you have to make sure it's the right name.*
*What's the right name?*
*I don't know.*

It was hot and sticky outside. The wind

swirled devils in the dust, caking the insides of Kamal's nostrils with mud boogers.

Nader usually walked Kamal home, but today he was still back at school, competing in a debate competition.

He was a shoo-in for the blue ribbon—he could've won it on looks alone.

Kamal thought the whole idea of debating was stupid.

*What's the point?*
*To be right.*

It takes a real asshole to get off on winning an argument, especially if you don't even agree with the point you're making.

It was true—Nader did get off on it.

And he *was* a little bit of an asshole.

Kamal took a shortcut through an empty lot where the Five Star Diamond Royal Garden Hotel used to stand.

Back in '22, the hotel had been state-of-the-art, complete with an in-ground swimming pool and electric elevators. But by the time a 7.3 earthquake leveled it in '57, the elevators were broken, and the swimming pool was filled with leaves.

All that remained now were massive mounds of crumbled cinder block and rebar, piled in the back corner of the lot.

Kids played pickup soccer games here, and on Sundays, the men held cockfights.

But today, the lot was empty.

Kamal kicked a glass bottle across the ground. It spun and skipped before coming to a stop in a pile of cement dust.

    Seemingly out of nowhere, a rusted white truck came speeding around the corner.
    The shocks were so loose the teenage boys in the back nearly bounced clear out.
    The truck screeched to a sliding stop.
    The bundle of young men piled out and lined up in front of Kamal like a firing squad.
    Kamal knew these boys. They used to be Nader's classmates before they quit school to work on their families' farms.
    He also knew why they were here.
    They weren't here to kick a soccer ball.
    They were here to make their cocks feel bigger.
    In a way, he felt bad for them.
    *The only reason they're doing this is because their own worthless fathers probably beat the shit out of them.*
    *And their fathers are only doing it because their lives are out of control.*
    *Shit flows downhill.*
    The strong control the weak.
    The weak control the weaker.
    The weaker take it out on themselves.
    The weakest load a gun and start shooting.

    The boy driving the truck was Abram.
    He was still pissed because Nader had beaten the shit out of him last week for tearing pages out of Kamal's notebook.
    They weren't particularly important pages, but that wasn't the point.

You don't fuck with Nader Poya's little brother.

Abram's eyes were swollen purple and black, and the bridge of his nose was crooked. It hurt to move his face when he talked.

"Where are you going, Kamal?"

Nervous energy built up in Kamal's gut.

The only way to survive situations like this is to go on the offensive right away.

"You know where I'm going."

*The strong control the weak.*

Sometimes you don't get a say in whether things are going down. All you can do is dictate the terms.

"Shouldn't you be out in the field sodomizing a goat or sucking on your father's dick?"

"The fuck did you just say?"

Adrenaline pumped through Kamal's veins, filling his body with blood.

*You are not weak.*

"I said, get the fuck out of my way."

Abram took a step toward him, the ground seeming to quake under his weight.

*Jesus Christ, this son of a bitch is huge.*

"Where's your brother?"

Kamal's right knee started to Elvis. His heart raced, endorphins flooding him like he imagined cocaine might feel—not that he knew what doing cocaine felt like.

*It's fight or flight.*

He'd read that term in a book: *Bodily Changes in Pain, Hunger, Fear, and Rage: An*

*Account of Recent Researches into the Function of Emotional Excitement.*
    The book made some good points, but some of it was bullshit. Especially the parts that rhymed.
    *Fight or flight.*
    He hated when people thought something was smart just because it rhymed.
    But here he was, rhyming like a goddamn moron.
    *Why are you thinking about fight or flight now?*
    *I don't know—it just popped into my head.*
    *Probably because it rhymed.*
    *Goddammit.*

    Their father always said, "It doesn't matter if you're strong ninety-nine percent of the time. You just have to be brave when it matters."
    That sort of motivational bullshit was almost as bad as rhyming.
    Three years ago, their father came home from work with a bloody nose and a missing tooth.
    When their mother asked what happened, he'd said, "I didn't run from the Soviets or the rebels, and I sure as hell wasn't going to run from these bastards. Poyas never run."
    He never clarified who "those bastards" were, but the point was clear.

    *Fight or flight.*
    *Stop rhyming.*
    *It doesn't matter if you're strong ninety-*

*nine percent of the time.*
*Don't be a fucking moron.*
*Poyas never run.*
Not even when you're twelve years old and staring down six teenage Neanderthals.

Just because Nader fought Kamal's battles didn't mean he couldn't take care of himself.

In fact, the opposite was true.

*Never pick on the kid brother of the toughest guy in town.*

Nobody bullies like an older brother does.

After years of getting your ass kicked by a gorilla, you turn into quite the bully trap yourself.

Abram should have known better.

*Fight or flight.*
Kamal clenched his fists.
"Poyas never run."
"What?" Abram laughed.

By the time Abram stopped laughing, Kamal had already made up his mind.

He picked up a rock and smashed it into Abram's broken nose, screaming, "Fight!"

One of the boys lunged forward to help Abram, but Kamal threw dirt in his face and gouged at his eye.

Another kid grabbed Kamal from behind, lifting him off the ground.

Kamal kicked and screamed like a wild animal.

The next thing he knew, he was on the ground with a knee pressed against his temple.

The walls of his skull pushed against his brain, ready to crack.
The other boys punched and kicked the living shit out of him.
Kamal felt his ribs crack.
Somehow, in the flurry of fists and boots, he managed to grab one of them by the leg and bite down.
"The little asshole bit me!"

The boys doubled down.
A boot landed square in Kamal's sternum, causing him to spit blood.
By the time his collarbone snapped, Kamal had already blacked out.

Nader stood on stage, dressed in his best tunic—a dark navy piece with gold embroidery. He'd gone to the barber the day before to get his hair freshly cropped for this moment.
You could tell he knew he looked good by the way his eyes smirked as he scanned the modest crowd.
His velvet baritone slipped effortlessly into the microphone. His words, half-formed and rambling, filled the courtyard.
"As it concerns the tribal population, we must be careful not to dismiss or mislabel their desire for an autonomous region as treason or the pipe dreams of poor farmers. We must remember—these men are still our brothers.
God does not see invisible borders; He only cares about the hearts of men.
If our country is to have lasting peace—"

he paused for effect, "I mean *truly* lasting peace—we cannot enter another ethnic war that will only further divide our fractured country.

We cannot be caught sleeping in our own hatred. It's time to wake up and see who our *true* enemy is."

Nader placed a hand on his chest, directly over his heart.

"Ourselves. Our greatest enemy is right here."

The crowd erupted into applause.

Nobody seemed to care, least of all the judges, that Nader hadn't once proposed a solution to the actual question: *How do we solve the issue of indigenous unrest?*

He smiled and waved at his admirers with the half-hearted grace of someone used to being adored.

As the applause ebbed, Nader spotted his best friend, Shafi, slipping through the green wrought iron gate at the far end of the courtyard.

Out of breath, Shafi pushed his way through the crowd, dirt and sweat streaking his forehead.

Shafi was a lazy son of a bitch, so if he was running, someone was either dead or close to it.

Nader leaned into the microphone.

"Shafi? What's wrong?"

By the time Nader got home, Kamal was already asleep, his body a battered patchwork of black, purple, and blue.

His left arm was bound against his chest to

keep it immobile.

Yellow drainage seeped from the wounds on his face, staining the fresh bandages.

Nader grabbed the wooden chair from Kamal's desk, careful not to let the legs scrape the floor, and placed it by his brother's bedside.

He sat down, staring at Kamal.

Kamal looked at peace—a rare and fleeting sight.

Even in his sleep, Kamal's mind usually ran a mile a minute, the wheels in his head always turning. But now, he was still.

It was like watching a snowflake melt: once gone, there would never be another moment quite like it.

Kamal's curly hair was matted to the side of his head in clumps of dried blood.

Seeing him like this filled Nader with both pride and jealousy.

When Nader woke up that morning, he'd known his purpose, who he was. He was the protector, and Kamal was the kid who was too smart for his own good.

They both had their roles.

But now?

Kamal had outgrown his "kid brother" costume, and Nader was too big to grow into anything else.

Leaning forward, Nader reached out with his King Kong-sized hand and gently brushed a clump of dried blood from Kamal's hair, as though handling a butterfly.

Kamal stirred, opening one eye.

"What are you doing?"

"Cleaning the blood out of your hair."

"Is it my blood?"

"How am I supposed to know?"

"I don't know. I guess I thought you'd be able to tell the difference."

"It's all red."

"Yeah, but one is family, and the other belongs to a fucking orangutan."

"I think an orangutan might be mad if it heard you comparing it to Abram."

"That might be the wittiest thing you've ever said."

"You're a real piece of work, you know that?"

"Why do you say that?"

"Because here you are with the shit kicked out of you, and you're still running your mouth."

"That's because I've got a free pass—you wouldn't hit a guy with broken ribs."

"I've done it before."

Kamal winced, trying to sit up.

"You wouldn't hit *me* with broken ribs."

"Don't sit up."

"I'm alright."

"Yeah, you look *real* alright."

"You should see the other guys."

"Yeah? What do they look like?"

"A lot better than me."

That small joke made Nader laugh. For a moment, he felt less useless—even if he hadn't done anything to stop it.

Kamal pointed at a lukewarm glass of water on the nightstand.

"Will you hand me that?"
"I'll get you a fresh one."
"Don't be stupid. That one's fine."
"There might be germs in it."
"Germs are the least of my worries."
"You say that because you've never had dysentery with broken ribs before."
"Have you?"
Kamal tried to sit up again.
"Don't sit up."
"Besides, you can't get amoebic dysentery from germs. Amoebas are parasites."
"Fine. There might be parasites in it."
"Just give me the goddamn glass."
"I'll get you a fresh one."
"I don't—"
But Nader was already halfway out the door, clinging to this small excuse to still matter.

Kamal stared at the ceiling, thinking about amoebas and how they could alter their shape by extending and retracting pseudopods.
*It would be nice to change your shape.*
He would've made himself a hell of a lot bigger when he fought Abram.

Nader returned with a fresh glass of water and a plate of orange slices.
"I'm not hungry."
Nader set the plate on the nightstand.
"Well, you might get hungry later."
Kamal took a small sip of water, wincing in pain, then handed it back. He was grateful, but he'd be damned if he said it out loud.

Nader set the glass down next to the plate.

"Why'd you fight those guys in the first place?"

"I didn't have a choice. It was—" Kamal stopped himself from saying *fight or flight*.

"What was I supposed to do, run away?"

"I didn't say that."

"What would you have done?"

"You're not me."

"Fine. What would you have done if you were me?"

"Not what you did."

That was a lie.

When Nader got home from school the next day, he went straight to Kamal's bedroom to drop off his homework.

He knew Kamal was the kind of weird kid who'd be waiting for it, even if it was so simple it bored him to death.

Kamal was sitting up in bed, scribbling in his notebook. But as soon as he saw Nader, he shut it and tossed it aside like it didn't matter.

"What're you working on?"

"Nothing important."

He said things like that to keep Nader from feeling stupid for not understanding.

Sometimes, it's better to lie than to hurt someone's feelings.

Nader set the homework down on the bed next to the notebook.

Kamal picked up his algebra workbook and flipped to the page the teacher had dog-eared.

"Do you believe in miracles?"

"You mean, like when God answers prayers?"

"No, not like that," Kamal said, shaking his head. "I mean miracles of science."

"What's the difference?"

"I'm not sure. But I know there's a difference."

Kamal mulled it over, fragments of thought swirling in his head like leaves in the wind. They didn't quite fit together, like puzzle pieces turned the wrong way.

"Okay, so, our planet is just one speck in the vastness of space, right? And as far as we know, Earth is the only one with life on it."

He looked up, his thoughts tumbling out faster than he could organize them.

"Think about it—if they ever found an ant on Mars—just one ant—the whole world would flip upside down. Countries would blow each other up over who owned that ant."

"Countries already blow each other up."

"You know what I mean. It'd be World War Three, and whoever won would slice the ant to pieces to dissect it or whatever."

"Yeah, probably."

"But it'd be the only other intelligent life we know of in the universe!" Kamal's voice grew louder, his ribs aching from the effort.

"Easy," Nader cautioned, "you're going to hurt yourself."

Kamal was already hurting, but it wasn't just his body—it was for that ant.

An ant that didn't even exist.

Or maybe it did.

"I guess what I'm saying is—who has the right to do that? If there's an ant on Mars, isn't that a miracle?"

"Yeah, I guess so."

"Then why do we squish ants here on Earth without even thinking twice? Why do we kill anything at all? Isn't everything that's alive a miracle?"

"Because there are billions of them."

"There are billions of us."

"Yeah, so?"

"So we don't go around killing people."

"Some people do."

"Yeah, but those people don't believe in miracles. Do you believe in miracles?"

Nader looked at Kamal like he was crazy. "Yeah, I guess so."

"No, you don't."

"Why do you say that?"

"Because it's a miracle. And you said, 'Yeah, I guess so.' Miracles are like love—if you only sort of believe in them, then you don't. It takes too much faith to go into it halfheartedly."

"You should do your homework. You've got too much time on your hands."

"I don't know why Mr. Ahmadi even bothers—I could do this shit in my sleep."

"Because you're in seventh grade, and everyone in seventh grade has to do algebra. I don't know what you're upset about—Dad already let you skip a grade."

"He should've let me skip six so I could be done with it already."

Nader laughed. "Look at the balls on this

kid. The only thing bigger than your brain is your ego."

"What's the point of school if you're not going to learn anything?"

"Because they don't give diplomas just for being smart. You have to show up and actually do the work."

"God, the whole thing is so mediocre."

Suddenly, Kamal felt so discontented that he wanted to blow his brains out.

"I'm tired," he muttered, laying back down. He wasn't tired. He was just tired of the conversation.

Laying a hand on his discarded notebook, he turned his face toward the wall.

Taking the hint, Nader stood and headed for the door.

"Right. I'll let you nap."

As soon as Nader was gone, Kamal sat up and grabbed his notebook again.

He felt bad for lying to his brother.

But not thinking about the things that mattered was giving him a headache.

And he had shit to do.

## Grandma and Grandpa Poya

Ahmed Basir Poya owned a modest textile shop.

He never sold enough to be comfortable, but he only dealt in the finest fabrics.

That ensured one thing: his wife, Maraye, was the best-dressed woman in town.

Maraye made her own dresses and *firaq partugs*. It gave her something to be proud of.

She was the sort of person who didn't care if there was food on the table as long as people envied her when she walked into a room.

She loved the feeling of imported silk and cerulean satin resting gently over her breasts and hips.

Ahmed loved it too.

The fine clothing gave them an air of importance that exceeded their means.

She was his greatest possession—his ant on Mars.

## The Epyllion of Yesal The Brave

Yesal ventured across the evaporated sea,
And tread upon the beach of ashes.
Climbing high into the beast's domain,
With his trusty sword, Rasti, at his back,
He crossed the black river
To the place where the silverbird sleeps.
He crept into the soot-stained cavern—
Blacker than the river,
Blacker than the monster's heart,
Blacker than his sweet daughter Kaameh's skin.
Only the glow of the silverbird's eye
Guided him to his destination.
His white bones wrapped around Rasti's grip,
As he raised the blade at his side,
Ready to slay the beast—or, if need be, die—
To avenge the death of Kaameh,
The lone gift his wife had left him when she died.
And now, Kaameh was gone too.

Creeping across the limestone shoal,

He found the beast resting atop a pile of bones,
　Its red eye taunting him,
　Its fiery tongue mocking.
　Charging the beast,
　He swiped his blade against its wing—
　Metal meeting impenetrable feather,
　Sparks bursting into the darkness.
　With a single flap of its wing,
　The silverbird flung Yesal across the den,
　Cracking his spine against a stalagmite.
　The beast breathed hot fire—
　Yesal rolled behind the giant spire for cover.
　The beast stalked,
　Its claws scraping across the cold stone floor,
　Calling out to him in the darkness.
　The terrible creature pounced upon the hiding rock,
　But Yesal was no longer there.
　He slipped through the shadows,
　Now at the back of the beast.

　The battle ensued—
　Rasti's blade struck against the beast,
　Sparks flying like fireworks on New Year's Day.
　The silverbird was upon him,
　Pinning him to the wet rocks with its talons,
　Its claws digging into the meat of his shoulder.
　Rearing back,

The beast prepared to consume him with fire.

But just as it did,
Yesal plunged Rasti's blade
Deep into the monster's throat.
The silverbird unleashed its blaze,
Killing both man and monster,
Engulfing their bodies in a sea of flames.

It did not bring Kaameh back.
But at least the beast was gone.

## Kosha: Part II

The sun gives way to the moon.
The firmament rises and spins on its axis.
The night glow is bright enough for Kosha to see without a flashlight, which is good because he doesn't have one.
His dad once told him why the stars twinkle, but he can't remember what he said now.
*How could you forget?*
*At the time, it didn't seem important.*
*You should have memorized every word he ever said.*
Kosha stares up at the celestial garden, wishing he knew why they twinkled.

He's tired and hungry. He hasn't eaten since yesterday.
The stars may be bright, but it's still too

dark to hunt. He has to keep moving through the night. Once day breaks, he can rest and try to find something to eat.

For now, all he can do is keep putting one foot in front of the other.

Things change once the moon sets.

The whole world disintegrates into nothingness before his eyes. It's hard to see more than a few feet ahead.

*I can't see where the path leads.*

Kosha creeps forward.

*I have to keep going.*

Seeing something terrifying in front of your face is one thing, but the uncertainty of nothingness is worse.

He inches along, glancing over the edge of the cliff. It's too dark to see the bottom, which means it's high enough to kill him.

*In the daylight, I'll find a way down. For now, I don't have a choice.*

He stops for the night. He won't sleep well out here, but then again, you never do when you're outdoors.

The heat of the early morning blasts across his face.

Kosha wipes the crusty sleep from his eyes, waiting for his vision to adjust.

His gut growls, but he has more immediate concerns.

Peering over the cliff, he sees that things aren't as dire in the daylight as they seemed last night.

It's about a hundred feet down, but it's not a straight drop. The slope is steep but gradual, slanting into a small ravine.
*If I'm careful, I can slide down on my butt without too much trouble.*
The real problem is on the other side, where an impossibly sheer rock wall stares back at him.
He'll have to find another way around.
*One problem at a time,* Ara always said. *You can't solve everything all at once.*

Sliding down the slope isn't hard work—gravity takes care of itself.
Once at the bottom, Kosha looks around, weighing his options.
A row of bushes stretches across the middle of the ravine, shrinking into the cracked clay of the riverbed.
It hasn't rained here in a long time.
But nothing stays dry forever—every river has a mouth that feeds it.
He'll have to follow it and hope it either bends around the mountains or, better yet, that the cliffs break and let him out.

*Which way to go?*
Both directions look equally daunting.
He has nothing to go on but his gut, and right now it's growling so loud he can't understand a thing it's saying.
Kosha looks at the broken earth beneath his feet.
The cracks in the sediment and the angle of

the bushes seem to show the direction the river once ran.
*Nothing cuts through stone like water.*
*If I can find the source, maybe it will break me out of here.*

Kosha walks over broken mud.
The mouth of the valley widens, and the cliffs climb higher on both sides, trapping him in the chasm.
He's screwed if this riverbed goes underground.
He doesn't want to waste a whole day backtracking, but he doesn't want to get stuck here overnight either.
The river might be dead now, but all it takes is one solid rain for a flash flood to roll over you.
He looks behind him.
It still looks just as bad as it did ten minutes ago.
*No use second-guessing. Pick a direction and stick with it.*

By midday, his worst fears are realized—he picked the wrong direction.
Kosha stares up at a three-hundred-foot stone wall, where the riverbed abruptly disappears into a tangled crag of rocks and branches.
Peering into the opening, he sees a drop of at least thirty feet to the bottom, with no footholds or ledges to climb down.
He picks up a pebble and tosses it into the

darkness, listening.

The sound of stone hitting stone rattles back at him.

There's no way to tell if the crevice drops off again further down.

If it does, there's no telling how far.

If he goes down there, there's no way back out.

His only option will be further down, further in.

*Going over a mountain is less scary than going under it.*

His mother used to say Iblis lived in the heart of the earth.

He doesn't know how far down you have to go to reach the heart, but he knows this much:

Even if Iblis isn't waiting for him, something else might be.

Until now, Kosha hasn't seriously considered the possibility that he might not make it out of this alive.

*Yesal went into the mountain and never came back.*

He was one of the bravest warriors of all time.

The shaft is about two and a half feet wide—just big enough for Kosha to wedge himself in and chimney his way down.

The first fifteen feet are easy enough.

But then the lactic acid sets in, burning through his legs as they scream for relief.

Kosha takes a deep breath, trying to calm

his nerves.
 His knee starts bouncing.
 *Calm down.*
 He presses a hand to his kneecap.
 His knee settles.

 Just before his legs give out, he reaches the bottom.
 The air is thick and wet.
 Kosha stumbles to his feet, looking down at his scraped, red palms.
 He spits into his hands and rubs them together, trying to clean the dirt out.
 His throat is parched. He hasn't had a drop of water all day.
 His stomach churns.
 Keeling over, he vomits—just bile and remnants of the last breakfast his mom made him.
 It splatters on the rocks, soaking into his shoes and pants.
 Wiping his mouth with the back of his hand, Kosha presses on.

 At one point, the grike narrows, and Kosha has to turn sideways, sucking in his gut to slide through.
 The damp karst scrapes against his belly.
 He looks back.
 The keyhole is almost gone now—a faint beam of white light casts against a bend in the wall, proof that the outside world still exists.
 Creeping forward, the roof of the cavern dips lower and lower.
 The beam of light disappears completely.

Kosha pulls Isah's matches from his pocket and lights one.

The small orange-yellow glow reveals the bleak path ahead.

Everything is damp.

If he doesn't find a way out, he's going to die down here.

*This isn't what I imagined the road to hell would look like.*

The moisture seeps through his clothes, chilling him to the bone.

He squeezes through the rocks as the ceiling presses tighter against him.

The match goes out.

The roof scrapes against his stocking cap.

He lights another match, his breathing shallow and panicked.

The flame illuminates the suffocating space.

He slaps the walls with his raw palms, feeling as if they're closing in around him.

*Am I claustrophobic?*

He never knew he was until now.

Kosha tries to go back, but it's too tight to turn around.

The match burns the tip of his finger. He drops it, and it hisses out in the water.

He can't keep this up forever.

*I have to conserve the rest.*

He lays his arrows on the ground in front of him, pushing them forward as he crawls.

It's slow, painful work.

The angle of his body tells him he's still going downhill.

Kosha strikes another match, but it doesn't light. The moisture has seeped into them.

He tries another.

This time, the flame sparks to life.

*I need to use these now, or they'll be useless.*

There's no sense of time.

In a cave, it's always night.

Kosha crawls through the darkness, lighting a match every ten meters or so, just to make sure he still knows where he's going.

But the matches run out fast.

Soon, he's down to his last one.

Peering ahead, he sees the descent leveling into a stagnant pool of saltwater that rises to his chin.

He has no choice but to go forward.

From here on out, he's in total darkness.

Arching his neck backward, he sniffs at the roof, just managing to keep his nostrils above water.

*I really wish I'd never come down here.*
*I wish I could go back the way I came.*
*I wish I'd stayed with Wali.*
*I wish I'd never gone outside in the first place.*

Inch by inch, he creeps forward.

The water rises over his lips, forcing him to move even more carefully.

He exhales; his breath bounces off the

stream and splashes back onto his face.
Running his hand along the manganese-coated walls, he feels it.
A dead end.
He's trapped.

The air down here is bad, quickly running out.
Desperately, he runs his hand under the waterline.
There—a trap below the surface.
The passage continues underwater. It's big enough for him to fit through.
But if it doesn't open up on the other side, he's going to drown.

*I don't want to die alone.*
*But then again, everyone's alone when they die.*
He doesn't know what happens after death.
*Whatever it is, you have to do it by yourself.*
Suffocation and drowning are the same in the end.
His only chance is to make the swim.
*Why put off the inevitable?*

Tears stream down his face.
"I don't want to die," he whispers.
His voice echoes in the silence.
"Help!" he screams, his chest tightening.
No one answers.
He clings to each foul breath.
"Help!"

*If you don't go now, you're going to die anyway.*
*I don't want to die.*
*It doesn't matter if you're strong ninety-nine percent of the time.*
*This one percent seems to be happening a lot these days.*
*Do it!*
*I don't want to die.*
*Do it!*

Taking one final breath, Kosha sucks all the remaining air out of the crawlspace and dives through the hole.
*I don't want to die.*
Squeezing his body past rocks and stalagmites, he kicks as hard as he can.
*I don't want to die.*
He can't see anything.
*I don't want to die.*
His chest burns. His head feels light.
*I don't want to die!*
Frantically, he claws along the wall, his body screaming for air.
*I don't want to die!*
The tunnel widens slightly, but he's still underwater.
*I don't want to die!*
He pushes upward, searching for air, but the roof presses against his back.
*I don't want to die!*
His lungs give out, the pressure unbearable.

*God, save me! I don't want to die!*
Everything is blacker than black.

Maybe this is how it is when you die.
Things just get darker and darker until you're gone.
*I'm going to die.*
Water floods his lungs.
He thought maybe he'd hear his mom's voice, guiding him.
But there's no voice.
No light.
Just water and darkness.
Both fill him.

He isn't thinking anymore.
He isn't feeling.
Everything shuts down.
And then suddenly, it's over.
Like nothing happened at all.

*Death is only monumental for the living.*
*The dead don't even realize it when it happens.*

The cold current of the underground river carries Kosha's body, letting it drift to wherever his final resting place will be.
He thought he'd at least see a white light or something.
*Something more than this.*
*This can't be the end.*
*This isn't eternity.*

He was supposed to be in paradise.
He was supposed to see his mother again.

*This is nothingness.*

*This can't be how it ends.*
*This isn't fair.*
He deserves better than this.

...
He was promised so much more.

Kosha wakes up face down on a flowstone shore at the edge of a massive subterranean lake.

A silver strand of moonlight filters through a small opening in the cavern's dome ceiling, reflecting off the black water.

Rolling onto his side, he coughs, forcing the remaining water from his lungs.

He wipes the snot and spit from his face.

Looking out over the still water, he sees his arrows floating in the middle of the lake.

For a moment, he sits there, catching his breath.

Then he swims back out to retrieve them.

This cavern looks like the kind of place where Yesal fought the silverbird.

He half expects to find their bones down here.

He's done with the underground.

Other than not dying with his family, coming down here was the dumbest thing he's ever done.

Scrambling ashore, Kosha crawls up a calcium slope and finds a six-foot-wide false floor.

The cavern wall runs along one side, but on the other, there's a sheer drop that descends into god knows what.

Massive stone pillars rise out of the darkness, disappearing into the ceiling.

Hugging the sweaty blue-brown wall, Kosha inches deeper into the cave.

It's too dark to see anything, so he tests the ground with each step to ensure it's still there before putting his weight down.

After about a hundred yards, the flowstone bench disappears entirely.

Dropping to all fours, Kosha stretches his arm into the black void, desperately searching for the other side.

His fingertips barely reach it.

The ledge is there—for now.

But he has no idea how sturdy it is, or how far it continues.

The moonlight dies behind him.

Acid churns in his gut, burning through his stomach lining.

*I don't want to die.*

He rears back and lunges forward, leaping into the darkness, unsure if his feet will ever touch the ground again.

He lands safely, gripping a handhold in the wall to steady himself.

Feeling around with the toe of his shoe, he assesses the ledge.

It's pretty much the same here as it was on the other side.

Inching forward, he continues into the darkness.

Kosha is used to the dark by now, but the silence is something else entirely.

When there's nothing to hear, everything sounds terrible.

The drip of water pierces like a switchblade.

The scurry of a single bug becomes a stampede.

*The devil's magic works best when you do the heavy lifting for him.*

*Give up.*
*You're never going to find your way out.*
*You're going to die down here.*
*The worms will crawl into your eyes and eat your brain.*

Even if he gets out, nothing has changed.

*You're alone.*

Kosha holds up his hand in front of his face.

He can't see it.

This is a new kind of loneliness.

It doesn't just feel like he's lost everyone he's ever loved—it feels like he's losing himself.

Like the universe is steadily erasing him.

He's afraid he won't recognize what comes out on the other side.

Somewhere along the way, he scratched his knee.
The blood seeps through his pant leg.
Just another wet thing in a wet place.

Hours later, Kosha is still hugging the wall, muttering to himself.
*A whale doesn't know what an apple tree looks like.*
*So?*
*So, if you've never seen it, is it still real?*
*Of course it's real.*
*Not to the whale it isn't.*
*You're going crazy.*
*No, I'm not.*
*Yes, you are.*

*What about blind people?*
*What about them?*
*They can't see anything, but that doesn't mean things aren't real to them.*
*Yeah, but whales don't eat apples.*
*What about colors?*
*What about them?*
*Do colors matter to blind people?*
*Probably.*
*Why?*
*Because blind people still want their clothes to match.*

*A single speck of orange light appears in the distance.*
At first, Kosha thinks it's a silverbird's

eye.
But the light grows larger with each step.
It's the morning sun.
The yellow-amber glow spills across the cavern floor, so bright it feels like a flashlight in his face.
Shielding his eyes, he sprints for the exit, afraid the mirage will disappear before he reaches it.

All that stands between him and freedom is a ten-foot pitch.
*Be careful. You're almost there.*
Double-checking each handhold, he begins to climb.
*Don't fall and crack your head open now.*
Slowly, he ascends out of the darkness.
*You're so close.*
The warm sunlight splashes against his face.
He's out of the cave.

## Ara: Part V

Ara fell asleep sometime after the moon set. Hours passed in what felt like a second, then a jolt from the road yanked her awake. Sunlight stabbed through a hole in the tarp, turning the space into an oven. Her sweat-sticky hair clung to her face. She wanted to peel the tarp back, let fresh air rush over her, but fear kept her still. They'd covered her for a reason.

She poked a finger through the hole. Cool morning air curled around her skin. The sky was a clear, pitiless blue. The air carried that acrid mix of old garbage and burning tires. They must be near the capital. She thought of the news footage from yesterday—Molotovs arcing through the air, bursting against police shields. That was before Abdul. Before she saw the president's smile.

A streetlight slicked in black ash flickered past overhead. Another followed. Then another. Then they multiplied until they marched in a never-ending parade. And then something truly spectacular—a building. Eight stories of ice-gray glass reflecting the sky.

The whole city hit her at once—a sensory flood. Honking horns. Growling mufflers. Police whistles. Shouting voices spilling from open windows. Street vendors haggling over prices. It was too much, too fast.

Abdul used to talk about the capital like it was Mecca. *They have everything you could ever want.* But he never let her or Rahil go with him. *It's no place for women.*

What he actually meant was: it was no place to bring your wife. Especially when you spent eighty percent of your time at bacha bazi parties.

The truck veered into an alley, the walls tight as a clenched fist. Lines of laundry flapped overhead. Then, a hard stop.

*Are we here?*

*Wherever here is.*

*Maybe it's just a pit stop.*

Her stomach knotted. Her neck ached. She wanted to stretch. *Am I allowed to sit up yet?*

The two men circled to the back, yanking the tarp away. They stared at her. She stared back, waiting.

"She's beautiful," one muttered.

"Can't blame the old bastard," the other said.

The first one turned to her. "Are you hungry?"

She nodded. He fished an apricot from his pocket and handed it to her. The moment she bit into it, she realized how empty her stomach was.

"Do you know who we are?" the second

man asked.

She nodded.

"Do you know our names?"

She shook her head.

"We know your aunt gave you money."

"She's not my aunt. She's my mother." Ara's voice was firm. "And I'm not supposed to give it to you until we get there."

"This is close enough."

Ara glanced around. This wasn't the kind of place her mother would have sent her. "Where are we?"

The second man yanked her bag from her arms.

"Give it back!" she shouted.

He ignored her, unzipping the bag, upending its contents—clothes, books, everything tumbling into the truck bed. His face twisted with frustration. "Where is it?"

The first man yanked down the tailgate, grabbed Ara by the ankles, and dragged her into the mud. She thrashed, kicked, fought.

"Help!" she screamed. "Help!"

"Shut up!" The man clamped a hand over her mouth, fingers digging into her cheek. His other hand plunged into her pocket. Empty.

*Don't just go with it!*

She bit down, hard. He yelped, jerking his hand back.

He shoved his hand into her other pocket.

*Not this time!*

She wriggled, twisted, fought—but he was too strong. His fingers brushed too close to things that felt like Abdul all over again.

Then he yanked his hand free, clutching the wad of money.

"I got it."

"Only half of that is yours!" Ara's voice cracked.

"Not anymore."

"That wasn't the deal!"

"Deals change."

At the end of the alley, a back door banged open. A middle-aged woman with coal-black eyes popped her head out, squinting at the commotion.

When she saw the men grabbing Ara, she took off at a full sprint, moving like a locomotive gathering steam.

"Hey—stop it, you sons of bitches!"

The two men jumped back in their truck and sped off.

"Give me my money back!" Ara shrieked after them.

But her voice was swallowed in the roar of the engine.

Her bag. Her books. Everything was still in that truck.

She lay in the garbage-soaked mud, the filth mixing with her tears, running down her face like mascara.

She'd never get to read *As I Lay Dying* now.

*As I lay dying.*

The words seemed laughably prophetic.

By the time the woman reached her, she was panting hard.

She was uniquely beautiful—not the kind

of beauty you could name, but the kind that made you pause.

She had the same wrinkles as any other woman her age, but they didn't make her look old.

She looked like a Persian princess wearing an old woman's mask.

Extending a hand, she helped Ara to her feet.

"You okay, sweetheart?"

"No." Ara's voice cracked. "They took my money. And all my stuff."

The woman's face darkened. She brushed away the translucent gray tears pooling on Ara's rose-cold cheek.

"Savages."

"Where am I?"

"You're in the capital. Where were you trying to go?"

Ara's lips quivered. "I—I don't know."

The woman rubbed her back, a feeble attempt at comfort. "Don't worry. You're safe now."

But Ara didn't feel safe.

She didn't know what to do.

The woman hesitated, glancing around the alley.

"Where do you live?"

As soon as she said it, she could see the answer in Ara's eyes.

Nowhere.

"Okay," the woman said, shifting gears. "Here's what we're going to do. Let's get you inside. We'll figure out the rest from there. How

does that sound?"
Ara had no choice.
She nodded.

Ara sat at the kitchen table, cradling a cup of chai. A soft wool *patu* was wrapped around her shoulders.
The woman busied herself over the *bukhari*.
"Have you eaten?"
"I had a bite of an apricot."
"That's not breakfast."
A plate clattered in front of her—sweet *roat* and scrambled eggs.
"Eat."
Ara tore off a piece of bread and nibbled at it like a mouse.
"My name is Fahima."
"I'm Ara."
Fahima smiled. "Nice to meet you, Ara."
She studied the frail girl, choosing her next words carefully, like the wrong one might shatter her into dust.
"When I asked where you live, it seemed like you didn't want to answer. That's fine. But tell me this—can you go back there?"
Ara lowered her head and took another bite.
Fahima reached across the table, resting a hand on hers.
"A simple yes or no will do. Then we won't have to talk about it anymore."
Ara swallowed hard.
"No."

Fahima nodded. "Okay."
"Do you have anywhere to go?"
Ara shook her head.
"Are you scared?"
She nodded.
"Is someone trying to hurt you?"
Ara hesitated.
Fahima rephrased. "Did someone already hurt you?"
Ara's eyes flicked over the room.
There were masculine items scattered throughout—a pulwar sword mounted on the wall, a *buzkashi* helmet and a pair of riding boots near the back door.
"Where's your husband?"
Fahima's voice grew heavy.
"He passed away two years ago."
Ara exhaled a quiet sigh of relief.
Fahima sipped her tea. "I know it's silly, keeping his things around. But it makes the house feel… less empty."
She looked at the skeletal girl before her.
She had a decision to make.
She wasn't sure if she was ready to make it.
But that's life.
Nobody asks if you're ready.
Things just happen. And you figure it out as you go.

Fahima tapped her teacup, thinking.
Ara stared back.
It was like looking into a mirror at a younger version of herself.

She didn't know this girl.
But she could tell she was trouble.
And she was alone.
Fahima had carved out some semblance of happiness in the silence of this house.
She wasn't sure if she wanted to inject life into it again.
Or if the house could bear it.

*How do you resuscitate a body that has already begun to decay?*
*Can half-rotten veins sustain the pressure of fresh blood?*
*Could the formaldehyde-soaked guts handle the swelling of new life?*
*Or would everything burst?*
*What would this Frankenstein family even look like?*
Some things aren't worth the risk.
Then again, some things aren't really your choice.

Fahima had lost her husband.
It nearly killed her.
She couldn't handle losing anyone else.
She could only bear the weight of losing one more.
If she lost this kid, it would be over.
She put down her teacup.
"You're going to stay with me."

That's it. She said it.
No going back now.

Ara smiled and took another bite of eggs.
Fahima smiled back.
The decision felt a little less terrifying.

"If you're going to live here," Fahima said, "I think we ought to know a little about each other. Don't you think?"
Ara, mouth full, nodded.
"What do you like to do?"
Fate has its ways, even if we don't understand them.
Sometimes you get kicked out of the back of a truck, mugged, and tossed in the mud—just so you'll end up exactly where you're supposed to be.
Ara didn't know it yet.
But this was the best place she could have crash-landed.
She wiped her mouth with the back of her hand.
"I like to read."
Fahima slapped the table so hard the next bite of eggs fell right off Ara's spoon.
"Well, you're in the right place then," she grinned.
"Because I just happen to own a bookstore."

## Ara: Part VI

The house was dark and full of cobwebs. Whole rooms were left untouched and stowed away like memories that are too painful to think about and too precious to throw away. Fahima's husband was a social anthropologist who was named after the thirteenth century mystic and poet Rumi. His greatest achievement was meeting James George Frazier at Cambridge in 1941. Rumi was twenty years older than Fahima, but he didn't die of old age— free thinkers never do. Other than dust and books, the house was filled with all the other clutter you would expect an anthropologist to own— skulls, tapestries, mosaics, etc. Fahima showed Ara to her new room. It was mostly used for storage up to this point. There was a steel shield with an English lion emblazoned across the front sitting in the corner. It was no doubt a souvenir from Rumi's time at Cambridge. It was solid and heavy, and oddly comforting to look at. Fahima cleared out all of the boxes and other oddities.

"You can leave the shield if you want."
Fahima smiled, "Good because I don't

think I could lift the damn thing if I tried."

When it was all said and done, the room was empty, save for the shield, a bed, and an empty bookshelf. Fahima exhaled and took a look around, "Don't worry, we'll fill it up in no time. If there's anything else you need, we'll buy it when we go out later."

"I don't have any money."

"Yeah, I was thinking about that— I'm pretty swamped at the shop— what do you say you work for me after school and on the weekends? I mean you would really be helping me out."

Ara smiled, "Yeah, that sounds good."

Fahima looked around the room, taking it all in, "Okay, I'll leave you to get settled then."

*Get settled with what? I don't have anything.*

*It's just something you say.*

Fahima started for the door, "I'm leaving for the bookstore in a bit, you're more than welcome to come with me if you want, but I understand if you're tired."

"No— I'll go with you," replied Ara a little too eagerly.

"Sounds good. How about we leave in thirty minutes? Does that work for you?"

"Sure."

"I'll leave you to it then."

"Wait—"

"Yes?"

Ara felt ashamed, "I don't have anything to wear."

"Don't worry, I have something you can

borrow for now, and then we'll go shopping this afternoon."
"I don't want a handout."
She didn't know why she said this— she regretted it the second it came out.
*Why did you say that?*
*Why can't you just let someone do something nice for you?*
*Why must you ruin everything by saying something mean?*
*Nobody does anything for free.*
*You're an ungrateful little beast.*
"I'm sorry, I shouldn't have said that."
"It's okay, I understand."
"What I meant to say is thank you for everything, but I'm going to work very hard to earn all of this— I promise."
The ludicrousness of it all made Fahima laugh, "I'm sure you will— you're a proud woman— it's okay, I am too. It used to drive my husband crazy— hell sometimes I made him mad on purpose— nothing feels worse than indifference."
Ara could think of a few things that felt worse than indifference. A little indifference and she wouldn't be here. She would be back home in her bed— surrounded by her things— with her mother.

Ara stood in the center of her new room— Fahima's oversized firaq-partug hung off her skin and bones frame in baggy heaps like a parachute. She took in the emptiness of it all.
*This is a new start.*

*You can be anyone you want to be here.*
*I want to be back home.*
*Home is gone. This is as close to home as you're going to get.*
*Be grateful.*
*It doesn't feel even close to home.*
*It never will.*
*It has to.*
*It won't.*
*It must.*
*I miss mom— we could go back.*
*We can never go back.*
*I don't want a new life.*
*Nobody asked you what you want— you get what you get, and you don't complain.*
*I miss mom.*
*Mom is gone.*
*Try and be grateful.*
*Fahima doesn't seem so bad.*
*Everybody puts on a good face in the beginning.*
*What would mom say if she saw you acting this way?*
*Mom is gone.*

## Kosha: Part III

Kosha stumbles along the cliffside.
The ridge rises gradually, but his head pounds like someone has their foot on it.
Waves of black overtake him. His knees buckle.
He's never fainted before, but he knows this is what it feels like.

At the top of the hill, the landscape shifts—lush flatland spreads before him, a sea of crimson poppies carpeting the green earth.
Bright red slashes through his blurry vision, snapping him back to life.
*Do colors matter to the blind?*
Who cares.
They matter to *him*.

He descends a small slope, the flowers brushing against his legs. The petals are so soft.
He could just lie down here and never get up again.
He didn't want to die in that cave—dark and wet and suffocating.
But here, among the flowers?

Here, it doesn't seem like such a bad idea.

He kneels, running his fingers over the odorless velvet petals.
*I'll just rest for a second. Catch my breath. But I won't go to sleep.*
*I can't sleep.*
The ground is warm.
His head drifts down.
*I'm only resting for a moment.*
*I can't stop.*
He closes his eyes.
*I have to get up.*
His eyes flutter open for a moment, then shut again.
He's *so* tired.

*I can't stop.*
*If I stop now, I won't start again.*

He dreams of his mother.
She's sitting in a beautiful garden, surrounded by unfathomable colors—hues and shades he's never seen before.
Sunlight trickles through the branches, catching in the white marble fountain, sparkling like golden champagne.
Three bronze cherubs stand at the fountain's edge, blowing victory horns.
White daisies and chrysanthemums line the walkway in perfect circles.
In the distance, a fifty-foot waterfall kicks clouds of mist into the air, birthing floating rainbows.

*This is what heaven looks like.*
*There* is *something after all.*
*It all makes sense now, if* this *is where good men go when they die.*
*That was never our home.*
*This is home.*

Ara sits peacefully on an ivory bench by the fountain.

Kosha runs to her.

"Mama!"

Panic grips her face when she sees him.

"Why are you here?"

He tries to climb into her lap, but she moves aside, stopping him.

"I want to be with you."

"No!" Her hands fly to her mouth as she chokes back tears. "You're not supposed to be here yet!"

Kosha doesn't understand.

Why would he have to leave?

*Everything is so wonderful.*

"It's not safe for you here," she pleads.

"I don't want to go. I want to stay with you."

She grabs his shoulders, shaking him violently.

"You have to wake up right now! Kosha! Kosha!"

His head snaps back and forth.

"Kosha, wake up! You're in terrible danger!"

No sooner do the words leave her lips than a shadow looms at the top of the waterfall.
A massive pair of wings spreads against the rainbow mist.
The light refracts off the creature's chrome feathers.
Kosha screams.
"Mama, watch out!"
The silverbird descends.
"Mama!"

The beast breathes fire.
All of paradise erupts in flames.
The rainbow mist boils into colorless steam.
"Mama!"
The silverbird's wings engulf Ara.
Its demonic red eye locks onto Kosha, measuring him.
It speaks.
*Come for me, boy, if you dare. But you can't save her. She's already gone.*
Ara's muffled voice calls from beneath the monster's grip.
"Kosha, wake up!"

The silverbird bares its dagger-like teeth and lets out an earth-shattering roar.
"You're not safe!" Ara implores.

In the real world, something flutters against Kosha's cheeks.

"Wake up!"

His eyes snap open.
He shoots upright, panting.
The wind moves through the poppies.

Then, he hears it.
A low, grumbling roar.
The same one from his dream.
But this time, it's real.
And it's *here*.

Hunched low, the unseen animal circles through the stems of the giant red flowers.
Boys and silverbirds aren't the only hungry beasts in the wild.

Kosha slowly pulls himself to one knee, drawing his bow.
His arms are weak. His fingers tremble.
He can barely pull the string back.
*You have to be brave—this matters now more than ever.*
That's how survival works.
The deeper you go, the more it matters.

A flicker of movement in the flowers.
Something long. Slender.
White fur. Dark spots.
The growling nears.
The moment will come.
He has to be ready.
His elbow wobbles under the tension of the bowstring.

*Hold steady.*
*This matters right now.*
Everything is silent.
*Maybe it's gone.*
The string cuts into the flesh of his fingers.
*Maybe it's gone.*
It's *not* gone.
It's *never* gone.

A rush of movement behind him.
The beast bears down.
Kosha spins, just in time to see the full-grown snow leopard lunging from the poppies, claws out, mouth wide.
There's no time to fire.

Falling back, more out of instinct than skill, Kosha thrusts the tip of his arrow forward.
The leopard sails overhead.
A claw rakes across his shoulder, tearing through flesh.

The beast lands.
It pivots, ready to charge again.
Then, it falters.
Blood spurts from its ribcage.

Kosha looks down at the broken arrow shaft in his hand.
Then back at the leopard.
The animal stares at him.
Red stains its perfect white coat.
It collapses, breathing shallowly.

Kosha has just done a terrible thing.

His father always said, *Never kill a leopard.*
"But what if they're attacking the sheep?"
"Even if they eat all the sheep."
"Why?"
"Because they are the ghosts and keepers of these mountains. The hidden gods who hate to be around men. Life is about rules, Kosha. Things you do and things you don't do. And when you mix them up, bad things happen."

Blood fills the leopard's lungs. Its breath comes in short, shallow gasps.
Kosha looks into its glassy, wet eyes.
There's nothing dangerous about this leopard anymore.
It's alone and scared like everyone else—ashamed of what it's done, of what it had to do, of what life pushed it to.
We're all ashamed of ourselves in the end.
Nobody lives a life they're proud of. Not really.
Kosha kneels, stroking its bristly white fur, soothing it as best he knows how.
"I'm sorry."
The leopard turns its gaze toward the cliffs. It lets out a weak, pitiful whimper—a final moment of longing, of similarity, a reminder that we're all in the same boat.
Then, it closes its eyes.
And it's gone.

Kosha rolls the animal onto its side, taking in the damage he's done.

Its ribcage is soaked straight through.

Whether bright red or coal black, death is just as terrible, no matter what color it comes in.

He never should have woken up.

He should have stayed in the garden with his mother—silverbird or not.

*Maybe that's what heaven is.*

*Maybe it's whatever you're thinking about when you die, and then it just goes on forever.*

No, that can't be right.

Nobody thinks of the same thing. If that were true, everyone would be alone.

And *Mama* wouldn't really be there with him—it would only be a dream.

If that's what heaven is, then she's still in their house.

Still burning.

That *can't* be it.

There has to be more.

More than anger. More than pain. More than burning.

*If heaven and hell are only in your head, then what else is there?*

*Nothing.*

But if there's nothing, then at least there's no fear.

*Fear is a construct of this life.*

Constructs need structure to exist.

There is no structure to nothingness.

Starvation drives people to brutal things.
He was hungry a day ago.
He doesn't even know what to call what he is now.
Fresh meat is less likely to carry parasites.

He presses his fingers into the hole in the fur, pushing the arrowhead deeper to get a grip.
Tearing the skin open, blood and water ooze down his wrist.
Working his fingers under the hide, he jerks it apart from the bone and muscle.
With both hands, he peels back the raw flesh.
The naked pink meat of the ribcage gleams under the sun.

It's slow, bloody work.
In time, he yanks the fur over the hindquarter, his fingers slipping between strands of tendon and muscle.
Tearing a strip of meat from along the spine, he bites into it.
It tastes like copper.
He pulls another chunk from the thigh.
Sinew dangles from the edge.
He sinks his teeth in, blood running down his chin, staining his shirt.
It's disgusting.
But he can feel his strength returning.

By the time he's full, the body is unrecognizable.

Wiping his face on the hem of his shirt, he looks down at the brown stains of dried and fresh blood.
Some of it's his.
Some of it's the leopard's.
It doesn't make a difference.
Blood is blood.

He nears the cliffs.
Below him, a small shaded vale stretches out.
The grass is sparse.
A single wild apple tree grows near the base of the rocks.
It's not big, but it's old enough to bear fruit.

His stomach twists.
*If I knew this was here, I wouldn't have eaten the leopard.*
It was *kill or be killed*, but it didn't have to be *eat or be eaten*.
He *chose* that.

As he moves down the slope, he notices a small dugout where loose rocks meet the tree's roots.
Bending down, he peers inside.
A wet black nose pokes out.
A pitiful cry follows.

It's the leopard's den.

A single fuzzy head wobbles through the

opening.
    The first of four baby snow leopards stumbles forward, its fur matted and dirty.
    The others follow close behind, tripping over themselves.
    Their eyes are barely open.
    They whimper, waiting for food.
    Waiting for a mother who isn't coming.

    *Kosha's fault.*

    There's nothing he could've done differently.
    She attacked him.
    There was no way he could have known.

    *It's not my fault.*

    *It's not the leopard's fault either. She was just trying to feed her cubs.*
    *She would have killed me.*
    *I didn't have a choice.*

    *I had to.*

    Sometimes, *what you have to do* outweighs *what's right.*
    But that still doesn't make it right.

    *You could've let her kill you.*
    Then she'd still be alive.
    And so would her cubs.

    *Is my life worth more than five leopards?*

His mother would have said yes.
The leopard clearly thought no.
Kosha isn't sure.

These cubs are going to starve.
It would be better to put them out of their misery now.

*It's better than starving.*
*Better than being eaten alive.*
*It's the right thing to do.*

He picks up the first cub, stroking its head.
"I don't want to hurt you."
It claws at his sleeve, its soft baby fluff squishing between his fingers.
It leans down and licks the dried blood from his hand.

Its mother's blood.

Kosha flinches, gently pushing the cub's face away.
Bracing himself for what must come next.
"I'll make it quick. I promise."
His hand tightens around the kitten's tiny muzzle.

*I don't want to do this.*
The cub squirms.
*You have to.*
It lets out a muffled squeal.
*But I don't want to.*
He cradles it against his chest, squeezing it

still.

*Tears well in his eyes.*

*It doesn't matter if you're strong ninety-nine percent of the time.*

*But I've already been strong today.*

This isn't quick.
He *promised* to make it quick.
But this is taking forever.
And it *hurts*.
The cub's pale blue eyes stare up at him—its mother's eyes.
Ara always said *he* had her eyes.

*What would Mama say if she saw this?*
*She'd say, Kosha, put that leopard down this second. Don't you dare harm that poor thing! It's already lost its mother today. Isn't that enough?*

*Isn't that enough?*

He swallows the lump in his throat.
He's going to be sick.
He *can't* puke up the cubs' mother in front of them.
No matter what, he has to *keep her in*.

*Losing your mother is enough.*
*You don't have to die too.*

He lets go.
The cub bites him hard.
Wincing, he drops it.
It lands awkwardly on its side before scrambling back into the safety of the den.

There's nothing else he can do.
The longer he stands here, the worse he feels.
And the harder it is to keep their mother *inside him.*
He hoped that sparing the cubs would stop their mother from churning in his gut.
But as the adrenaline wears off, the realization of what he *almost* did starts to settle in—
*I'm the only person they've ever known besides their mother.*
*And I killed her.*

*I am their silverbird.*

Everyone is someone else's silverbird in one way or another.
Even if it's just our passive silence to the tragedies around us.
We all have a part in someone dying every day.

A few weeks ago, Kosha was sitting on the arm of his father's chair, reading the newspaper over Kamal's shoulder.
There was a story about two men caught poaching and selling snow leopard furs.

They had four pelts in their possession when the police found them.

*If you count the cubs, I've killed more leopards than those guys did.*

Kamal shook his head and sighed as he read the story.
"Goddamned savages."

*You're a goddamned savage.*

He screams into the den, trying to mean it—
"I'm sorry!"

But it's hard for a savage to mean anything.

It's the difference between *living* and *surviving*.
When you're in survival mode, every ounce of energy is focused on sustaining your own life.
There's no room for personhood in survival.
Everything inside Kosha is either dying or already dead.
Soon, he'll be numb, and none of it will matter anymore.

He looks down at the den one last time.
*I'm sorry.*

The soles of his shoes feel like they're

made of lead.
One foot in front of the other.
The earth shifts beneath him, sending small rocks somersaulting down the rust-colored cliffs.

He wants to stop.
He wants to let his legs catch their breath.
He wants to get there *already* and get whatever is coming *over with.*

He needs to silence the beast.
Not the one that took his family.
The one in his chest.
The one that's eating him alive.
The one that says—
*There is no forgiveness for you.*
*You will always be lost and never found.*

Being angry all the time doesn't do you any good.
You can't see anything with tears in your eyes.
The best warriors don't fight angry.
Anger gets you blindsided with a bullet to the brain.

*Don't stop.*
You have to keep walking.

## Kamal: Part II

Kamal and Nader walked through the market. Passing a fruit cart, Kamal swiped a pear and slipped it into his pocket. The whole thing was over in less than two seconds. Nobody saw.

Nobody except Nader.

They turned down a narrow side street, brick buildings closing in on both sides. Kamal pulled the pear from his pocket and took a bite.

"You want some?"

"You shouldn't steal."

"Suit yourself." Another bite.

"The Holy Scripture says you're not a believer at the time of stealing."

Kamal chewed, swallowed. "Sorry, I didn't know you were an *imam* now."

He held up the pear.

"What about now? Technically, I'm not stealing anymore—I'm eating. Can I be a believer and eat at the same time?"

"That's blasphemy."

"No, it's a disagreement." Kamal took another bite, then ditched the core into the gutter. "I think, therefore I am. I'm hungry, therefore I eat."

"Don't say things like that. People might hear you—"

"Who's going to hear me? The *Mullahs*?"

"Not just them. Normal people will turn you in faster than anyone else."

Kamal laughed. "What about you? You going to turn me in? They don't get more normal than you."

The moment it came out, he regretted it.

But you can't *unsay* things.

"That's not what I—"

Nader's jaw tightened. "No, you meant it. But it's okay. I get it."

A week later, they came home from school and found their father sitting at the kitchen table, drinking tea. His eyes were bloodshot from crying.

It was one of the most terrifying things they'd ever seen.

Nobody had *ever* seen their father cry.

Not even their mother.

Hell hath no fury like a woman's scorn. But life hath no fear like a father's tears.

Maraye was in the next room, crying too.

Kamal glanced through the doorway. She sat at the sewing machine, stitching together a loose-fitting black dress. Plain woven cloth.

No embroidery.

None of the *panache* she was known for.

Ahmed stared down at the knitted coaster on the table.

"Please, sit down," he said.

He tried to smile. It didn't work.

His voice was soft, his eyes still fixed on the coaster.

"I have something to tell you."

The words stuck in his throat. The silence carved out little holes in their hearts, making room for the pain that was sure to come.

Nader and Kamal cleared their own throats, bracing themselves. Ahmed's hands trembled.

He had to set his cup down before he spilled tea everywhere.

Fumbling with his reading glasses, he pulled a half-crumpled piece of paper from his pocket.

Unfolded it.

Stared at it.

Checking one last time to see if the words had changed.

Kamal felt like his chest was caving in.

Ahmed focused harder on the paper.

But the words weren't changing.

They never would.

Snatching his useless glasses off his face, he wiped his eyes on the sleeve of his shirt.

They needed to be clear for what he was about to say.

"The last few hours have been a whirlwind," he began.

His voice was steady. Forced.

"I just finished telling your mother what I'm about to tell you."

He exhaled.

"There's no easy way to say this, so I'll just come out and say it— I went to the doctor a few days ago. Had some tests done. They gave me my results this morning."

A pause.

It was only a moment, but it was one last moment before everything changed.

"They found a lump in my chest."

The word *lump* hung in the air.

Nader clung to hope. "Lump? What does that mean?"

Kamal knew better. "It means he's sick."

*No.*

Their father *couldn't* be sick. He was never sick. Never showed weakness.

But now, as they watched him, the cracks started to show.

Nader forced a laugh. "But you're going to get better, right?"

Kamal said what nobody else could.

"He's trying to tell us he's dying."

Nader's stomach lurched.

The word *dying* sat wrong in his mouth, like it wasn't supposed to be there.

Like saying it out loud would make it real.

"But Mom's sewing a black dress," Kamal continued, voice hollow. "She's getting ready."

It doesn't matter how old you are. You're never ready for your parents to die.

"No." Nader shook his head. "You're crazy. It's not true."

He turned to their father.

"Tell him it's not true."

Ahmed's face was unreadable.

"Your brother is right."

Nader felt the floor tilt beneath him.

*No. No. No.*

His father was *immortal*.

The singular constant they had built their lives upon.

If you pulled him from the base of the pyramid, everything collapsed.

"It must be a mistake."

Ahmed shook his head.

"It's not a mistake."

"But what are we supposed to do without you?"

Ahmed exhaled.

"You'll do what you've always done— You'll be strong— And you'll make me proud."

Kamal clenched his jaw.

He wanted to prove he was strong too.

That Nader wasn't the only one worth being proud of.

He fought back the tears clawing at his throat.

But it was no good.

There's no hiding *that* kind of sadness.

His father saw it.

Nader saw it too.

Ahmed started crying again.

Then they were all crying— collapsing into

each other's arms.

Ahmed crumpled beneath the weight of their touch.

Kamal fought to compose himself.

"Poyas never run."

Ahmed nodded, barely able to speak.

"I know."

"Then act like it."

Everything seemed *gray* after that.

There was a constant shadow over the house.

Maraye's extravagant dresses—the pride of her life—felt useless now.

Material things no longer mattered.

In the nearness of death, she and Ahmed finally fell in love. She found love in the way she stroked his hair at night. In how he became a kind and gentle lover for the first time in their marriage. In how they allowed themselves to be scared in front of each other.

It was in the spaces carved out by their breaking hearts that love finally had room to grow.

They had been married eighteen years.

But none of it mattered.

Not until they could count the minutes

until it ended.

## Kosha: Part IV

Within an hour, his legs are running on fumes.
He stares up at the sheer cliff before him.
Flat-faced stone.
Almost no crags.
Almost nothing to hold onto.
He wants to quit.
His legs just need to catch their breath.
*Turn back.*
*I can't.*

If he quits now, the beast will never leave him.
He must silence the one within and the one without.
Because there will be others.
More families.
More mothers.
More fathers.
More uncles that you don't care about, but still don't want to die.

*It's impossible.*
*I have to do it anyway.*
*You're not strong enough.*
*You have to be.*

The cliff is high.
He is small.
But *body be damned,* breath or no breath—
He is climbing this mountain.
Then he is finding that silverbird.
And then he is driving an arrow straight through its heart.

*I'll skin it and eat it like I did the leopard.*
*I won't feel bad about it.*
*I won't even think about whether it has babies.*

This is how you survive in the wild.
You *become* it.
Hatred blinds you, but it also makes you strong.
He must learn to walk as a blind man.
To *become* the rock and the earth.
To stalk the bush and scale the wall.
To do it all with his eyes shut and a fist in his heart.
Leopards and silverbirds do not self-loathe.
They hunt. They eat.
Then they do it all over again.

Tearing a strip of cloth from his shirt, he ties his two remaining arrows to the riser, pulling the knot tight.

Slinging the bow over his shoulder, he looks up at the stone face one last time.
*You have to climb this cliff.*
Grabbing the first rock, he pulls himself up.
His feet scramble for footing—kicking, searching in the dirt.
*Don't stop.*
He wedges his left shoe into a V-shaped crevice.
Pushes himself higher.
His arms scream.
But he keeps climbing.

His fingers search the stone, feeling for something solid.
A three-inch hole.
Good enough.
He sticks his fingers inside and pulls.

The next rock gives way.
His foot slips.
Loose soil and sand trickle down into the abyss below.
His stomach lurches.
*Don't fall.*

His fingers ache.
His shoulder feels like it's being yanked out of its socket.
Frantic, he searches for another handhold.
Finds a root.
It's slimy and covered in moss.
He tugs on it.

*If it breaks, you're a goner.*

It holds.
He shifts half his weight onto it.
Thank God.
Another ten meters.
More frantic climbing.
Then, finally— A small incline in the wall.
Enough to lean into.
Enough to rest.
*Don't get tired.*
*I'm already tired.*
*No, you're not.*
*Yes, I am.*
*Do you want to die?*
*No.*
*Then you're not.*
Maybe I should climb back down.
*There's no going back. Only falling.*
Maybe I should fall.
I could just let go.
It would be easy.
Then it would all be over.

*Stop being scared.*
*What would Mama say if she were here?*
But she's *not* here.
*Exactly. So keep going.*

His eyes want to fill with tears.
But he won't let himself cry anymore.
His knee wants to bounce from the adrenaline.
But he won't let it.

He will be *steady like the mountain.*

Taking a deep breath, he gathers every ounce of strength left in his little body—
And climbs higher.

*I should've stayed at the bottom.*

*Don't look down.*

He looks down.

The rocks below look tiny.
*I'm gonna fall and die.*

*Don't stop.*

*I have to make it.*
*I have to kill the silverbird.*

Endorphins flood his body.
He grits his teeth.
Grunting, he wills himself up the mountain.
At last, he reaches the top.
Rolling onto his back, he gasps for air.
Spits dirt.
His chest is burning.
His sides are cramping.
His back is cold against the giant slab of stone.
The bend of the bow digs into his shoulder blade.

Low and thick, the clouds swirl around him.
They slip through the valley, veiling him in mist.
Baptizing him.

Rolling onto all fours, he pushes himself up and peers out from the crown of the world.

Below, the valley is separated like a yin-yang.
Scarred earth and bleeding wounds on one side.
Lush orchards and civilization on the other.

The fog rolls in.
Following the river's path.
A snake twisting through the mountains.
Erasing everything behind it.

He can't see where the poppies grow anymore.
He can't see where the leopard died.
He can't see the cave.
The road where he saw the old man with sad eyes is gone.
Like his burnt house.
Like everything.

All that's left is *what's in front of him.*

When he wakes, the world is still wet with

dew.
    His nose drips from the cold.
    His cheeks are pink from the wind.
    He's never felt so *sore* and *empty* in his life.

    The morning sun salutes him through a broken cloudline. It's as bright as his mother's face.
    He can still hear her voice waking him up—
    "Kosha, my darling, it's time to get up."

    He used to roll over.
    Pull the covers over his face.
    Hope she'd let him sleep a little longer.
    But she never did.
    She'd brush his hair back and say—
    "Come on, it's raining today. You need to get ready for school."
    "I don't want to," he would groan.
    "You've already missed two days this week."
    "But—"
    "No buts. Get up, your breakfast is getting cold."

    *It's important to do things even when we don't want to.*

    He picks up his bow.
    Pulls his aching body to its feet— wipes the crust from his eyes, and begins the long climb down the ridgeline.

This side of the mountain is dead.
Nothing but beige desert as far as the eye can see.
Bracing himself between two boulders, he lowers down onto the plateau.
He's starving.
He needs food soon.
Crouching low—*like his father taught him*—
He slides down the loose slope.
The brush rubs against his pants.
He watches his feet, careful not to step on too many twigs.
He doesn't want to alert his prey.
Slowly, he swings his bow around front.
Pulls it over his head.

The hunt begins.

## The Squirrel

    Nearby in the valley, a squirrel is going to town on some scattered juniper berries.
    Stuffing his gullet, he scurries around, tossing leaves and twigs, making a real mess of things.
    But his efforts pay off.
    Beneath a pile of dead pine needles, he finds the *motherload*—
    A pale green walnut.
    Big as his head.

    The squirrel's eyes grow wide with wonder and lust.
    He holds it up to the sky like a pagan god.
    His whole life has led to *this* moment.
    Saliva drips from his tongue.
    The nut is perfect.
    Golden and round.
    Thick with promise.

    He should take it home.
    Save it for winter.
    Savor it slowly, piece by piece.

Because once it's gone, he'll long for just one more taste—
With every breath.
Until the day he dies.

*If only for that reason,*
*To avoid the torture of paradise lost,*
*He should wait.*

But temptation is stronger than foresight.

He turns the nut in his hands, adoring it.
It *calls* to him.
Begging to be tasted.

He can't take it any longer.

Smashing it against a rock, he cracks it open.
Peeling away its green outer shell.
Revealing the honey-colored heaven inside.

The divine aroma rises, filling his nostrils.
His tiny body shudders with ecstasy.
*This is it.*
*This is what divinity tastes like—*

FWIP.
An arrow rips through the branches.
Tears through his skull—
In one side, out the other.
Pins him to the dirt.

Kosha leaps from his position.

Runs to inspect his prize.

The squirrel's body twitches.
Blood drips into the cracked walnut shell.

The golden god of his tiny world, now splattered in brain matter.

The squirrel stretches out his arm, reaching for heaven.

Just beyond his grasp.

His black eyes widen—
*He was so close.*
So close to everything.

Then they turn dull.
Gray.
Empty.
And he's gone.

## Kosha: Part V

Kosha yanks the arrow from the squirrel's head and wipes bits of brain off on the dead grass.
A line of fire ants emerges from a hole, swarming the blood-specked ground. They gather the tiny scraps of brain matter.
Winter is coming.
Even the smallest creatures prepare.

Using the tip of his arrow, Kosha slices open the squirrel's stomach.
Peels back its flesh.
A squirrel is *a lot* easier to skin than a leopard.
You just have to be careful not to break the bones—
They're so much smaller.

Eating squirrel isn't like eating leopard.

*"You have to cook a squirrel really well before you eat it,"*
His father's voice lingers in his head.

*"They have worms and prions."*

*"What's a prion?"*
*"A type of protein that mutates in your brain and kills you if you eat it."*
*"That's why you never eat the brain of a squirrel—that's where the prions are the worst. If you eat squirrel, you have to burn it to a crisp first."*

Autumn brush makes for great kindling.
There's plenty of it here.
But he has no matches.
He lost Isah's book back in the cave.

*He'll have to make fire another way.*

He saw Wali use a bow drill once.
Thinks he remembers how it's done.

Walking to a nearby tree, he snaps off a juvenile branch, about as thick as his index finger.
Sits down.
Takes off his shoe.
Pulls out a shoelace and strings it into a bow.

He searches until he finds a large strip of dry bark and straight, hard stick. Using the flat side of a stone, he shaves the end of the stick into a sharp point.
Notches a V-shaped groove into the bark.

He gathers beard lichen and twigs, forming a bird's nest.
Places it beside him.

Using the stone as a socket, he sets the stick in the bowstring and begins sawing back and forth.

His arms were tired before he started.
Now, it feels like they might fall off.

It's *hard* work.
But he *can't* stop.

It hurts.
The heat from the friction grows.

*You can't stop.*
*But it hurts.*

The ember smokes to life.

Kosha carefully lifts it into the center of the bird's nest.
Blows on it.
Gently.
Coaxing the flame into being.

It flickers.
Catches.
Grows.

He adds twigs, one by one.
The smoke stings his eyes.

*He's tired of the smoke.*
But he keeps going.

    Breaking dead branches over his knee, he builds a small pyre over the flame.

    He finds a long, straight stick and snaps off the tip to make it sharp.
    Shoves it down the squirrel's throat.
    Rests it over the fire.

*Squirrels look strange with no fur.*

    Fat and grease drip off the meat.
    Sizzle in the flames.
    It smells like they smelled.

*Don't think about it.*

    Forty-five minutes pass.
    The squirrel is charred black.
    The prions were probably dead fifteen minutes ago.
    But he wants to be sure.

    He doesn't like looking at it.
    He closes his eyes.
    Eats as fast as he can.

    When it's done, he tosses the bones into the fire.
    Kicks dirt over the embers.
    Puts it out.

It's not safe to leave it burning this close to the border.

He needs to put earth under his feet while he still has strength in his legs.

## Ara: Part VII

The scent of moldy pages struck Ara the moment she stepped inside.
The sheer *multitude* of books filled her with a strange kind of wanderlust.
Fahima, standing in the middle of it all like a proud queen, gestured at the shelves.
"What do you think?"

The place was packed floor to ceiling.
In the back, piles and boxes of forgotten titles sat collecting dust—books that had never lived up to their authors' aspirations or their publishers' investments.

"It's fantastic."

Ara sat crisscross applesauce in the center of the store, surrounded by stacks of paperbacks like a fairy circle.
She had read most of the titles.
The ones she *hadn't* were garbage spy novels with names like—
*A Dangerous Agenda*
*The Agenda Game*

*Spy Danger*
*The Spies' Agenda*
*A Dangerous Spy*
*Game of Spies*
*The Agenda of Spies*

And so forth—
Always the same plot.

A disavowed protagonist, framed by his own government in a plot to sell nukes to the Russians.

Then there were the romance novels.

Pulp-paperbacks that played out like muscle-bound, popcorn versions of *Pride and Prejudice*— books about a brooding boy from the wrong side of the tracks who falls madly in love with the minister's daughter. But no matter how hard he tries, her father will never approve— books with titles like—

*A Stable Boy's Promise*
*Hot Arctic*
*Passion For Rent*
*Boyfriend or Boytoy?*
*Passion's Game*
*A Game of Love*
*Lovers' Passion*
*A Game of Passion*
Etc.

Beneath the stacks, one book stood out. A spine red-orange like *faded blood*.

It wasn't thick, but it wasn't *Fahrenheit 451* either.

Something about that *color* pulled her in.

She lifted the book.
Its cover was curled and torn at the top, showing brittle yellow-brown pages underneath.
The image on the front was of a boy wearing a red cap backwards, with a matching scarf, carrying a brown leather suitcase. A beautiful blonde woman in a blue waistcoat stood behind him, lighting a cigarette.

*Where is he going?*
*Where has he been?*
*He looks young.*
*Why is he carrying a suitcase?*

A neon sign hung behind the woman— partially blocked by the boy's head.
Something about Rosemary... a club, maybe?
Beneath it, grainy images of women.
Prostitutes? Strippers?
She couldn't tell.

Bold black letters stretched across the bottom:
"This unusual book may shock you, will make you laugh, and may break your heart— but you will never forget it."
All the words were in black, except for the words—*This unusual book* and *You will never forget it*. Bothof them were in the same faded blood red as the spine.
Fahima's voice appeared behind her.

"Have you read that one?"
Ara jumped.
"No."
"You should—it's good. Go ahead, take it."
Ara wanted it.
More than she wanted the clothes on her back.
More than the roof over her head.
She was a reader.
But pride is a tricky thing.
It's hard to accept the kindness of strangers when you're doing everything you can just to keep your chin up.
"No, it's okay. Thank you, though."
"Don't be silly," Fahima waved her off. "That bookshelf in your room isn't going to fill itself. Besides, it's a really popular book in America. I'm sure we have another copy lying around here somewhere."
That last part was a lie.
There were no other copies.
"Don't say no," Fahima added.
"When you refuse a gift, you're stealing someone else's blessing."
Ara hesitated.
Then, at last, she relented—setting the book aside.
She didn't know it yet.
But this book—
*This book was her favorite.*

Ara lay in bed with the dim yellow light of the lamp tilted toward her. She held the book in her hands, staring at the cover. The boy was looking away from her. She touched his face. The pages were stiff, as if they hadn't been turned in years. Cracking the cover open, she began to read.

 Holden was the first boy Ara ever fell in love with—not because he was a whiny, angst-ridden little bastard, but because they were both lost. Sure, he pissed and moaned a lot, but at his core, he was just a kid who wanted to be seen. He wasn't wise, but he was real in a fake sort of way.

 Holden, when you think everything is phony, it only exposes you for the faker you are.

 She never found what she was looking for in him, but she found something in herself through him, and that was almost the same thing. Before him, she felt like *The Old Man and the Sea,* talking to herself, gripping the line as it slowly cut through her hands. But with Holden, she was at ease—even if nothing was easy.

 She stood behind the shop counter, reading about how Holden didn't have the guts to go through with it with Sunny. The book said she had blonde hair, but when Ara pictured the *young as hell* girl standing half-naked in Holden's hotel room, she pictured herself.

 *If I was standing there with my clothes on the floor, would you still stop, or would you keep going for me?*

 She kept reading, infuriated at Sunny—infuriated at herself—for jacking up the price just because her elevator pimp told her to. Holden stood there, realizing now more than ever

that he was a virgin who just wanted to talk.
Holden was a virgin. Sunny wasn't.
Neither was—
*Do you still want me even though I'm not pure?*
They were both just lost kids, feeling sorry for themselves in an adult world, and there wasn't a damn thing they could do about it. When Maurice punched Holden in the gut, she *felt* it—like she was the one who got slugged.
She was Sunny.
She was Holden.
She was also the fist.
The pain was hers on all sides.

The sky was gray as the first frost of winter crept across the store windows. On days like this, you were going to freeze whether you built a fire or not. The walls of the building were just breaking the wind. If you stood close enough to the glass, you could see your breath, like you were smoking. She had never smoked before, but Holden made her want to.
*You're a bad influence on me.*
They were young and in love—too dumb to realize real rebellion was more than bitching and breaking rules.
Fahima walked into the shop, peeling off her gloves. Her hands were pink and stiff from the cold. Ara set the book down and went to fetch her a cup of tea. When she returned, she set it in front of Fahima.
She wrapped her hands around the steaming cup, breathing it in. "Mmm—thank

you."

"They say there's going to be freezing rain later."

"Wouldn't surprise me. How's the book?"

"It's okay."

That was a lie. Or a half-truth, which was the same thing. She didn't know why she said it. Holden was rubbing off on her.

"It gets better toward the end," Fahima said.

"The part I'm on now is good."

The heat of the tea resonated through the cup. "Have we had any customers today?"

"Just an old man looking for a cookbook."

Fahima smirked. "His daughter must be getting married."

"I don't know."

"I guarantee it."

"He didn't say."

"Men only buy cookbooks when their daughters are about to get married. It's an insurance policy so their husbands don't come back demanding a refund." She laughed dryly. "The truth is, there's only one thing a man cares about, and once he stops caring about that, he doesn't care if he's married or not. Then he just wants a maid to clean up after him."

There was a time that would have made Ara blush. But Holden may have been too nervous to go through with it, while *she* wasn't.

Not anymore.

*It doesn't matter if you hate Abdul—you still did it.*

She played the conversation out in her head

as if Holden were real.

    A: *If it would have been me, you would have gone through with it.*

    H: *How do you know?*

    A: *I just do.*

    She wouldn't have minded if it had been Holden. He wouldn't have had to force her or give her money—she would have been okay with it just because it was *him*.

    She accepted him, scars and all, and she hoped there was an outside chance he would do the same.

    Thinking about this brought Abdul's hand back to her thigh. The stench of his stale, smoky breath, cauterized beneath her skin. As if she was still on his lap, his yellow fingers sliding across her belly and up her shirt.

    *Fuck him.*

    She didn't want to think about Abdul anymore.

    She tried to replace his face in her memories.

    Tried to make his scruffy cheeks young and soft.

    Tried to make his violent groping *tender and nervous.*

    Tried to make it Holden's hand between her legs.

    Holden's lips on the back of her neck.

    Her stomach hurt, like Maurice had just punched it.

    Holden would never have thrown her on the floor when he was done with her.

    He would have been sweet.

If it had been him, she would have been *happy*.
But no matter how hard she tried, she couldn't make it Holden's face in her mind.
It would always be Abdul.
And because of that, she could never be Sunny.
Even if she met Holden in real life, she'd be too nervous to let him touch her.
Even if it was what she wanted.
Every man felt like Abdul.
Where there was love, she saw hunger—she was afraid of being *devoured* again.
That's what it felt like when a man looked at her.
Like somebody was trying to *eat* her.

The silver-matte sky gave way, shedding its icy skin in mercurial flakes that pranced in the wind like moon dust. Ara wore a brand-new red scarf, one she bought to match Holden.
The frigid air chapped their cheeks—too cold to talk. Fahima and Ara pulled their jackets tight around their bodies.
The weather worsened over the next few blocks. Wind kicked up clouds of white, let them settle back down, then kicked them up again like some holy rebirth.
Visibility was nothing. The whole world turned to mush.
The traffic cops had long since retreated indoors, but it didn't matter. There wasn't a car on the road in the entire city.
They were alone.

Flickering in and out of sight like a spark from the tip of a Bic lighter.

By the time they reached the house, the walkway was already coated in an inch of ice. The frost crunched beneath their boots. The doorjamb was frozen shut. Fahima had to throw her whole body into it to bull it open.

Inside, Ara knelt in front of the bukhari, stoking the fire. Ice melted off their clothes in slow drips, soaking the rug. They stood with bloated muscles, rubbing warmth back into their hands.

"You should get out of those clothes before you catch a cold," Fahima said.

Ara unwrapped her scarf. Her ice-locked hair fell in clumps down her back. She wrapped a fresh towel around her head, wrung the permafrost from it, and went to her room to change.

Dinner was unremarkable.
A few pleasantries.
A "please pass the salt" and not much more.

Afterward, they sat in front of the fire to read. The room was painfully cold despite the flames licking their feet. Fahima picked up two books from the end table, flipping them over in her hands.

"What's wrong?"

"At a certain age, it becomes hard to be *well read* and *to read well*," she mused. "There just aren't many new books worth picking up."

Ara couldn't imagine such a thing, but Fahima had been reading three times as long.

She held the books up with a smirk. "Be careful, my dear. You just might be staring at your future."

## Ara: Part VIII

About a month later, Ara walked into the store to find Fahima frantically running around, cleaning the place like Jesus was coming to dinner. She set her books down. "What's going on?"

"He's coming."

"Who's coming?"

Fahima was so out of breath she could hardly speak. "President Al-Ghwayway."

Sweet Jesus, the messiah was coming to dinner. "What?"

"The President is coming to our shop—I... I still can't believe it."

"Wait—are you serious? Why is he coming here?"

"I don't know—his people called this morning and asked if they could use our store for a press conference. See that guy over there?"

Ara followed her gaze to a tall man in a

suit, six-three, with dark eyes and cropped hair. Even from across the room, it was obvious—ex-military. He still carried himself like a soldier, the kind that never skipped a workout.

"Yeah."

"That's the head of his security detail."

"What's he doing?"

"I'm not sure. Getting things ready, I suppose."

"What does that even mean?"

"Who cares, just *look* at him—God, he's handsome."

This was the first time since Abdul that Ara saw a man and thought he was physically attractive. He was no Holden, but Holden was different. Holden *got* her. This man was something else entirely. No boyish softness. No nervous energy. He looked immovable, like each step he took grew roots.

"They didn't say what the press conference was about?"

"No, just that he'll be here at five."

The man whose big-toothed grin got her through the worst moment of her life was coming *here*. Ara disappeared into her memory.

"Maybe he's coming to buy a cookbook."

President Parsa al-Ghwayway entered the

shop, surrounded by a gaggle of reporters. The endless strobe of camera flashes was blinding, but Al-Ghwayway didn't blink once. He was conditioned, impervious to the limelight. His frame was massive and spellbinding.

    He looked big on TV.

    In person, he was *mythical*.

    No wonder they called him *The Bull*.

    She understood now why men would kill for him. He was intoxicating.

    "Education is the most pressing issue facing our country today," he said, brandishing his iconic grin. His lips moved, but his teeth stayed perfectly still for the cameras. "If we want to lift our people out of poverty, the first step is ensuring all youth have access to quality education. The only way to build an independent and prosperous nation is to do away with the laborer mentality. We must raise our children to be teachers, doctors, and engineers—not servants. How can we expect them to do this if they don't even know how to read?"

    His eyes scanned the room.

    Looking for a *patsy*.

    Before Ara knew what was happening, he already had his arm around her.

    She wanted to die on the spot.

    *The President's arm is around me.*

Her body grew flush.

His hand was so big, it covered her shoulder down past her bicep.

Might as well have been the *hand of God.*

"This girl here is exactly what I'm talking about."

His eyes burned with self-importance. His breath smelled like mint.

She could feel the warmth of his sweat soaking through his suit jacket.

She was sweating too.

*The President sweats like everyone else.*

That was the thing about Presidents. The aura faded once you realized they weren't gods.

They couldn't save a nation on their own.

Al-Ghwayway was just a man. A man with a few good ideas and powerful friends.

Leaning down, he whispered in her ear, "What's your name, sweetheart?"

The bass of his voice vibrated through her skull.

She covered her mouth like a child.

"A—Ara."

"Standing here today, with my good friend Ara, I'm pleased to announce a new education initiative we are calling *The One in a Million Program.*"

Squeezing her shoulder, he flashed his teeth again.

"Over the next two years, our goal is to identify and educate one million of the estimated four million illiterate women and girls in this country. Education isn't just about math and science—it's about critical thinking, about equipping people with the tools to build a strong, independent society. Isn't that right, Ara?"

She whispered back, *"But I already know how to read."*

His grip tightened.

She was a bird in his palm.

"Who cares," he gritted out of the side of his grin, before turning his attention back to the cameras.

"We have been a nation at war for far too long. But now, *peace* is upon us. We must look our battle-weary faces in the mirror, wipe the blood and dust off our cheeks, and see our true reflections again.

*The war is over!*

*This is our moment of victory!*

I challenge you all—put down your guns and pick up your pencils.

We alone must choose our path.

Will we remain a feudal nation of warring tribes?

Or will we become an enlightened society,

full of educated and prosperous people?"

The *chorus of cameras* went insane. The flashes strobed so fast, it was *blinding*. The lights. The voices. The heat of his body against hers.

He was *holding her so tight.*

A sharp pain shot down her side.

But in this program, she could attend the national university.

The electricity in her veins burned brighter than the pain.

He was her savior.

She could have stayed in his arms forever.

*Just promise me you won't tell Holden.*

Fahima stood in the back, tears in her eyes. When she was ten, her father called her a whore and beat her with a wooden rod because their male neighbor had taught her to read.

*The One in a Million Program* wasn't just about literacy. It was about giving girls the power to *transcend* the preposterous, misogynistic bullshit of their society.

Politicians made empty promises all the time.

But for some reason, *she believed him.*

## Kosha: Part VI

After about a half mile of stumbling downhill, Kosha comes upon a dirt road cutting through the mountains like the dead river. Normally, he'd stay off the road this close to the border, but he's wrecked, and the thought of returning to the wilderness feels like a fate worse than death. He'd rather be blown to hell and back than climb another damn cliff.

The first hour is uneventful. Then, things get real.

In the distance, a pitch-black pillar of smoke twists into the sky.

Kosha knows what this means—
Someone's house is on fire.

He needs to get off the road. Quickly, he marches through sixty feet of brittle yellow sagebrush, climbing just far enough into the mountains to conceal himself behind a line of boulders—close enough to the road to keep it as a guide, but far enough to avoid being seen. It's slow going, but it's a mile better than being eaten by a silverbird.

The smoke draws near.

The whole thing is all too familiar.

A middle-aged woman kneels in front of her burning house, wailing—begging God for mercy. Praying for an impossible miracle. Beating her chest, she cries out in anguish,

"Take me!"

She rips at her hair in fistfuls, choking on each broken sob.

"Take me!"

But it would be too easy if we got to die with everyone we loved.

No one is that lucky.

The howl of unrestrained grief taints each cry escaping her mouth.

"Oh God, why didn't you take me too?"

Life is a lot of things, but one thing it isn't is *easy*.

If it were, it wouldn't be *life*.

The holy scriptures say that if you save one life, it's as if you have saved all of humanity.

So then what does it mean when you *lose* somebody?

Kosha creeps closer, wedges himself into a cleft of rocks, and covers the entrance with an armful of dried bracken—leaving just enough of

a hole to see out. In this position, he's safe from the preying eyes above.
    And so he waits.
    And waits.
    And waits some more.

    The woman's lamentations flood the empty sky, filling the vacant valley, drowning this country of orphans.
    *I wonder if the silverbird is still out there.*
    It all comes rushing back—
    The pain.
    The fire.
    The screaming.
    The loss.
    The guilt.

    The woman is still crying.
    She's *him*, and he's *her*, and they're each other, and they're both alone.
    It feels like she's been crying for hours.
    Kosha just wants her to stop.
    Enough already.
    It's not *her* fault.
    I can't take it anymore.

    The thesaurus is jam-packed with a bajillion words that all mean the same goddamned thing.
    It doesn't matter if she's wailing, or caterwauling, or screeching—
    It's all just crying.
    She's a bajillion words worth of sadness.
    Kosha's a bajillion words worth of

remembering.
    He wants to comfort her, but he doesn't know how.
    He wants to cry with her, but he won't let himself.
    Please stop.
    Please, somebody just *make her stop.*
    He doesn't even know who he's talking to—
God, maybe.
    It would be easier if she had died too.
    The less empathy you feel for someone, the easier it is to forget about them, to carry on like you don't give a damn.
    He *wants* to hate her.
    But the harder he tries to despise her, the more he just wants to *hold her hand.*

    *It's okay if you cry.*
    Please cry.
    I wish I could cry with you, but I can't.
    Please cry.
    It makes it easier if you just get it all out.
    I know because I'm holding everything in.
    Try to remember what their smiles looked like.
    It makes it easier if you can remember their faces.
    But please, just *keep crying.*

    Somewhere between guilt and exhaustion, listening to her grief, he drifts off to sleep.
    The sun falls asleep too.

## The King of The Silverbirds

The King of the Silverbirds
Lives in a castle across the shining sea,
With white halls,
White walls,
White lords,
And white ladies-in-waiting—
All who bend their knee.
But if you do not walk in his white glory,
There is no God on this earth or beyond to save you from his fallen seraphim.
Come and have dinner with me, he says, a seduction curled in his smile.
He seems a just king, but his reach is long—
If you refuse him, he will not forget.
He will remember,
To the third and fourth generation.
He laughs as his enemies choke,
Raises his glass to the widows' wails.
Until there is no one left to put in the cold ground—
Only ashes in the wind,
Smoke in the sky,

And an empty space where a people once stood.

## Kosha: Part VII

The wailing woman is gone by the time Kosha wakes up. The moon is already setting. The clouds move in, swallowing the stars. It's one of those nights where your eyes never get used to the darkness—like the whole world has been scribbled over with a black crayon.

His ankle twists a few times in potholes as he makes his way down to the smoldering rubble of the woman's house. It looks just like his own did. If you've seen one charred pile of rubble, you've seen them all. This house could have been anything—a church, a mosque, a synagogue, a home, a daycare, a hospital, a school. It's all just broken bricks and rebar. The only difference is the size of the *nothing* that's left behind.

There's a well beside the ruins. A wooden bucket with a rope tied to its handle sits next to it. He lowers it into the murky water, draws it back up, and drinks deeply. The water tastes like mud and gravel, but he's so damn thirsty it doesn't matter. The cold liquid spills down his cheeks and splashes onto his shirt. Cupping more in his hands, he washes his face, arms, and the back of his neck. His bloody palms sting. Yellow pus gathers at the edges of his scabbed-over wounds. Dipping his hands back into the water, he pushes on the raw, inflamed skin, letting the infection seep out. He tears a few more strips from his ruined shirt and wraps his hands.

Then—headlights.

Far in the distance.

Coming fast.

A truck barrels toward the ruins, kicking up billows of dust, a brown fog spreading across the low night sky. The lights crest one hill, disappear, then reappear atop the next.

No one good comes rushing into the countryside in the middle of the night.

Aid workers wait until morning so their shiny new SUVs can be fully appreciated by the woebegone souls they've chosen to grace with their benevolence.

Only the military and the militants storm in at this hour.

And it doesn't matter which they are.

They'll ask him where his parents are. Why he's alone. If he tells the truth, they'll send him to an orphanage. If he lies, they won't believe him, and then they'll *try* to take him home—until they realize he doesn't *have* a home.

Then they'll send him to an orphanage.

His only chance is to run.

Scrambling into a nearby ditch, he slides down seat-first into the shallow ravine, ducks between the walls, and peeks over the top. The truck slows and rolls to a stop. The headlights burn in his direction. He can't make out the men

inside—just their crude silhouettes as they climb out. But he knows what that shadow is in the truck bed.
 A .50 caliber machine gun.
 His stomach twists. He still can't tell if they're military or militants.
 Not that it matters much.

 He once asked his father, *"Whose side are we on?"*
 *"We don't have a side."*
 *"Why?"*
 *"Because it's safer that way."*
 *"Why?"*
 *"Because we don't know who's going to win. So it's better if we wait until after the fact and just choose then."*
 *"After what fact?"*
 *"What?"*
 *"You said 'after the fact.' After what fact?"*
 ...
 *"The fact that even the safer of two choices still isn't safe."*
 *"So we're never really safe?"*
 *"Correct. Even when people tell you they're on your side, that doesn't mean you can trust them."*
 *"But if they're on our side—"*
 *"They can still be dangerous."*
 *"Like if they lie to you?"*
 *"Yes."*

 The men in the truck are young. The oldest is barely past twenty-one, but Kosha can tell he's

in charge by the way he cusses and bosses the others around.
"Alright, you goddamned bastards," he shouts. "Spread out and don't come back until you find him."
The other four hop out. They're all dressed like Uncle Nader was the night he came home. AK-47s slung over their shoulders. But the commander is the only one who looks like he's actually seen combat. The other four are too green, like they just shot up from the soil.
The men spread out, flashlights sweeping over the ruins. The commander steps toward the well, kneels, and dips his fingers into the patch of wet dirt left behind from Kosha's drinking.
"He's here."

*He?*
*Who's 'he'?*
*Me?*

Almost as if he can hear Kosha's thoughts, the commander shines his flashlight directly into the ditch.
Kosha ducks.
His back presses into the cold dirt wall. His breath stills.
The commander follows a trail of small footprints with his light.
They lead straight to the ditch.

*What if they're the good guys?*
*There are no good guys.*
The commander takes another step toward

the ditch.
*He can't just sit here.*
*Dad was a good guy.*
*Dad is gone.*
The moon isn't out. He has the darkness on his side.
*How do they know who I am?*
The commander's boots scrape over the dirt.
He's too close.
Kosha springs up and runs.

The flashlights whirl.
"There!"
"He's running!"
The beams chase his heels, but Kosha's legs are filled with adrenaline now. He doesn't cramp. Doesn't slow. He looks back—
The lights are getting smaller.
They aren't following him.
But he keeps running anyway.

Kosha's name rings through the darkness like a gunshot—when it hits him, the sound of his own name nearly knocks him over.
*What the—how do they know my name?*
His feet slow for half a second.
*Maybe I should go back.*
*You can't trust them.*
*But what if they're on my side?*
*Nobody's on your side—it's just you.*
*But how do they know my name?*
*It doesn't matter.*
*It matters to me.*

*It's too dangerous.*
*Maybe they can help.*
*You can't go back—they will stop you.*
...
*You can't stop.*
...
*I don't want to be alone anymore.*
...
*That doesn't matter.*
...
*It matters to me.*
...
*What matters to you doesn't matter anymore.*
...
Kosha looks back toward the man who knows his name.

The man screams again.

"*Kosha!*"

He never thought he'd hear someone say his name again.

"*Kosha!*"

It's nice to hear someone say your name, even if you don't know who they are. It means that you're not completely forgotten—that you still exist.

"*Kosha!*"

That you still matter to somebody.

"*Kosha!*"

He doesn't know why he matters to this person, but he knows he can't go back and find out. It is what it is.

The truck is still on the road. They won't leave it behind. At some point, he has to turn back. If he pushes far enough into the brush, he'll be able to lose them.

*Once you reach the hills, you can climb out of here and sneak back into the mountains.*

The commander follows Kosha's footprints until they disappear at the end of the crevice. He exhales sharply through his nose, staring into the dark wild ahead.

One of his men—green as the earth in spring—pulls a crooked cigarette from his fatigues and lights it. "Where did he go?"

The commander snatches the cigarette from the man's mouth, takes a deep drag, and exhales into the night.

*"Into the mountains."*

The soldier shifts uneasily. "Are we going after him?"

The commander stares ahead, smoke curling from his lips, eyes sharp as flint.

*"No."*

A pause.

*"He has to make his way back down to the road at some point. If he's going where I think he is—"* he flicks the cigarette to the dirt, crushing it beneath his heel.

*"—we need to get there first."*

## Ara and Kamal: Part I

Ara's world had changed at the Capital City College of Arts and Sciences. It was a place where skepticism wasn't just tolerated—it was expected. You weren't a zealot, a Bolshevik, or a bohemian—you were just you. Free thought wasn't a sin, it was the standard.

Her course list was heavy: comp 101, lit 101, algebra 101, history of the East, Eastern state philosophy, introduction to physics. Between classes, she had little time for Fahima's shop and even less for Holden. She still reread him as often as she could, but she knew him forwards and backwards now. There was no mystery left. She could predict, with absolute certainty, the way he would comb or not comb his hair, how many cigarettes he would smoke after lunch, how he would watch television with an ever-present scowl, but never bother to change the channel.

At some point, even love wears thin.

She had spent so much time shaping her life to fit within the walls of his, constricting herself into the space he could fill. But life wasn't something you could put borders around. The more she tried to hold onto him, the further behind he fell. Each time she reached back to pull him forward, her fingertips drifted further from his, until at last, they weren't even close enough to hold hands anymore.

She needed him to evolve with her, but he couldn't. He was who he was. And who he was had once been exactly what she needed him to be. But she wasn't that broken girl anymore.

A: *You drink too much.*

H: *I can't sit in a corny place like this cold sober,* he said, trying to hurt her, as if his words still had the power to do so.

A: *Why can't you just grow up?*

H: *Because I don't give a damn, except that I get bored sometimes when people tell me to act my age. Sometimes I act a lot older than I am—I really do—but people never notice it. People never notice anything.*

A: *But I'm not other people, Holden. It's me. I love you.*

Each time she put herself out there, he retreated twice as far into himself.

H: *Oh, Christ. Don't spoil it. I'm twelve, for Chrissake. I'm big for my age.*

A: *I'm leaving you, Holden.*

He didn't say anything. He just sat there, trying to feel some sort of goodbye. She walked out the door and turned off the light behind her. The sun was setting, but he couldn't see it because the curtains were drawn.

H: *That's the thing about girls, every time they do something pretty, even if they're not much to look at, or even if they're sort of stupid, you fall in love with them, and then you never know where the hell you are. Girls. Jesus Christ. They can drive you crazy. They really can.*

And then he cried big goddamned tears, because he knew he had been phony with her when she was honest with him. She deserved better than an imaginary boy stuck in the pain of the past. She may have left him, but she also took him with her wherever she went. Love isn't always enough. But that doesn't mean it can't last forever.

Ara didn't talk to another boy for six months. It wasn't just that she didn't have time for them—she didn't have space in her life. But life has a way of forcing you to make time for things you don't want, especially when you're better off alone.

One afternoon, she was standing outside the female entrance to the college, waiting for the bus, when a scrawny young man with a nervous energy about him leaned against the white cinder block wall and lit a cigarette. He wasn't ugly, but he wasn't much to look at either. A scar on his cheek pulled at the left side of his mouth, giving him a permanent half-smirk. His black slacks and white linen shirt were wrinkled. The only thing he had going for him was that he was clean-shaven—she detested beards on men. They made them look sloppy.

He looked lost inside of himself.

Ara knew what that felt like.

His hands fidgeted constantly—he couldn't

stop flicking the ash off his cigarette, even when there was no ash left. He flicked it anyway, accidentally sending the severed cherry flitting to the ground.

"*Shit,*" he muttered to no one. He pulled out a silver lighter and relit his smoke.

The air was warm. Jasmine crept through the cracks at the base of the wall. He snubbed out his cigarette and slid the butt into his shirt pocket. Then, pulling a notebook from his bag, he leaned against the wall for support and started writing.

"Hey," Ara said awkwardly.

The young man looked up and stared at her. She stared back.

Most men didn't speak to women who weren't in their family. In some places, it was lewd for a woman to speak to a man at all. Ara rarely wore a veil anymore. She preferred Western-style skirts that cut just above the knee, paired with white stockings. Her light pink button-down was neatly pressed, though she had rolled up the sleeves earlier in physics class, leaving her bare arms out in the open for everyone to see.

Nowadays, this was enough to get you locked up. Or worse yet, labeled a whore and beaten.

But things were different back then.

In those days, a woman could dress how she wanted.

"Hey," she said again.

"Hey," he answered.

She wanted to ask about the scar on his

face, but that would have been rude. He noticed her trying not to stare.

"I saw you put your cigarette butt in your pocket."

"Yeah."

"Why?"

"I always do that."

"Yeah, but why?"

He thought for a moment. He knew the real answer, but he didn't want to say it. He wanted to say whatever she wanted to hear. He looked down at the crumbling wall—at the flowers pushing their way through.

"I don't know—because the jasmine won't grow if it's buried beneath a pile of shit."

She smiled.

He had said something right.

"Don't flowers grow quite well in fertilizer?"

He liked that she called him out. "You're right. I don't know why I said that."

"Because you're trying to impress me."

He smiled. "Yeah, I am."

"So impress me then."

He looked down at the flowers. "*Jasminum officinale*. That's their binomial name. Binomial means scientific."

"I know what binomial means."

"Oh."

"You're going to have to do better than that."

"What if I told you I've seen you before?"

"That's funny. I don't remember you at

all."
"That's because I'm forgettable."
"No, you're not."
"Why? Because of the scar?"
"No, that's not what I meant."
"I'm just messing with you."
"I really didn't mean it like that."
"I know. I was just trying to throw you off balance."
"Why would you want me off balance?"
"Because you make me nervous, and it evens the playing field."
"Why do I make you nervous?"
"You sure do ask a lot of questions."
"No, I don't."
"Yeah, you do. That was your fifth question."
"Are you trying to throw me off balance again?"
"Maybe."
"Well, here's another one—why do I make you nervous?"
"That's not another one. You just repeated the last question."
"That's because you haven't answered it."
"Do I really need to? Look in the mirror, you're stunning."
She blushed—he won. She was off balance.
"Okay, I give up. Where do I know you from?"
"You don't. I've just seen you around, that's all."
"Well, where?"
"I don't know—on the street, in the coffee

shop, at the bookstore you work at."
"Are you stalking me?"
"No, I just tend to notice beautiful things."
"Oh—that's probably why I've never noticed you."
"Ouch."
"I'm joking."
"Well, you noticed the scar on my face."
"That's not fair!"
He didn't know why it was so easy to talk to her.
She didn't know why it was so easy to talk to him.
"My aunt owns the bookstore—well, adoptive aunt. I work there—sort of—never mind."
He smiled. "That makes sense." He pulled out another cigarette and lit it.
"Aren't you going to ask what I meant?"
"By what?"
"When I said adoptive aunt? Doesn't that sound weird to you?"
Why did you say that?
Do you want him to know what happened to you?
"I guess it does. Aren't you going to ask me how I got my scar?"
"No, that would be rude."
"Exactly. You don't ask me how I got my scar, and I won't ask how you got yours."
But I want you to ask me.
He felt comfortable.
She took a step toward him. "Why haven't you ever said hi to me before now?"
"Because you never saw me."

"I see you now."
"Hi."
"I'm Ara."
"Nice to meet you, I'm Kamal."

## Ara and Kamal: Part II

After that day, Ara saw him everywhere. Sometimes peering sheepishly from behind a bookshelf in the store, other times waiting for her in the stairwell outside class. They walked together—sometimes going somewhere, sometimes going nowhere at all. He thought about things nobody else thought about.

When Ahmed died, he left just enough money for one son to go to college. Nader insisted Kamal take it. Kamal hadn't been the same since. He was quieter now. Less brash. Less arrogant. As if Ahmed had taken all the words with him when he died. Every son wants to make his father proud—Kamal had nobody left to show off for. Until now.

When we're young, our minds are like the big bang—exploding with unruly ideas too wild to form coherent concepts. But with age and introspection, we suck the chaos back in, compress it down into a single articulate black hole of a thought. For Ara and Kamal, conversations weren't about winning. They were about truth.

"What is truth?"
Kamal thought for a moment. "Anything that's not fake—even if it's not real."
They never touched. Society had rules about that. Plus, Kamal was scared shitless. He wanted to, but wanting and doing were two different things. Ara liked that he wanted something he couldn't have. He knew everything else there was to know in the world, but he didn't know the softness of her cheek or what her lips tasted like. He spent endless nights longing to hold her, scheming ways to make it happen without disrespecting her. He didn't even know if he loved her yet, but he would have married her if it meant he could touch her.
Kamal saw his parents kiss on the lips exactly once—begrudgingly, for a staged anniversary photo. A week later, chemo took the last of Ahmed's hair. The kiss had been obscene. Flesh on flesh. A performance. So fake it bordered on pornographic. No one should have to demean themselves to appease a hungry crowd. It was the most dishonest thing Kamal had ever seen. He swore he'd never do that—especially not with Ara. It had to be the real deal or nothing at all.
The yellow paint on the stairwell railing flaked, revealing brown-red rust beneath. Kamal dug his fingernail into it and looked at her.
"Hey."
"Hi."
There was a slight smile in the left-hand corner of her mouth. She could feel his confidence resting on her skin like morning dew.

He pushed off the railing, and they began walking. He was different today.

"What?"

He just smiled.

"What?" she asked again.

"Nothing. It's just—you're happy to see me."

"I'm always happy to see you."

"No, you're not."

"When have I ever not wanted to see you?"

"The day you failed your physics exam."

"What makes you think I didn't want to see you?"

"I could feel it. You were in a bad mood and wanted to be alone."

"I had never failed an exam before."

"I know."

"Okay, Mr. Smarty Pants—how do you know I'm happy to see you now?"

"Because your reptilian brain controls emotions and connects to your left frontal lobe, which is also where higher thinking happens. You smiled in the upper left-hand corner of your mouth when you saw me, which means my face triggered your happiness receptors and made you think about me. Whatever you thought about—that's what made you smile."

"A simple *it was the way you smiled at me* would have sufficed."

"What were you thinking about when you saw me?"

"That I like you a lot better when you're quiet."

A week later, Kamal asked her to come over to his apartment. "Come by around midnight."
"I don't know."
"Please. There's something I want to show you."
It was an odd request. She had never been to his place before. Hell, they still hadn't even kissed—yet here she was, sneaking out at eleven o'clock at night.
She walked down the alley where Fahima had first found her. It wasn't safe for a girl to be out alone this late. If anyone saw her, they'd assume she was a *bazari aurat*. She avoided streetlights and main roads as much as possible, which only made things more dangerous. At one point, she had to run for her life from a pack of street dogs. The darkness of the city played games with her mind.
*What if you run into Abdul? Or another man like him?*
She heard his footsteps in the shadows, imagined him around every turn.
*You can't stop. You just have to keep going.*
An hour later, she stood shaking in front of Kamal's door.
*This was a bad idea.*
There was still time to ditch this whole thing and go home.
*And walk all the way back across the city alone?*
Electricity ran through her body.
*You should just leave.*

This wasn't like Holden—
*What about Abdul?*
Fuck Abdul. Kamal was different.
*You should just leave.*
She wanted to stay.
*You should just leave.*
She knocked on the door.
*You should just leave.*
The door opened.
*Leave now.*
Too late.
*Run.*
"I was afraid you weren't going to come."
*This is a bad idea.*
"I was afraid I wasn't going to make it."
"Did something happen?"
"No—yes—no—never mind."
"Wait—what? Are you okay?"
"I don't want to talk about it. Are you going to invite me in, or leave me out here on the doorstep all night?"
"Sorry—yes, please, come in."
*This is a bad idea.*

He led her up to the rooftop where a telescope waited. He was behaving strangely, fumbling over anything he touched. The night before, he spent hours trying to relocate the unnamed star he'd found as a kid, but now his hands shook too much to bring the telescope into focus. He peered one last time through the eyepiece to make sure it was there.
"Here, take a look."
She had never looked through a telescope

before. The dim, flickering, yellow-blue orb came into view. Something so far away, impossible, suddenly brought near, placed in the palm of her hand. "It's beautiful—what's it called?"

"I've checked all the star maps. It doesn't have a name."

"How is that possible? I thought all the stars had names."

"They do—at least the ones we can see."

"Then how did this one fall through the cracks?"

"I don't know—but I'm glad it did."

She could tell by the way he was looking at her that he wasn't just talking about stars anymore.

He leaned in.

She instinctively backed away, knocking the telescope over. Lunging, Kamal caught it just before it crashed into the unforgiving cement rooftop. In doing so, he accidentally touched her hand.

She didn't pull away this time.

He looked into her eyes.

She smiled out of the left side of her face.

He smiled out of the left side of his.

She wasn't thinking about Abdul, or the president, or Holden—only him.

He was terrified, but he didn't move his hand. He left it there, lingering.

Her whole body grew flushed.

Slowly, Kamal set the telescope upright.

She never wanted him to stop touching her. If he could just leave his hand on hers forever—

"You should give the star a name."
"I already have."
Taking her hand, he placed it back on the gear and refocused the lens. It had taken months for him to work up the courage to do this. She could feel his breath on the back of her neck. Lowering her head, she peered through the eyepiece again.
"Say hello to *Pulchra Ara Minor*."
"What?" She turned into him.
He slid his hands down around her hips and turned her back around. "Don't look away just yet. Stare at it a little longer. *Pulchra* means beautiful."
"I know what *Pulchra* means."
She didn't. But he was such a know-it-all that she wanted him to think he wasn't the only one in the world who knew useless things like that.
He kept her grounded.
Wrapping his arms around her waist, he continued, "I've known this star was out there my entire life, but I always refused to name it."
"Why?"
"Because if I was going to name it, it had to be the right name."
She started to say, *Are you sure my name is the right*— but he cut her off.
"Marry me."
"What?"
She felt at home in his embrace.
"You heard me. I love you."
She loved the feeling of his arms wrapped around her waist. It felt like scrambled eggs on a

Sunday morning, or a warm cup of coffee. She wanted to be his Sunny. No, she wanted to be more than that.

"I love you too."
"Then marry me."
"Okay."
"'Okay' isn't a yes."
"Yes."

He kissed the back of her neck, and it didn't feel pornographic at all. It was more than lips meeting flesh—it was truth meeting life.

Love, unshackled, set free from its cage.

She would never pull away from his touch again.

## Kosha: Part VIII

Kosha cuts through the dense vegetation of the mountains until morning. Up above, a star bearing his mother's name flickers, though he doesn't know it. He stays more or less parallel to the roadside. The mountain peaks disappear beneath a half-put-together jigsaw puzzle of thunderclouds, blocking out the chartreuse and salmon dawn. Another miserable day ahead. His stomach growls louder than the storm. It hasn't even started raining yet, and already he can see his breath in front of him. It reminds him of last winter when his mom caught him out back with a stick in his mouth, pretending to smoke.

He mock-inhaled deep frozen puffs of breath and exhaled them, trying to look like a real badass. He knew that if you wanted to look like you knew what you were doing when you smoked, you had to say the right things. His dad never smoked in front of him, but the men at the market always did, talking about one of three things—sex, politics, or God. He didn't know much about any of them except God. He knew people got easily offended on God's behalf, and when they got offended, it was usually because someone was talking about sex or politics. Politics made them angry. Sex made them laugh. Either way, they looked around to make sure no one else was listening.

He knew all the words they said and mostly how to put them together—even if he didn't understand them. Taking another drag of winter air, he said all the things he didn't understand:

*"I took her in the bedroom after her husband left and had sex with her—"* He took another drag. *"You're an offense to God."* Another drag. *"Her husband is a member of the jirga. You know those guys. They only care about the bacha bazi."* Another drag. *"You're a devil!"* Another drag. *"I don't fucking care."*

Out of all the words he didn't understand, one stood out the most.

Fucking.

Two syllables long. Starts with *fu-* like fun, or full, or fungus. Ends with *king*.

Fun. King.

The king of fun.

Fun king.

Fucking.

He smoked his fun king stick like a real fun king sonofabitch and said all the fun king words he didn't know the fun king meaning to—until his mother overheard him from around the corner, and it was all over.

Materializing like a fun king phantom, she snatched him up so fast the fun king stick fell out of his mouth and hovered in the air for a half-second like a cartoon. There's nothing pretty about the first time your mother catches you

saying *fuck*. Dragging him by the back of his shirt, she slapped the shit out of him and tossed his ass into his bedroom at goddamned light speed—*which, according to his father, is 299,792,458 meters per second.*
"*Where did you hear that word?*" she demanded.
"*I don't know.*" He had a small scratch on his lip from where the stick fell out. It burned and bled a little. "*I made it up.*"
"*No, you didn't.*"
"*Yeah, I did,*" he doubled down on the world's worst lie. "*I swear.*"
"*Don't lie to me.*"
Sometimes lying is better than the alternative. "*I'm not lying.*"
"*Yes, you are.*"
Trying in vain to squirm free from her grip, he squealed, "*You're hurting me!*"
"*If you think that hurts—*" she took her size seven-and-a-half shoe off and landed it square on his backside, "*those are the filthiest words in the world.*"
Bent over the bed, he pleaded for mercy. "*Mama, stop!*"
But his pleas fell on deaf ears.
"*Smoking will give you cancer, and you'll die.*"
"*Mama!*"
"*Is that what you want? Do you want to die?*"
Mothers have a way of making everything feel like the end of the world. She was hurting him, and he was hurting her too. She didn't want

to do it, but you can't be soft on your kids in a world like this or they'll never make it. When she was done, she hugged him tight against her chest.

"*I never want to hear you say those disgusting words again. Do you hear me?*"

Mothers are always *never* wanting to see you do things again. It's a wonder you get to do anything at all. Still, Kosha felt bad for making her angry.

Don't lie to Mama anymore.

And don't say filthy words unless you're sure you won't get caught.

Find out what fucking means, but don't let Mama know that you know.

He spent the rest of the day grounded, but that was okay—it gave him a chance to make a list of all the ways he'd heard *fuck* and *fucking* used.

WAYS TO SAY FUCK
1. You can yell *fuck* when you're angry.
2. *I want to fuck.*
3. *He fucked me.*
4. *I want to fuck her.*
5. *Fucking Jesus H. Christ.*
6. *We were fucking.*
7. *We fucked.*
8. *Don't fuck me over.*
9. *I don't give a fuck.*
10. *Buttfuck or buttfucking.*
11. *What the fuck?*
12. *Who the fuck are you?*
13. *Fuck off.*

14. *Fuck you.*
15. *Fuck me.*
16. *I give no fucks.*
17. *Fucktard.*
18. *Fucking fuck.*
19. *Fuck everything.*
20. *Fuckton.*

    Folding up the piece of paper, he hid it in an old mint tin. Once he was ungrounded, he buried it behind their house—close to where his mother is buried now. His own private treasure. Sometimes, when no one was looking, he'd dig it up and read it. Sometimes, he even added new ways he'd heard it used—

21. Clusterfuck.
22. Bumfuck.
23. Fuckflaps.
24. Fuckwad.
25. Mindfuck.

    He used to love how strong it made him feel.
    It doesn't make him feel strong anymore.
    Even though he can say it all he wants now—he could fucking yell *fuck* at the top of his fucking lungs if he fucking wanted to—but he doesn't.
    There's no fun in *fucking* if there's nobody there to catch you saying it.

    The clouds open up with the coldest damn rain he's ever felt. Muddled gray sheets of water fall thick enough to chew, turning the dusty plains into sloppy ash-muck. There's nothing you can do when winter spits like this—just pull up your collar and press on.

But something still gnaws at him, worse than hunger, worse than the storm.

How did those men back there know my name?

He really wishes his legs would just catch their breath already. His skin is pink from frostbite—fingers, toes, the exposed sliver of belly where his shirt tore. He probably has hypothermia. It wouldn't surprise him if it started snowing soon.

*Is there anywhere in the world where it's not cold right now?*

*I bet it's not cold in Egypt.*

*I bet it's warm there.*

Kamal used to tell him facts about the pyramids.

"They were built to line up with the North Star—but it was a different North Star then."

Kosha doesn't remember how we got a new North Star or where the old one went, but he does remember how it felt, sitting on his father's knee, listening to him explain things he was too young to understand. He shields his eyes with his hand and fights through the sleet and wind. His shoes are soaked through. His breath hangs in the frigid air, waiting for him to grab it and shove it back down inside himself. The water in his joints turns to ice, cracking and shattering with each step.

Hours pass, each moment feeling like his last—he takes one more step—
*This is my last step.*
He takes another step.
*I can't go any further.*
He takes one more.
*I can't—*
He goes on like this, dying and resurrecting with every step, until at last, after who knows how many hours, he suddenly looks up and finds himself standing at the border of *The Land of the Silverbirds.*
His heart sinks.
He knows he should be happy that he's finally made it, but it's not just some angry daydream or tightness in his chest anymore. It's real. Right in front of him. An actual place—soil, sky, rocks, and trees.
*You don't have to be brave 99% of the time—you just have to be brave now.*
*Poyas never run.*
His father's wisdom wills him forward.

## Kosha: Part IX

The sky is clear on this side of the border. Kosha stands at the edge of the rust-colored field, staring into the endless flatland. Everything is dry and lifeless. The rain vanishes behind him, locked away with the mountains, as the pale, infant sunlight spills over his face. The warmth is startling, a contradiction to the ice still clinging to his bones. His joints don't feel like they're breaking anymore. He's scared, but he doesn't want to be.

*They'll burn you up with their fire until there is nothing left.*

He isn't scared. He can't be.

*You have to be brave now.*

He needs to be impenetrable, just like they are.

He's terrified, but he won't let himself feel it.

*Poyas never run.*

Kneeling, he presses two fingers into the dirt. It crumbles like ash. He studies the sky—clouds breaking apart and rolling back toward the peaks. Everything is clear blue, stretching past the horizon to Musaqara. The silverbirds will be hunting soon.

He's starving, but hunger doesn't matter anymore. Nothing does. Not revenge. Not regret. Not anger, or love. The only thing that matters is doing what he came here to do.

The black earth shifts beneath his feet as he steps forward. To his right, a shallow ditch snakes through the field, carved out by years of erosion. A thin metallic pole juts out at an angle—rusted, gray-black, dull. Kosha stumbles toward it, peering into the furrow.

Three corpses lie tangled in the dirt, twisted and frozen by rigor mortis. Their skin is sun-sucked and pulled tight over their skulls, their teeth jutting out as if their lips had been carved away. They are dressed like Uncle Nader and the men in the truck. Two still clutch AK-47s in their stiff fingers.

Kosha inches closer.

Their bodies are defiled, but he can't help himself—he bends down to inspect them.

One is shorter than the others, his shoulders slighter. Younger. Kosha has never fired a gun before, but this dead boy isn't much bigger than him. Reaching down, he pries the weapon from the corpse's grip—brittle fingers snap like twigs.

This is the first time he's held a real gun.

His father hated guns so much he never even kept a wolf rifle.

The magazine is half-empty. It's lighter than he expected.

The empty sockets of the dead men stare up

at him, indifferent. At least their skin isn't burned. Something else must have killed them. There's more than one kind of monster in this wilderness.

He adjusts the butt of the gun against his shoulder. It doesn't feel right. He isn't sure if he's holding it correctly. Squinting down the barrel, he aims at the vacant distance.

*You have to be brave.*

The sun is sinking. He slides his finger over the trigger, but before he can pull it, gunfire shatters the silence—four shots, ringing from the mountains behind him.

Kosha whirls toward the sound.

Everything is still.

Then, eight more shots.

*Be brave.*

He squints into the horizon, shielding his eyes from the sun. The air ripples with heat, bending and distorting the light. His nightmare materializes before him.

The beast soars low, gliding through the windless sky, heading straight for him.

His chest tightens.

*Is this real?*

A cold sweat spreads down his back.

*I'm brave. I'm not scared. I'm brave. I have to be.*

His hands tremble so violently the gun barrel rattles in his grip. He almost squeezes off a shot by accident.

He takes a deep breath. *Calm down.*

He raises the gun back to his eye.

The silverbird is flying no higher than a

hundred feet. He always thought he'd have to sneak up on it while it was sleeping, slit its throat before it could burn him alive. He never imagined he'd have to shoot it out of the sky.
    It's an impossible shot.
    His arms are exhausted. The rifle only weighs nine pounds, but it feels like a hundred. The silverbird grows larger. Faster than he thought it would be.
    He tries to focus through the glare.
    *I want to look it in the eye.*
    He's come this far. He deserves to see it.
    He wants to say *This is for my family* and all the other things you're supposed to say at moments like this. But at this distance, he won't get the satisfaction.
    *This is for my mother and father. For Uncle Nader, who was still family even though nobody liked him. For Isah, who I never knew. For all the others who are dead because of you.*
    His arms are burning, but he doesn't fire.
    *Don't let the breath go out of your arms. Hold it just a little longer.*
    He has to wait until it's right on top of him.
    *Don't shoot yet.*
    It moves so fast, its shape distorted in the flickering waves of light.
    *Now.*
    He squeezes the trigger.
    The rifle kicks like a mule.
    A flurry of bullets scream through the air—
    One of them hits.
    But it's not enough.

The silverbird keeps coming.
He fires again. The gun clicks.
*Empty.*
Throwing the rifle to the ground, he scrambles for his bow—
The beast emerges from the waves of sunlight.
What the—
It's not the face from his nightmares.
It doesn't even have a face.
It isn't silver.
It's matte gray.
It doesn't breathe fire. It doesn't roar.
It just shoots missiles from its wings.
It isn't even alive.
What the—
The silverbird flies overhead.
It's a plane?
No.
It's a U.S. MQ-9 Reaper drone.
The realization hits like a rock to the skull.
It's all so unsatisfactory.
Kosha is speechless.
Thoughtless.
Overwhelmed.
Underwhelmed.

## Silverbird Pilots

Inside the dimly lit command center—a cluster of repurposed shipping containers—three twenty-something U.S. Air Force pilots huddle around a panel of monitors. One of them, Bailey, sits in a light-brown leather chair, guiding a drone toward a possible target.

"I don't think he can do it," one says.

The other scoffs. "Of course, he can. Bailey's the G.O.A.T."

"Bullshit. They'll see him before he gets the drop—plus, at that height, they'll be able to take him down."

Bailey toggles the controls, steady and precise. "I can do it."

"See? My dude can do anything."

"Twenty-five bucks says he can't."

"Why not double it?"

"Fine. Fifty."

"What's his ceiling?"

"Seventy-five feet."

"Make it a hundred fifty."

"Ninety."

"Ninety's too low—one hundred."

Bailey smirks. "I can do ninety."

"Fine—fifty bucks, hundred-foot ceiling."

"You sure about this?"

Bailey doesn't hesitate. "The terrain's flat to the eastern ridgeline. I'll swing through the valley—they'll never see me coming."

"Deal—fifty bucks."

"Just hurry up. The CO will be back soon."

"We're fine. McMaster called the Captain into his office—they're prepping for Washington's inquiry into the hospital situation."

"God, that whole thing was fucked."

"I bet Johnson's shitting himself right now."

"Doesn't matter. It's not our job to care about the target. We just execute the mission."

"Yeah, but it was a fucked-up mission."

"You don't know that."

"It was a hospital."

"So they say."

"What does that mean? It was *definitely* a hospital. You saw the reports."

"A hospital being used as a base of operations."

"So they say."

"There's footage of them shooting SAMs off the rooftop."

"That intel was *months* old."

"Wait—what's that? Is that the target?"

"No. Just a kid."

"What the hell's he doing out here?"

The screen flickers as the camera zooms in. The child looks straight up, right at them.

"He's looking right at us."

"Of course he is. There's a giant-ass drone

over his head."

"What's he holding?"

"Looks like a rifle."

"Probably just a stick."

"No—see, right there? That's definitely a chopper."

On the screen, the kid lifts the rifle.

He squeezes the trigger.

"Holy shit."

"The little bastard just shot you."

"He sure did."

"Better send the jarheads to check it out."

"Fuck it. He's just a kid—"

"It's protocol."

"I fucking hate those pricks. All they do is talk shit."

"Yeah, but do you really wanna be the guy who let a kid with an AK and a suicide vest waltz right up to our gates?"

But it's not even the pilot to blame. It's the man piloting the pilot. The one deciding who lives and who dies. Who matters, and whose parents are reasonable collateral damage in the quest to assassinate a high-value target.

Somewhere in a quiet office on the other side of the world, an analyst with coke-bottle glasses works out the political-military calculus of it all.

MOTHER = M
FATHER = F
8 Y/O CHILD = C
NADER POYA (TARGET) = T
M + F + C > T = NO KILL ORDER

But—

M + F - C < T = KILL ORDER

So it turns out, in the end, Kosha *is* to blame for his parents' deaths. If he'd just stayed inside, none of this would have happened. They weren't authorized to kill a kid on this mission. They needed him *out of the way.*

In the Western World of White Privilege-ocrats—

A CHILD'S LIFE > ADULT LIFE.

Why is that? Sentimentality? A way to sleep at night with the blood still on our hands?

At some point, we have to factor in other variables.

The average family in Kosha's valley has 4.6 kids.

4.6 KIDS + M + F = FAMILY / STABLE COMMUNITIES (FAM)

4.6 KIDS - M - F = NOT A FAMILY / UNSTABLE COMMUNITIES (NFAM)

NFAM = 6.6 ORPHANS

4.6 ORPHANS + LACK OF SECURITY + WARZONE = 4.6 AT-RISK YOUTH

4.6 AT-RISK YOUTH × EXTREMISM = 4.6 POSSIBLE TERRORISTS

Even if their parents *were* terrorists, taking them out means an increase of 4.6 terrorists per household.

Extremists think they're the good guys. Show me *one* orphan who believes the person who murdered their parents is a hero. But that's still just emotion.

In the end, strip it all down, and you'll

find—
    WHAT I WANT > EVERYTHING ELSE.
    At any cost. Even if it means burning the whole world to the ground.
    And why not?
    They don't look like us.
    They don't think like us.
    They don't even believe in the same things we do.

My Fellow American's

To white America, everything in the developing world looks *weird*—getting their adventure voyeurism rocks off watching people bathe in the Ganges. CNN and Anthony Bourdain made millions off it, and now that he's gone, they'll churn some new semi-adventurer into his slot to keep the global poverty-porn industry rolling.
    A group of sorority girls sit in front of their TV, watching a rerun of *Parts Unknown*.
    "Oh my God, look at them."
"My sister's friend was in the Peace Corps, and she went there—she said it smells terrible, and there's, like, dog shit and garbage everywhere."
"Gross, stop—how do they *live* like that?"
"My pastor went there on a mission trip, and he said most of them have never even heard of Jesus."
"What are they eating?"
    Sniff. A rail of coke disappears up the nostril of a nineteen-year-old bleach blonde.
    "That's disgusting."
"Shut up and pour another line, I'm starting to come down."

OUR WAY = BEST WAY
BEST WAY = ONLY WAY
OUR WAY > YOUR WAY

The show is interrupted by *BREAKING NEWS* on CNN.

Standing at the podium in the White House press room, the President stares into the camera.

"My fellow Americans, yesterday we received intel on the whereabouts of a high-profile target in the war against terror. After careful consideration of all our options, I, with the support of the Joint Chiefs of Staff, gave the go-ahead to execute a strike at 1:30 AM Eastern Standard Time via an MQ-9 Reaper drone.

Thanks to the tireless efforts of the men and women of our U.S. armed forces and intelligence agencies, I'm proud to stand before you today and announce that *Operation Firestorm* was a resounding success—

*Nader Poya*, the architect behind the 2012 Yankee Stadium bombing, and more recently, the U.S. Embassy bombing in Paris this past March, has been confirmed dead.

We got him!"

The press room erupts—reporters thrusting their hands in the air like Pentecostals on Sunday morning.

The President calls on a chubby, half-bald man from *The New York Times*.

"Yes, John."

"Mr. President, how did you obtain the intelligence regarding his whereabouts?"

"We received information from a local informant. Knowing we had a small window of opportunity, I ordered the strike without delay."

"Seems like quite the stroke of good luck—after five years of no idea where he was, he just *pops up* all of a sudden?"

"I wouldn't say we had *no* idea where he was—we just didn't have firsthand, on-the-ground confirmation until now."

"It just seems... fortuitous that an informant would call you up out of the blue."

The President's smile tightens. "First of all, it wasn't *out of the blue*—we're in constant contact with our people on the ground. Look, I know what you're fishing for, but you won't find it. To answer your actual question—*no*, we did not obtain his location through torture. There was no waterboarding, no sleep deprivation, none of those 'enhanced interrogation' tactics you people love to write about."

A moderate chuckle ripples through the room.

"Sorry to disappoint you, but Guantanamo had nothing to do with this one."

Another chuckle.

"That sort of thing may have happened in previous administrations, but not on my watch. Next question."

A tired-looking woman with thick glasses from *The Washington Post* raises her hand.

"Yes, Pamela."

"Mr. President, where was Poya when the attack occurred?"

The President doesn't wince at *attack*—

he's good at this game.

He clears his throat and reframes. "He was staying with relatives at the time of the *operation*."

"What do we know about these family members?"

"We know they had strong ties to extremist organizations. The home belonged to Nader Poya's brother, Kamal, whose own son, Isah, was spotted at a terrorist training camp in Sudan in 2015."

"Were there any other casualties?"

"Kamal Poya and his wife are confirmed dead as well."

A bald, African American man from *The San Francisco Chronicle* raises his hand.

"Yes, James."

"Mr. President, after all this time in hiding, why do you think he chose to surface now?"

"Our intelligence indicates he was injured in a recent clash with coalition forces. We believe he went to his brother's house for medical care."

"Were you able to recover his body?"

"It was a *Reaper* drone." The President chuckles. "What body?"

The press room laughs again. He's *killing* this.

This was his *moment*. His high-water mark. He's going to *enjoy* it.

"Next question. Yes, Lisa."

A twentysomething reporter from *USA Today* stands, trying to look like she belongs in a room full of people twice her age.

"Mr. President, your administration has been criticized for being weak on terror. With reelection around the corner, wouldn't you say this is *good* timing? Do you think this will silence your critics?"

The President barely conceals his smirk.

"I think it's *always* a great time to kill terrorists and those who seek to tear our republic apart."

He leans into the podium, voice swelling like a third-act monologue.

"Listen, this isn't just a great day for *me*—this is a great day for *America*. A great day for *democracy*. A great day for *little girls around the world* who want to go to school without the fear of grown men bursting into their classrooms with machine guns.

This is a great day for *everyone* who wants to live free of tyranny.

This isn't about me.

This is about every person in America standing up and saying, in one voice, that no matter what you do to us—*we will not live in fear.*

You might sucker-punch us here and there, but watch out—because we're coming back, and when we do, it's gonna be with a sledgehammer."

The room *erupts*.

Lisa isn't done. "But wouldn't you say they've hit us more in recent years than we've hit them?"

The President doesn't miss a beat. "No, I wouldn't. Not at all. If you look at the advancements we've made over the last twelve months—at some of the strongholds we've taken—I think it's clear we *are* winning this war."

"But still," she presses, "your administration *needed* this, didn't it?"

The President smiles.

"Next question."

## Kosha: Part X

The drone flies overhead like Kosha doesn't even exist. Like his pain doesn't matter. Kosha doesn't know his uncle's face is on the front page of every newspaper in the world—but even if he did, it wouldn't change anything. This was never about his uncle.

He tries to remember his mother's smile. He doesn't want to forget it.

A massive explosion erupts in the distance behind him. He turns just in time to see black smoke coil into the sky. Bailey must have found his target.

There's a crater in the mountains now—deep, charred, final. At the center of the blast radius sits what's left of a pickup truck, a few mangled body parts, and some unsorted scraps of meat. Nothing recognizable.

It was a fool's errand from the start—just creeping up on the border of The Land of the Silverbirds is enough to get you killed. But he had to try.

He was trying to save his little brother's life.

Back in Washington, the POTUS calls

another press conference to announce his new victory.
    He's up twelve points in the polls this week.

## Ara and Kamal: Part III

Ara and Kamal sat on the roof, staring at the stars—the ones in the sky and the ones in each other's eyes. They talked about almost everything. She told him about Abdul, but not Holden.
*It's rude to talk about old lovers.*
Darkness faded into morning light, and he told her how he got his scar. Things had changed between Kamal and Nader since their father died. He pulled a cigarette from his pocket and lit it.
"It started slow," he said, the smoke curling from the tip and disappearing into the peach and purple sky like a forgotten memory. "Nader had a hard time finding work after graduation—he was used to people laying down laurels wherever he went, and now he couldn't even get a foot in the door."
He took a drag, exhaling away from her. "With nothing better to do, he just sat in his room all day, listening to those religious programs on the radio." Another drag. "You know how those bastards are. They take a dummy with no future and promise him the fucking world. Tell him he'll be a boss, a leader of

men—that he's enforcing God's law."
    The moment took a hard left turn. Ara suddenly felt less like a lover and more like a therapist. The long ash at the tip of his cigarette threatened to fall. He flicked it off.
    "I mean, who wouldn't sign up for that shit?" He wasn't just explaining—he was apologizing for his brother, trying to rationalize it all in real time. "Soon he forced my mom to don the full veil, which she never did before."
    "What did you do?"
    "What could I do? He was the man of the house. It was his call."
    Kamal broke away from her, drifting somewhere restless in his mind. There was more he needed to tell her, but saying it made it real, and he wasn't sure he could stand the weight of it. It made him sad, scared, ashamed.
    Regret filled him like cement—regret that he let it get this far, that he hadn't stopped it, that he hadn't done anything *until it was too late.*
    One memory, scarred thick, festering beneath layers of infection. It took up too much space inside him. He needed to drain the wound.
    Kamal took a breath, cut into the deep pain, and let the pestilence flow out—

## Kamal: Part III

It was a Saturday afternoon during Kamal's first year at university. He had traveled home for the weekend, but as he neared the house, a thick column of black smoke rose from the backyard. His mother was waiting at the door. Through the slit in her veil, he could see she was crying.

"I'm sorry—I couldn't stop them."

"Couldn't stop who?"

Disintegrating into a puddle of sobs, she fell into his arms. "I tried—I'm sorry."

He grabbed her, harder than he meant to. "Mother, what have they done?"

But this only made her cry harder. Shoving past her, Kamal sprinted through the house and into the backyard. Sixteen men, clad in camouflage, stood around a bonfire. Kamal's books were burning. At the center of the circle stood that mouth-breathing piece of shit, Abram. And beneath the pomegranate tree their father had planted, presiding over it all, was Ishmael al-Hadafi—a prominent radio cleric, his gray beard fading into his black *pakol* in a gradient that matched his stone-colored eyes. The men fired rounds into the sky like exclamation points in his sermon.

Nader was standing beside Ishmael, a place of honor. He wasn't holding an AK-47 like the others, but he was thrusting his fist in the air, pretending to be a real revolutionary. And then Ishmael stopped speaking and placed an arm around him like they were old friends.

Ahmed never said *I love you,* but sometimes he came home with a new book for Kamal, and it almost felt like the same thing. And now, every fledgling attempt at love was fluttering into the midday sky in hot flakes of orange. Kamal couldn't remember a single word Ishmael said that day, but he remembered the scent of his father's love burning.

Fucking Abram.

Of all the assholes in the world, why *him*?

And how could Nader go along with this?

But he already knew the answer. Nader wasn't the biggest bully anymore—people will do anything to fit in.

Kamal clenched his fists at his sides. Abram saw him and grinned. He knew he had won.

Motherfucker.

Kamal wanted to knock that goddamn smile off his face. They'd kill him for it, but he'd make

Abram spit blood first. Instead, he did something only a man with a death wish would do—locked eyes across the flames and silently mouthed, *Fuck your mother.*

Abram's grin vanished. His face contorted with rage.

"This *kafir* dares to insult God in the presence of His holy soldiers and the Prophet Ishmael!"

Before anyone knew what had happened, Abram was around the fire, toe-to-toe with Kamal. He grabbed him by the back of his shirt and shoved him to the ground.

Kamal bounced back up almost instantly, shoving Abram hard—almost sending him into the fire. Abram reached for his gun.

"Abram, no!" Nader shouted. He rushed forward and grabbed Abram's arm just before he pulled the trigger.

Futilely trying to wrestle free from Nader's grip, Abram bellowed, "He denied God!"

"No, I denied *you!*" Kamal shot back.

Nader could hear the pain in his brother's voice, but he had no choice—his devotion to God had to be absolute. That's what Ishmael had taught him. If a prophet speaks the will of the Lord, and the will of the Lord is infallible, then so is the prophet.

Nader pleaded, "Kamal, stop!"

"How *could* you?" Kamal screamed. He

wasn't just angry. He was begging his brother to *see* him.

"Our love for God must be absolute."

"Those books weren't yours to burn!"

Ishmael finally spoke, his voice calm, chilling. "They were in his house. And what happens in a man's house is his responsibility."

"I wasn't talking to you," Kamal spat. He turned his venom back to Ishmael. "*Fuck* you and your bullshit lies."

Ishmael smiled. "Easy, boy. Talk like that will get your head cut off."

"Kamal, don't talk to the Prophet like that," Nader said, trying to deescalate the moment—trying to save his brother's life. "I'm sorry, Brother Ishmael, he's just a kid. He doesn't know what he's saying."

"I know *exactly* what I'm saying."

"No, you don't," Nader replied, more like a parent giving an order than a brother. He walked in close and whispered, "You need to apologize. They will *kill* you."

Kamal still had so much to say, but sometimes the truth isn't worth dying for.

Nader begged, "Whatever's on your mind, keep it to yourself. *Please.*"

Fuck this guy.

Do it for Nader.

Do it to save yourself.

I don't fucking care.

Do it for Nader.

But my books—

Fuck your books—do it for Nader.

But—

Shut the fuck up and just do it.

Kamal got down on his knees. "I'm sorry, Brother Ishmael. Everything you do is for the glory of God."

Ishmael's face remained cold. "I should kill you."

Kamal swallowed hard. "I call upon your mercy—in the name of God, please spare me."

"The problem is," Ishmael mused, "if I let this go unanswered, who will respect me?"

Nader knew what that meant. He stepped forward, desperate. "Brother, nobody doubts your righteousness. Please, I beg you, have mercy on the boy."

"Our love for God must be absolute."

Ishmael unholstered his Makarov pistol and handed it to Nader.

If Nader refused, Ishmael would kill them both. There were too many men to fight their way out. Kamal was dead either way. The only variable Nader controlled was his own life.

*It's okay to do terrible things if you're doing them for God.*

Nader held the gun in his shaking hands, staring down at it. It was heavier than he expected. Serious things carry serious weight. His finger hovered over the trigger.

"What are you doing? *Put the gun down!*" Kamal screamed. "Nader, *goddammit!*"

His brother's voice cracked wide open, full of betrayal.

Nader swallowed hard.

"I'm sorry."

"Nader! *Oh, fuck! Nader!* I'm your brother, goddammit!"

"If you love God, you must pull the trigger," Ishmael said smoothly.

"He's *lying to you!*" Kamal cried. "*Don't do this!*"

Ishmael lifted Nader's hand, pressing the barrel against Kamal's cheek.

The scent of metal and gunpowder filled Kamal's nostrils. He couldn't bear to look down the barrel—at his brother's twitching finger.

*Fuck.*

*I don't want to die.*

*Fuck.*

*I don't want to fucking die.*

*Fuck. Fuck. Fuck. Fuck. Please. Fuck!*

Nader squeezed his eyes shut, trying to block out his brother's pleading. Trying to block out *everything*.

"Nader, don't!"

"Open your eyes," Ishmael commanded. "You must see the work of your hands. It is not a sin to kill an unbeliever."

Nader opened his eyes. His grip tightened.

Kamal saw it before it happened.

"No! *Nader!* Fuck! *Wait!* Wa—wait! D— don't! Don't! Don't! Stop—"

A single shot rang out, singing Cain's song.

Kamal remembered nothing after that.

## Ara and Kamal: Part IV

Ara's star had long faded from the morning sky, but it still twinkled in her eyes. Kamal lit another cigarette. "I woke up in the hospital a week later. The bullet went in through my mouth and out the left side of my jaw." He turned his cheek, pointing to the scar that had caught her eye the day they first met. "Three surgeries, two blood transfusions, a couple of skin grafts, and six fake teeth later, they managed to put me back together. My mother had to sell our home to pay the hospital bills."

"Where is she now?"

"She's living with her cousin and her husband. I tried to get her to move in with me, but she refused—says she doesn't want to be a burden. But I think she just feels guilty. I don't see her often, and when I do, she can't even look at me anymore." He exhaled a plume of smoke, shaking his head. "God, if my father were here to see us now—to see how we've all fallen to pieces."

Ara wanted to cry for him. She reached up, tracing his scar with her fingertips. "I'm sorry."

Kamal turned his face toward her and

kissed her hand. "It's okay."

"No," she whispered, trying to keep it together. "It's not."

"Why haven't you ever asked me about it before?"

"I don't know. I figured it was rude."

"You're too polite."

"Can I ask you something?"

"Yeah."

"You don't have to answer if you don't want to."

"There you go again."

"I'm sorry."

"Just ask me."

"What happened to Nader?"

Kamal stared out at the city below. "He's up in the mountains somewhere with Ishmael and the rest of his men. I haven't heard from him since."

Ara hesitated. "Can I ask you another question?"

"You don't need permission."

"Sorry."

"You don't need to apologize either."

"Sorry."

"What do you want to know?"

"Do you hate him?"

Kamal took a long drag, thinking. "No. I mean, I sure as hell don't like him. But I don't hate him—I can't."

"But he shot you in the face."

"Yeah, but he didn't want to. My brother is a naïve little lamb. When a wolf eats a lamb, you don't blame the lamb."

"But lambs don't kill people."

"My brother didn't kill me."

"He tried."

"Yeah." Kamal rubbed his scar. "But if you give anyone a gun and tell them they're a hero, they're bound to do something fucked up. That doesn't mean they're bad people. Ishmael isn't recruiting people like you or me—we have too much to lose. We'd tell him to go fuck himself. You can't beat radicalization with guns. The more shit you blow up, the more desperate things get for the people most vulnerable to it. War only creates low-hanging fruit for Ishmael to pick from. The wealthy don't die for their causes—they pay the poor to do it for them."

And just like that, the last fleeting breaths of romance evaporated from the night.

*You fucked up—you never should have brought up Nader.*

But wasn't this the kind of conversation that built intimacy? Wasn't honesty supposed to bring people closer?

*You should have started fighting the moment you walked into that backyard. You waited until they put the gun in Nader's hand. You should've made those cowards do it themselves. You provoked them. You should've kept your mouth shut then, just like you should've kept it shut tonight. Why can't you ever just keep your goddamned mouth shut?*

## Ara and Kamal: Part V

It was Thursday afternoon. Ara and Kamal sat at a little café, finishing their tea. Ara borrowed the restaurant's telephone to call Fahima, already late for her shift at the shop—she was supposed to be back by one. It was already 1:05.
"I'm sorry, I'll be there as soon as I can."
...
"I know we lost track of time."
...
"I know you have plans."
...
"I'm sorry."
...
"I know."
...
"I said I was sorry."
...
"I'll be there in fifteen minutes, I promise."
...
"I know."
...
"You're right."
...

"It's not his fault."

...

"He actually wanted to get takeout."

...

"Because it was a nice day and I felt like sitting outside."

...

"I know. I should have listened to him."

...

"Okay, I'm leaving now."

...

"Okay."

...

"Okay."

...

"I'm sorry. I'll be there soon."

...

"Bye."

Fahima had already hung up. Kamal could see the frustration on Ara's face. Tossing cash on the table for the bill, he stood.

Wiping a strand of hair back from her face, she picked up her handbag. "We need to go."

"Is everything okay?"

"Yes. No. I don't know."

"What's going on?"

"She's mad because she's supposed to go to a matinee with her friends, and now she's running late because of me."

"Oh. Did you know she had plans?"

"Yeah, I just lost track of time."

"We should get going then."

"Yeah, I know," she snapped, taking it out on him. "Let's go."

Kamal grabbed their jackets off the back of their chairs, but by the time he turned around to help her put hers on, she was already out the door and halfway down the street.

It took him a full block to catch up. "Did you forget something?" he asked, jogging up behind her, out of breath.

She snatched the coat from his hands. "Thanks."

"I was referring to your fiancé."

She exhaled, the tension softening just a little. "I'm sorry."

She seemed to be apologizing a lot lately. Too much. She hated it. Partly because she wanted to stop screwing up, but mostly because she hated feeling like she owed the world something. Just once, she wanted to not care. To say, *fuck it, it's about me this time.* But when you're in a relationship, it's never about you. Not unless the other person makes it about you first.

"I didn't mean to take it out on you," she admitted. "I'm just really frustrated with everything."

"It's okay. I get it."

He didn't get it, but he said he did. That's what you do when you want things to be okay again. He hated tension. He'd do anything to make things fun again, like they were ten minutes ago—like they were a block ago, on the terrace of their favorite café, before she made that phone call.

Spring was restless and newborn, the air thick with the scent of blooming trees. Light green buds tipped with brown, still too young to know that someday they'd blossom, then die.

They turned onto Park Street, but as they reached the intersection at Butcher Street, they saw the mob.

A sea of men waving black flags, banners slashed with Ishmael's insignia.

"What are they getting ready for?" Ara whispered.

A march?
A riot?
Worse?

"That doesn't look good," Kamal muttered.

He took her hand, doing his best to hide his apprehension. "I wouldn't worry too much. Most of these things fizzle out before they even get started. It's just an excuse for assholes to get out in the street and blow off steam."

*The rest of the time, you get shot in the face.*

He was trying to make her feel safe. She appreciated it. But there was no way around the crowd. They had no choice but to go through it.

"We better go," she said. "Fahima's waiting."

Kamal led the way. Ara pulled a scarf from her purse and covered her head.

*All it takes is one yahoo in the crowd and it's over.*
*Don't wait for them this time—throw the first stone.*
*If they lay a finger on her, you'll have to kill every last one of them.*

There were at least two hundred men. A

ridiculous prospect.
*You have to die trying.*
*You can't survive to see what they'd do to her.*
He could feel her hand gripping his. But then, just as they stepped into the crowd, he let go.
*As soon as he let go, she felt like she was floating in space, untethered and out of control.*
*Keep your eyes down.*
She just wanted his hand back. Something to anchor herself.
*Act like you don't exist.*
They stayed close, but not too close. Not close enough to be noticed.
*Don't notice us.*
*We don't exist.*
*I'm here.*
The mob chanted: *"Death to the infidels!"*
Someone with a megaphone screamed: *"Kill the bourgeois pigs!"*
The noise was overwhelming. She couldn't feel Kamal behind her anymore. She wanted to turn, but she couldn't risk it. He wanted to reach out and grab her, to let her know he was still there. That he'd keep her safe—even if it was a lie.
*We're invisible.*
*We're not here.*
*I'm here.*
A flag caught fire. The crowd roared in approval.
She pulled her scarf over her mouth to block out the smoke.
*Don't cough.*

*If you cough, they'll see you.*
*Keep walking. I'll protect you.*
She felt the heat of the flames on her face.
The mob grew restless, voices rising:
"God is great! God is great!"
*I just want to hold his hand.*
*If they stone me, let it be in his embrace.*
*If it comes to it, let me die in his arms.*
*Let his lips press against mine one last time.*
*Let him be the one who kills me.*
*Better to die from true love's mercy than at the hands of hate.*
*It's okay. I'm here.*
*I don't want to die.*
*Just keep walking.*
*I'll protect you.*
*I don't want to die.*
*I'll kill for you.*
*I just want to hold your hand.*
*I don't want to die.*
*I don't want to die.*
*Just keep walking.*
*Just keep walking.*
*I'm scared.*
*I'm scared.*
*Just keep walking.*
*Just keep walking.*

Emerging on the other side of the mob, they ran as fast as they could, disappearing into the safety of Butcher Street.

The moment they turned the corner, Ara gasped, "I'm sorry—I don't know what got into me back there."

"It's okay," Kamal said. He wanted to kiss her.

And just like that, things were back to how they were two blocks ago.

When they got back to the store, Fahima was already halfway out the door, purse in hand.

"About time," she huffed. "I won't be back until after close. Make sure you sweep and take out the trash. I'll count the register when I get back."

"Fahima, wait."

"What?"

"I don't think you should go."

"I don't have time for this. I'm already late."

"I'm serious—there's a mob forming around the corner. It's not safe. Tell her, Kamal."

"It's true. They've already started burning flags."

Fahima rolled her eyes. "People have been burning flags and marching in these streets for a hundred years. If I changed my plans every time some zealot tried to stage a revolution, I'd never go anywhere."

"I have a bad feeling about this one."

"I'll be fine. They're probably heading toward the American embassy anyway. These things only get loud when they know the cameras are rolling."

"But you have to pass right by there."

"I know you're trying to help, but I'm going." She kissed Ara on the cheek. "Don't forget to break down the boxes in the back. I'll

see you in a few hours—I love you."
And then she was gone.
Ara watched through the dirty shop window as Fahima hustled down the street, hips pumping like an engine piston. At the corner, she turned and disappeared.

Kamal placed a reassuring hand on Ara's shoulder. "She'll be okay."

He didn't believe it, but it felt like the right thing to say. Ara could tell. Just like that, things were back to how they were before they were back to how they were two blocks ago.

For the first time, she wished Kamal was more like Holden.

Shrugging off his touch, she tucked her curls behind her ear and grabbed a stack of books to restock. Kamal knew better than to follow. He wanted to, but she needed to sort this out on her own.

She didn't even want him in the store anymore. If he tried to touch her again, she would have pushed him away—but she was mad that he didn't try. She wanted to be alone but needed him to grab her and not let go, no matter what. She wanted him to pin her arms when she tried to slap him, to tell her everything was going to be okay.

She had already lost two mothers, goddammit.

He was trying to do the right thing, but he was doing it the wrong way.

She hated him.

No, hate was too strong of a word. But in that moment, she thought she hated him.

She just wanted him to leave.
But the last thing she wanted was to be alone.

They spent the next half hour in silence. Ara stocked shelves. Kamal flipped through a copy of *The Dragons of Eden*.
"She should be there by now."
Kamal looked up. "Huh?"
"Her movie started ten minutes ago. Are you even listening to me?"
"Yeah, of course I'm listening."
"I hope she made it okay."
It felt like an opening. An opportunity to close the gap between them. Had enough time passed for both of them to let their guards down? Could they go back to how things were two blocks ago?
Setting his book down, Kamal walked over and wrapped his arms around her waist.
She didn't push him away.
"I'm sorry for being so difficult today," she said.
"It's okay. It's been a difficult day."
"Thank you."
"For what?"
"For being you."
"It's all I know how to be."
"Well, I like it."
"Just like?"
"Love."
"I love you too," he said, a sly smile creeping onto his face. "What movie are they seeing?"

"The American one about the alien."
"E.T.?"
"Yeah."
"I hear it's good. Maybe we should check it out sometime."

Fahima and her four friends, Ida, Aatifa, Omira, and Bakhtawar, sat in the front row of the balcony. The silver light of the projector flickered through the dust, settling onto the heads of the audience below.

On screen, little Drew Barrymore knelt beside the rubber alien.

"Phone," she said in a sweet, emphatic voice.

E.T. bumbled his thick fingers over the buttons.

"Phh—phooonnnee."

The audience chuckled.

Elliot came home and found his sister hiding E.T. in the closet, dressed in women's clothing. The whole theater erupted in laughter.

Fahima giggled a little harder than she meant to.

The amusement was short-lived.

The theater lights snapped on.

A column of men filed in.

Thirty of them. Maybe more.

Some in fatigues. Some in street clothes, like they had just gotten off work or finished a soccer game.

Some carried guns.

Some held wooden clubs.

Some had nothing but their fists.

That's how hysteria works. It only takes a few instigators to convince ordinary people to burn the city to the ground.

Fahima's heart sank.

You never believe this sort of thing will actually happen.

Until it does.

It's an out-of-body experience.

Not here.

Not me.

Ara.

The projector operator had fallen asleep upstairs.

The first gunshot into the ceiling jolted him awake.

He scrambled out the back door, running as fast as he could.

The film kept playing.

The light from the screen washed over the militants, blinding them.

"Somebody get up there and turn that thing off!"

E.T. pointed at the sky.

"Phh—phooonnnee hoommme."

Another gunshot.

The projector cut off.

The theater went silent.

Fahima just wanted things to go back to how they were.

To how they were an hour ago.

To how they were when they were just watching a movie.

Abram's voice rose from the front of the theater.

"This cinema is an affront to God."

Back at the shop, it was past six. Fahima still hadn't returned.

Ara counted the register, stopping every few seconds to look out the window.

She wasn't sure what she expected to see.

Just something.

Anything.

"She should have been back by now," she muttered.

"I'm sure she's fine," Kamal said. "They probably just went out for tea after the movie."

Ara slammed the register shut. "Don't do that."

"Do what?"

"Lie to me just to spare my feelings. I'm not a child, Kamal. If it's bad, then it's bad. But don't lie to me."

"I'm not lying."

"Yes, you are."

Kamal walked behind the counter, reaching for her.

"Don't do that either."

"What?"

"Try to hold me every time I'm mad at you. Hugging me doesn't fix everything. Stop treating me like I'm fragile."

"I don't think you're fragile."

"Yes, you do. You're always trying to protect me."

"I know you're strong. I never said you weren't."

"Then be honest with me. If you think

something's wrong, say it."
Kamal exhaled. "Okay—I think something's wrong."
"Thank you. So do I."

Ara and Kamal were in the stockroom, on the phone with the police, when the bell over the shop door jingled. Rushing out, they found Omira standing in the doorway, wringing her scarf, fresh red scratches running down her face.
"Omira! Thank God—" Ara exhaled the breath she'd been holding for hours. "We were worried sick. Where's Fahima?"
Omira fumbled with the brass buckle on her handbag. There was something she didn't want to say.
"They took her," she whispered.
Ara's stomach dropped. "What? Who took her?"
"The men in the theater."
Kamal put an arm around Ara. This time, she didn't push him away. "What happened?"
Omira broke down. "I'm sorry. I did all I could."
An old wound split open inside Ara, bleeding hot and fast. "What did they do to her?"
Omira sobbed harder. "I'm sorry. I'm sorry."
Ara lost patience. "Where is my mother?"
It was the first time she had called Fahima that. She had felt it for a long time but never had the guts to say it.
Omira could only whisper, "I'm sorry," before she turned and ran, vanishing into the

cold, dark, bitter, fucking horrible night.

    They lined up everyone at gunpoint in the theater lobby, splitting them into two groups. Abram, swaggering in his self-appointed authority, checked identification cards and interrogated them on their religious and political affiliations. If you passed, you went to the right. If you failed, to the left.
    People started snitching to save themselves.
    "She's lying! I've seen her wear makeup when her husband isn't around."
    "I saw him drinking beer at his birthday party!"
    Truth didn't matter. Survival did.
    The right side shrank. The left grew.
    Six more were sent left. Ida, Aatifa, and Bakhtawar among them. Some wept silently. Others screamed. Those who screamed were dragged out the back. A gunshot rang out. The men who took them returned, laughing as they wiped the blood from their hands.
    "Next time, do it further away—I don't need her brains on me like I need a bullet to the head."
    It was Omira's turn. She panicked. Betrayal isn't always a choice—sometimes it's just fear.
    Before Abram could speak, she pointed at Fahima.
    "She owns the bookstore off Butcher Street—sells Western books and pornography!"
    Fahima's breath caught. "Omira, what are

you doing?"

Omira kept her eyes down. "They executed her husband because he was an atheist."

"That's a lie! She's lying!"

It wasn't a lie.

"Her adopted daughter is pregnant out of wedlock."

That was a lie.

"You stupid bitch," Fahima snarled, ripping Omira's scarf off and clawing at her face. Abram's men wrenched them apart.

"I'm not lying!" Omira shrieked.

Fahima spat at her. "Do you have any idea what you've done?"

"It's all true! I swear to God!"

"What do you know about God? You haven't prayed since your husband *died!*"

"She's lying!"

"Enough," Abram said.

He studied them. Stared Fahima in the eye. "Is this true?"

His breath was hot against her lips.

Her whole body trembled.

"No."

"Was your husband an atheist?"

She steadied herself. "No."

She wished she could go back to two hours ago. She should have listened to Ara. At least she got to say "I love you" before she left.

Abram held the pause long enough to stretch eternity. Then he pointed.

"I don't believe you. Go to the left."

He turned to Omira.

"You can go to the right."

Fahima's stomach dropped.
This isn't real.
This can't be happening.
Who have I ever hurt?
How have I ever offended God?
This can't be happening.
Maybe they'll let us go home.
They never let you go home.
Bakhtawar took her hand.
"Maybe they'll let us go home."
"Maybe," Bakhtawar said softly.
Wishful thinking.
But it was all they had.

They were never seen again.
Eighty-seven people, gone. No explanations. No bodies to bury.
A community doesn't recover from something like that. The wound never heals—it just lingers, inflamed, reopening every time someone walks past the street where the cinema used to be.
Kamal wanted to go into the mountains to find Nader.
Ara stopped him.
"What good will that do?"
"He can at least tell us where they put the bodies. He owes me that much."
She had just lost her third mother. She wasn't losing her fiancé too.
"They'll kill you this time."
"Probably," Kamal admitted. "But you deserve to know."
"I deserve to have my fiancé in one piece."

He didn't go.
But it ate at him every day.
Poyas never run.
And yet, here he was. Sitting on his hands.
Doing nothing.
For her.

## Operation Gatekeeper

Wali stood in front of the mirror, straightening his tie. He had been up for two hours. Checking his watch—4:45 AM—he had to be in al-Ghwayway's suite by 7:30. He wasn't nervous yet.

He slipped on his suit jacket, picked up his lukewarm tea from the nightstand, and drank. The room was dark, the curtains drawn. The beige plastic hotel phone rang twice. He didn't pick up.

It was time to go downstairs.

Stepping into the hallway, he looked both ways. Pressing the elevator button, he waited, watching his muddled reflection in the steel doors. The elevator opened. A young man inside smiled.

"Good morning."
"Morning."
"Going down?"
"Yeah."

They rode in silence. When the doors slid open in the lobby, the young man stepped out first.

"Have a nice day."

"You too."

The girl behind the front desk looked half-dead from exhaustion, struggling through the last hour of her shift. A maid adjusted the orange and green velour throw pillows on the lobby couch. The concierge leaned against his desk, reading a newspaper. Wali approached. The concierge set the paper down.

"Good morning, sir. How may I help you?"

"How's the weather?"

"The forecast calls for rain."

"Are you sure? That's too bad, I left my umbrella upstairs."

"Here, read it for yourself." The concierge handed him the newspaper. "Have a nice day, sir."

Rolling it up, Wali shoved it in his suit pocket. "You too."

Back in his room, he flipped through the pages. On the back, in pencil, the words: Taste left, turn right.

Lighting a cigarette, he tore off the message and ignited it, watching the edges curl into black.

Taste left, turn right.

He checked his watch—5:30 AM. Two hours to decide. No going back. He pulled open the curtains. The city was quiet. Streetlamps cast golden halos on wet pavement. A feral dog darted across the road.

Taste left, turn right.

By 7:20 AM, Wali was back on the elevator. The numbers climbed. He still didn't know what he would do. The doors opened.

Agent Zubair greeted him. "Morning, Wali."

They had come up together in the academy. No one in their line of work had friends, but Zubair was close as it got.

"How was last night?"

"Same as always."

Not good.

"What time is Baddar relieving you?"

"Any minute now."

"Good. Get some rest."

Wali walked down the hall to the presidential suite. Agent Sinpai stood at the door. The youngest member of the detail, built like a tank.

"Good morning, sir."

"Morning. Is he awake?"

"Yes, sir. Up early."

"How did he sleep?"

"Not well."

"Okay—"

"Sir—"

Wali stopped. "Yes?"

Sinpai hesitated. "I hope I'm not out of line, but last night—he was talking to himself again. Yelling. The things he was saying... I think he's getting worse."

"He's fine."

"But—"

Wali's look was enough. You're not over the line, but your toes are touching it.

"Sorry, sir."

Wali entered the room.

Al-Ghwayway sat at the breakfast table, drinking tea, flipping through the newspaper. The news played on the TV in the background. The charred remains of the movie theater filled the screen.

Wali stood by the door, waiting.

Al-Ghwayway sighed and turned to the sports section, smiled, then folded the paper. "Wali, my man. Good morning."

"Good morning, Mr. President."

"You don't look well."

"I'm fine, sir. Thank you."

The screen showed a mob burning an effigy of him. Al-Ghwayway barely glanced at it.

"What do you think about all this?"

Wali followed his eyes. "Disrespectful."

"Not that. They've been burning dolls of me for ages. I meant the theater. I remember the day it opened. Me and my younger brother—may he rest in peace—went to see *Like Eagles*. Seeing our own countrymen up on that screen—it was amazing."

"I have no doubt you'll find those responsible and bring them to justice."

"I'm sure we will. But it won't bring the theater back." He sighed. "I suppose I'll never get to see *E.T.* now."

"I can locate a copy, set up a projector—"

"No. It's not the same."

A knock at the door.

"That must be your breakfast, sir."

Wali peered through the peephole. Agent Sinpai stood on the other side with the room service cart.

Taste left, turn right.

He opened the door, let Sinpai in.

"Thank you," Wali said, taking the cart.

"Will there be anything else, sir?"

"No, you may go."

Sinpai nodded to Al-Ghwayway. "Mr. President."

Wali wheeled the cart over. Lifted the cloche. A lamb, garlic, and tomato omelet. Bolani. Cucumbers. Half a pomegranate. The same breakfast every day.

Taste left, turn right.

Sweat gathered at his collar. His palms were wet.

Al-Ghwayway unrolled his napkin, set it in his lap. "What do we have today?"

The joke landed wrong.

Taste left, turn right.

Wali's heart pounded. He cut from the left side of the omelet, raised the bite to his mouth. Al-Ghwayway watched him.

He knows.

He chewed, swallowed. Then the bolani.

He knows.

"Would you like me to try the cucumber and pomegranate?"

Al-Ghwayway's stare burned through him. "Yes. Please."

Taste left, turn right.

Wali ate them. Then, slowly, rotated the plate right. "Is there anything else I can do for you, Mr. President?"

He knows.

Al-Ghwayway studied the food. His instinct screamed. Setting his fork down, he sipped his tea.

"How long have you worked for me, Wali?"

"Ten years, Mr. President."

"Since the beginning."

"Yes, sir."

"I trust you with my life. Your job is to protect me."

"Yes, sir."

"At all costs?"

"Yes, sir."

"And you have done this every day for ten years?"

"Yes, sir."

The silence pressed. Wali's throat was closing.

"You are very good at your job."

"Thank you, Mr. President."

Al-Ghwayway smiled. Picked up his fork.

"Is this food poisoned?"

Run.

Al-Ghwayway cut into the right side of the omelet.

Run.

He raised the bite to his mouth.

"Mr. President—"

Al-Ghwayway stopped. "Yes?"

"Maybe you should skip breakfast today."

"If you think that's what I should do."

"I do."

Al-Ghwayway set his fork down. "Fine. I wasn't hungry anyway."

Wali snatched up the plate, set it back on

the cart, and wheeled it into the hallway. Sinpai was waiting.

"Is everything okay, sir?"

"The President isn't hungry."

"But he always eats breakfast."

A switch flipped in Wali's head. If he wasn't going to kill him, he had to do whatever it took to protect him. If he had been compromised, nobody could be trusted.

"Not today—take this away."

Agent Sinpai glanced around, ensuring nobody was listening. Leaning in, he whispered, "Are you—"

"That's an order, Agent Sinpai."

A hesitation. Then, "Yes, sir."

Wali reentered the Presidential Suite.

Al-Ghwayway was pacing, rubbing his temples as if his skull were splitting apart. Wali had heard about the President's episodes, but he had never witnessed one firsthand.

"Are you okay, sir?"

Al-Ghwayway banged a fist against his forehead. "I'm fine."

"Can I get you a glass of water?"

"I'm not sick."

"Of course not, sir."

The President stopped pacing. "Be honest with me—what's going on?"

Wali hesitated. Treason came with a firing squad. If there were others in on this, they wouldn't stop. Another attempt would come. He had to get al-Ghwayway to safety. But where? If Wali couldn't be trusted, no one could be.

"Your life is in danger, Mr. President."

Al-Ghwayway froze. His ghost left him. "How do you know?"

Wali grabbed his arm. "We have to hurry—"

Al-Ghwayway wrenched free. "Tell me how you know they're trying to kill me."

No way around the truth. Al-Ghwayway wasn't some fragile politician. He had survived trenches and guerrilla warfare. He could spot a lie before a man even thought of telling it. You don't take down a man like al-Ghwayway with a knife in the back. If you wanted him dead, you had to go toe to toe.

"Because I'm the one who was supposed to kill you."

A beat.

"You?"

"Yes, Mr. President."

The bear inside al-Ghwayway woke. He grabbed Wali by the throat and slammed him against the wall. "And what about now?"

Wali clawed at his fingers, his face turning red. "Now—I'm trying to save your life."

"Don't lie to me."

"I'm not."

The President's grip tightened.

Wali choked out, "I swore to protect you. That's what I intend to do."

Al-Ghwayway studied him, looking for the lie. Stepping back, he rubbed his temples again. His head felt like it was being pulled apart. "Of all people—why?"

"It doesn't matter anymore."

"Tell me."

"You know why."

Al-Ghwayway clenched his jaw. "It's not true—I'm fine."

"I don't care if it's true. Stick close to me. Don't engage with anyone. If something happens to me—"

"We'll cross that bridge when we get there."

They slipped into the hallway. Sinpai and Baddar stood a few meters down, whispering. This is about to get ugly.

"Don't look at them," Wali said.

They turned away, heading down the corridor.

Sinpai called out, "Excuse me, sir!"

"Ignore them."

"Sir!"

"Don't look back. Keep going."

They picked up their pace.

Sinpai rested a hand on his gun. "Sir, where are you going?"

"We're fine. The President wants to take a walk."

"Sir!"

"I said we're fine."

"Stand down!"

Al-Ghwayway spoke up. "He said we're fine."

Wali quickened his steps. The stairwell was close.

"Agent Wali, stop!"

Sinpai and Baddar drew their weapons and sprinted after them.

Wali threw open the stairwell door just as Sinpai fired.

Glass shattered.

They tore down the stairs.

Footsteps pounded above.

Bang! Bang!

Wali fired two rounds back up. Bullets ricocheted off metal railings.

Sinpai and Baddar returned fire.

Third floor.

They burst into the hallway, scanning for cover. An open storage closet.

They slipped inside.

The stairwell door opened.

"You go left, I'll go right. Meet in the middle."

Al-Ghwayway's breath was hot against Wali's neck.

Agent Baddar moved toward them, checking every door handle.

The closet door had no latch. Wali braced against it, holding it shut.

Footsteps.

Baddar stopped at their door.

The handle turned.

Wali let it twist—then, slammed his body into the door.

Baddar stumbled back.

Wali sprang forward, tackled him, and put two rounds in his chest.

Grabbing Baddar's sidearm, he tossed it to al-Ghwayway. "Ready?"

The President gripped the gun like an old friend. "Yeah."

Gunfire erupted down the hallway.

Sinpai.

The elevator chimed open.

Three more agents spilled out.

Nobody knew whose side they were on.

Sinpai fired wildly. "God is great!"

Bullets splintered the walls.

Al-Ghwayway returned fire, forcing Sinpai into cover.

"We have to move!"

The President kicked open the door across the hall.

They sprinted inside.

Three more agents charged in.

Wali tackled the first, slammed a pistol against his face, and shot the second point blank.

The third barreled through—

Al-Ghwayway grabbed him, shoved him into the bathroom, and bashed his skull into the mirror.

The agent crumpled into the shower.

Blood webbed across the tile.

Al-Ghwayway turned—saw Wali struggling on the floor.

Gun to the eardrum.

Bang.

Sinpai entered, still firing.

Wali and al-Ghwayway spun and cut him down with five rounds to the chest.

Sinpai fell to his knees, blood foaming at his mouth.

The fight was over.

Wali staggered up. "You okay, Mr.

President?"
　　Al-Ghwayway wiped sweat from his brow. "Yeah."
　　Wali poked his head into the hallway. Silence.
　　Curious guests peeked from their doors.
　　"Back inside. Lock your doors."
　　One by one, locks clicked shut.
　　Al-Ghwayway let out a breath. "So this is what being usurped feels like. I always thought there'd be more tanks."
　　"You still have friends in this city."
　　"The grass is always greener on the other side of the revolution."
　　Wali chambered a fresh round. "Are you ready?"

　　Stepping into the hallway, they moved toward the stairwell. Wali pushed the door open, and they started down the first flight.
　　Then—
　　Bang.
　　A single gunshot exploded from the stairs above, ricocheting off the concrete walls in an echoing cackle.
　　Red mist filled the air.
　　Al-Ghwayway's massive frame lurched forward. Falling. Tumbling. Crashing.
　　Wali watched him hit the steps, roll, and land in a lifeless heap at the bottom.
　　Blood trickled down the stairs.
　　Wali wiped his cheek. Wet. Warm. Sticky.
　　He looked down at his palm. Red.
　　A piece of flesh stuck between his fingers.

Fragments of the President's brain.

He turned.

At the top of the stairs stood Agent Zubair. His gun was still raised. Dark splatter flecked his sleeve.

Wali's stomach twisted. Of all people.

Zubair clenched his jaw. "Drop your gun."

Wali's weapon clattered to the floor.

"Zubair—why?"

"You know why."

"He was the President."

"He was a madman."

"We swore to give our lives for him."

"And I would have. But I wouldn't give him the soul of our country."

Silence.

Ten years.

A decade of standing shoulder to shoulder. Through war. Through chaos. Through blood and fire.

And now this.

Wali swallowed. "So what now?"

Zubair's grip on his gun tightened. "Go into the mountains. You'll be safe there."

"I'm not running."

Zubair exhaled. "I already killed my President today. Don't make me kill my friend, too."

Wali looked down.

Al-Ghwayway's body lay twisted at the bottom of the stairs, his blood spreading like ink.

How many bodies had he seen in his life? Too many.

But never one that mattered this much.

Wali lifted his head. "You really think things will be better now?"

Zubair hesitated. "I don't know. But something had to change."

Wali's legs felt like they might buckle. Slowly, he turned and descended. Step. Step. Step.

At the bottom, he stepped over al-Ghwayway's body.

In the basement, he found an abandoned housekeeping cart. He grabbed a towel, wiped the blood from his face, and slipped out the service entrance into the cold morning air.

## Poya's: Part 0

There weren't many people at the wedding. Kamal's mother came, but she refused to sit in the front row, taking a seat in the back with her cousin instead. Nader wasn't invited for obvious reasons. Only one person attended on Ara's side—Omira. She cried through the entire service and slipped out before the reception. On her way out, she left an unmarked envelope on the gift table with fifty thousand rupees inside.

They stayed in Fahima's house for a while, but then came the news: President al-Ghwayway had been assassinated by his own bodyguard. Presumably the same one who had once followed him into the bookstore. After that, the city was too dangerous to stay in. They left the day the military seized control and moved in to eradicate "the rebel element."

War swallowed the streets whole. Boots stomped where car horns once honked. Beautiful garden avenues filled with roadblocks. Bullet holes pockmarked the immaculate ivory walls of the financial district. Explosions churned up the earth like volcanic ash. Charred skeletons of cars lined the roads. The porcelain tiles of shop fronts were ground to pink dust beneath soldiers' heels, so fine it filled your nostrils. The schools shut down. Professors were hunted in broad daylight. The hospitals overflowed, their parking lots turned into graveyards where the wounded lay on blankets, dying of infection in perfectly treatable wounds.

    They abandoned the bookshop. Nobody was buying property, let alone a bourgeois bookstore. In one of Ishmael's most incendiary sermons, he condemned "all Western materials" as decrepit and against God's law. Art was outlawed. Clothes deemed improper by the moral police became crimes. A famous symphony conductor was dragged into the street and shot. Sixteen singers had their tongues cut out. Five renowned authors were tossed from a cliff—their skulls bursting on the rocks below, spilling the stories they would never tell. The state-run television studio and cinema burned. Headless corpses dangled from streetlights, swaying under the midday sun.

    But the most infamous of the dead was Franco Milleagas, the half-Spaniard poet and painter revered for his bold, almost abstract take on cubism. He had returned home only to care for his dying mother. The irony was that she outlived him. His body was found strung up by his ankles outside the liberal arts building. The dawn rose over the university lawn like the blood-washed hues of his masterpiece, *Apricot in Rhapsody*. The sun spilled into his gouged-out eyes, filling the hollow caverns with morning light. His fingers were severed because he loved the piano. His nose was hacked off because it *looked* too Jewish. A pile of his teeth lay scattered in the wet blood below. Ishmael bragged about his murder over the radio: "Even the most revered in hell are not safe from the wrath of the Holy One." The men who killed him had once been his students. Ishmael called them "Knights of Heaven."

Ara and Kamal found a fragile peace in the high wilderness on the far side of the country. The men there were shepherds and farmers, uninterested in city politics but quick to pick up a gun if a wolf came for their herd. Even Ishmael knew better than to enter these tribal lands.

Kamal was a city boy. He didn't know the first thing about farming, but he did his best. He spent all of Omira's hush money on a small slice of land full of more rocks than soil. Instead of fighting the earth, he raised sheep. His herd was small but healthy, which was what mattered.

At night, after Ara went to bed, Kamal stood outside and looked at the stars. Astronomy kept his mind from dulling, but it wasn't enough. Steel needs something to sharpen against, or it rusts.

Ara's first pregnancy was a troubled one. No outward signs, but she could feel it—something was wrong with the child. There was no hospital up here, so Kamal fretted day and night, over-preparing for the birth. He childproofed the house. Stocked up on enough medical supplies to furnish an emergency room. He'd read countless books on childbirth when he was a kid—but that was so long ago. The details were gone. He recounted the medical supplies for the thousandth time, a ritual to soothe his own

nerves.
One container of Sudocrem.
One bottle of prenatal vitamins—one hundred count.
One bottle of ibuprofen 200mg—one hundred count.
One bottle of acetaminophen 250mg—one hundred count.
One bottle of paracetamol cough syrup 125mg per 5ml.
One bottle of ibuprofen cough syrup 100mg per 5ml.
Amoxicillin 500mg—twenty-one count.
One bottle of opium tincture syrup 10mg/ml.
One bottle of bupivacaine 0.25%.
One packet of cough drops.
Six 25-gauge syringes.
Alcohol.
Hydrogen peroxide.
Four rolls of gauze and various bandages.
Scalpel.
Triple antibiotic ointment.
One box of latex gloves.
Surgical wash.
Iodine.
Six packets of size-zero surgical sutures and needle.
Baby powder.
Three bags of 0.45% saline sodium chloride fluids with IV.
One bulb syringe.

    He knew what each item did. But having what you need and being ready to use it—those are two different things.

The baby kicked hard, day and night. Ara rubbed her belly, wincing, "My love, I wish you wouldn't hurt me so much."

The baby kicked harder.

She loved him more than she ever thought possible—even more than she loved Kamal. Another sharp jab in the ribs. She smiled, wincing. "You're going to break my heart, aren't you?"

She walked through the hilltop market, wind tugging at her scarf, forcing her to keep pulling it back up. People were more conservative here than in the city, and strangers—especially women—were watched. Eyes everywhere. Old ones, jaundiced ones, cataract-clouded ones. Keen eyes, ready to spot the slightest misstep.

Especially if the misstep belonged to a woman.

Especially if she was young.

Especially if she was beautiful.

Even pregnant, she drew glances. Hands brushed her in the crowd. Not by accident. Never by accident. She ignored them. Stopped at a vegetable stand, bought a bundle of undersized carrots, three anemic onions, and a crisp head of cabbage. A rarity. She placed them in her basket and covered them with linen to keep out the dust.

She took a shortcut down a tarp-covered alley. More phantom hands, more bumping crotches pressed against her. It was disgusting. But it was normal.

She passed the toy vendor, the knife seller, the silk merchant.

"Psst."
She ignored it.
"Psst."
Sharp, like air escaping a tire.
Turning, she saw him—a gangly, weathered man leaning behind his stall. It was cluttered with second-hand rugs, a glass case of knock-off Zippos, used auto parts, and other random objects that didn't seem to belong together.
"Psst," he hissed again, beckoning her closer.
Ara folded her arms. "Why are you psst'ing me?"
The man grinned, half his teeth yellow, the other half black. "Come, take a look. I have the best things in town."
She glanced at his stall, unimpressed. "I doubt that."
"Please," he said, bowing theatrically, ushering her toward the pile of junk. "What do you like?" He lowered his voice. "Movies? I have movies."
Pulling a rug aside, he revealed a small storage hole with a few battered cardboard boxes. He pulled one out and lifted the lid, showing off a collection of Betamax tapes.
"I don't own a TV."
"What about music? I have tapes. Records." He dug through another box. "The Monkees? Pink Floyd? The Beach Boys?" He started singing under his breath. "I wish they all could be California girls—"
"No, thank you."
He frowned. "What do you like? I have it."

"Johnny Cash."

His hands rifled through the collection, growing desperate. "I don't have Johnny Cash. What else?" He brightened. "You like negro music? I have James Brown."

"No, thank you." She turned to leave.

"Wait!" he called, scrambling for something, anything. "Books! Do you like books?"

Ara stopped. "What kind of books?"

"Everything," he said, pulling out another box—half-wet, splitting at the seams. "Please, take a look. I have what you're looking for."

She hesitated, then bent down to peer inside. Mostly romance novels.

Digging deeper, she found a few battered classics—Bleak House, missing its back cover. A couple of Hardy Boys mysteries with pages torn out. And then—

She saw it.

A red-orange spine.

A worn-out suitcase.

A stupid red hat.

Her hands trembled as she reached for the book. He was looking away from her, just like he always had.

Her fingers brushed his shoulder.

"Hey, Holden."

His voice was bursting at the seams with goddamn regret—

H: Hey is for horses.

When she was still at the university, she found a story about his childhood in the library. She also found one that talked about when he

died.
It's a big deal to know when someone is going to die.
She didn't know if she should tell him. She wanted to. Needed to. But if his future was already written, what difference would it make? Would you want to know, even if there was nothing you could do to change it? Could you ever forgive someone who knew and didn't tell you? How would knowing change the way you lived your life?
She wanted to scream, Don't do it, Holden. Don't join the military. It will break Vincent's heart when you go missing.
Can't you see the ocean is full of bowling balls?
They'll shoot you up. You'll bleed out in a crater somewhere. Your beautiful arms will get blown off, and they'll take your legs with landmines. How are you going to lug around that stupid suitcase without any goddamned arms?
No one will ever even know how you died. You just disappear. But not like when you're crossing the street—this time it will be for real.
Don't go.
There's no honor in getting shot full of holes. They have parades for the dead, but you won't be there to see it. You'll be gone. And for what? For nothing. Don't do this to Vincent. Don't do it to me. Who will keep all the children from running off the cliff when you're gone?
But she didn't say any of that.
He was going to go off to war.
And he was going to die.

She picked him up. He could tell she missed him—
H: Don't ever tell anyone anything. If you do, you start missing everybody.
Turning to the shop owner, she asked, "How much for this one?"

## Isah: Part I

It happened in the middle of the night. The baby wasn't due for weeks. At first, Ara thought she'd peed the bed. Reaching down, she felt the sticky warmth between her legs. Her water had broken.

The amniotic fluid had already soaked through Kamal's pajamas before she let out her first scream.

It wasn't supposed to be this painful, this fast.

And then came the first contraction.

They said childbirth hurt, but no one told her it would feel like someone was stabbing her uterus with a butcher knife.

This isn't right.

She felt the baby panicking inside her, crying in a way that had no sound.

Kamal was scrambling. The books he'd read as a kid were useless now—this was Ara.

This was their child. Ara buried her face in his shoulder, squeezing his bicep so hard it went numb.

"The baby—something's wrong," she gasped.

Kamal had no idea what to do, but he had to say something. Anything. "Okay—take a deep breath—"

"Don't tell me to stay calm."

"Remember your breathing—"

"The baby is dying—get it out of me!" She gritted her teeth, arching her back as a new wave of pain tore through her. "If you let my baby die, I'll never forgive you."

"I'm not going to let the baby die."

"Promise me."

God, he loved her. He squeezed her hand, brushed the damp hair back from her forehead.

"Listen to me—I won't let anything happen to you or the baby. I promise."

And he meant it.

She screamed into the pillow.

Focus, goddammit. What's the first step?

Determine the baby's position.

Kamal placed his shaking hand on her stomach. "This is going to hurt. I'm sorry."

He pressed down.

Ara screamed.

To Kamal's horror, a tiny foot kicked back through the skin of her belly.

Fuck. The baby is breech.

And what he didn't know yet—what neither of them knew—was that the umbilical cord was wrapped around the baby's neck, lynching it inside the womb.

Little mounds of frantic skin protruded from her belly as the baby kicked and punched, trying to escape.

I don't know what to do.

Yes, you do. Take a deep breath.

I can't.

You have to. The baby has to be born cesarean.

I can't.

You studied this. You know the principles.

That was a lifetime ago.

You have to remember.

What if I do it wrong?

Then she dies.

I'm scared.

So is she.

Owning a scalpel and using it were two different things.

Make an incision in the lower belly, but be careful not to harm the baby or other organs.

Easier said than done.

Ara clawed at him. "Please—get the baby out!"

What if I do it wrong?

"Promise me," she panted. "No matter what—you won't let my baby die."

He knew what she meant.

If it came down to a choice between saving her or the child—

"I promise."

He never made promises he couldn't keep. But he wasn't ready to lose her.

"I need the medical kit—I'll be right back," he said, disappearing into the next room.

When he returned, his eyes were red, his hands shaking. Slipping on latex gloves, he rolled her onto her side. "I know it hurts, but try not to move."

Ara bit her lip hard enough to draw blood.

Kamal pulled out the vial of bupivacaine and a syringe, drew 8 mg into the needle.

"Okay, baby. I need you to hold very still—I'm going to give you an injection in your spine. It'll help with the pain."

The first successful cesarean birth—where both mother and baby survived—was performed in 1500 by a Swiss pig-gelder named Jacob Nufer. His wife had no anesthesia.

The medicine worked instantly—Ara couldn't feel anything from the waist down.

She looked at her belly, at the tiny fist pressing against her skin.

"Hurry," she begged.

Kamal fought to keep his hands steady.

"Everything's going to be okay. I won't let anything happen to our baby."

A lie. But she needed to believe it.

He laid out the IV fluids, the scalpel, the surgical wash, the sutures, arranging them neatly on a clean towel.

Jacob Nufer used a steel knife.

Kamal at least had a scalpel. And antibiotics.

And a promise.

*Being prepared and being prepared to do what needs to be done were two different things.*

The scalpel was sterile, but he soaked it in alcohol anyway.

Ara wasn't in pain anymore, but she was still crying.

Taking her bone-thin hand in his, Kamal searched for a vein in the dim light. "I'm going to put the IV in now."

*I can't see a fucking thing.*

There was nothing he could do about the darkness. It was night, and they were out of candles.

*You fucking idiot—of all the reasons to lose a child—because you forgot to buy more fucking candles.*

Ara sensed something was wrong. "What's wrong?"

"Nothing. Everything's fine."

"Then just do it."

*Just do it.*

He pulled the skin on her hand tight. The books said the veins should be right there—but he couldn't see a goddamn thing.

*If you can't even find a vein, how the hell are you supposed to perform a C-section?*

*Shut up and do it.*

Mrs. Nufer didn't have IV fluids when she

had her child cut out of her stomach. But Ara wasn't Mrs. Nufer.

Ara flexed her fist. The faintest line of purple rose beneath her skin, flickering like a beacon from the ocean floor. Bracing her hand, Kamal slid the needle in, watching the catheter slip into place. The bag hung from a coat hook next to their bed.

*Now came the hard part.*

*He picked up the scalpel.*

"I love you, Ara."

"I love you too."

"I'm going to make the first incision. Are you ready?"

Ara tried to hold back her tears. "No, but just do it."

*It doesn't matter if you're strong ninety-nine percent of the time—as long as you're brave when it matters.*

*She had to do this for the baby.*

*He had to do this for her.*

*His hands were shaking.*

*They were supposed to have a long life together. It couldn't end already.*

*Taking a deep breath, he ordered himself—Calm the fuck down.*

*Be brave.*

*Just for today.*

*You can be a coward tomorrow.*

*He saw the fear in her face. He couldn't let her see the fear in his.*

*Rolling a towel, he placed it between her teeth.*

"Bite down."

*She was a Poya now.*
*Poyas never run.*
"I won't let anything happen to you or the baby."
*She believed him.*
"No matter how much it hurts, you can't move," he warned. "You don't want to accidentally hurt the baby, do you?"
*She clenched the towel in her teeth, tears spilling down her cheeks. I won't move, I promise.*
*Kamal made the first incision.*
*He sliced through the thick outer layer of her stomach. Blood spurted hot and fast like water leaking through a crack in the wall.*
"Are you okay?"
"No."
"Does it hurt?"
"Just keep going."
*She could feel it. Not all of it—but enough.*
*You calculated the medication wrong.*
*His heart dropped. He grabbed the bottle of bupivacaine. The label read 0.25%.*
*He had dosed her for 0.5%.*
*Which meant she had only half the anesthesia she needed.*
*You fucking idiot.*
*How could you be so stupid?*
*It doesn't matter now.*
*Ara was open on the bed. Bleeding.*
*Keep your goddamn hands steady.*
*If you shake, she dies.*
*He examined the incision. He'd been careful—not cutting too deep.*

*He reached inside.*
*Pulled the two sides apart.*
*Ara gritted her teeth. She couldn't scream. She wouldn't.*
*She wouldn't risk the baby.*
*She clawed the bed sheets into tight fists as another wave of pain ripped through her.*
*If you move, the baby dies.*
*He mopped up the blood with a towel. Then another incision.*
*Small, precise nicks through the muscle.*
*Another.*
*Then another.*
*He was in.*
*Through the stomach.*
*He could see the uterus.*
*Ara trembled. Kamal was sweating.*
*He reached in with both hands and pulled hard.*
*Now came the scariest part.*
*Cut into the uterus. Get the baby out.*
*Keep your hands steady.*
*If you shake, she dies.*
*Blood poured out.*
*More than there should be.*
*Grabbing another towel, he wiped it away.*
*Move fast or you'll lose her.*
*He sliced.*
*The uterine wall opened.*
*He yanked it apart.*
*A tiny blue foot pushed through the hole.*
*"I can see him—I see our baby."*
*"How is he? How is my baby?"*
*Kamal reached inside, fingers sliding*

*through blood and warmth, and pulled out a second tiny leg. And then—there it was. The tiniest little penis, staring back at him.*

*A son.*

"It's a boy," he choked. "We have a son."

*He reached deeper, searching for the child's head— and then he felt it. The umbilical cord, wrapped tight around the baby's throat. A noose.*

*His heart sank.*

*Ara could see it on his face.* "What's wrong?"

"Nothing."

"Don't lie to me."

*But he couldn't answer. He had to move fast. His hands worked blindly, feeling for the direction of the twist. Carefully, he turned the baby, trying to unwind the fleshy rope. Too tight. The baby wasn't moving. Too still.*

*If you move, he dies.*

*Ara sobbed between shallow, gasping breaths.*

*Kamal pressed his palm against the back of his son's head, twisting gently, pulling him out of the womb— legs first.*

*She arched back against the mattress, her hands clawing at the sheets. She didn't care about the pain.*

"Don't let my baby die."

*Her vision flickered. Dark. Light. Dark.*

*She saw Kamal's hands moving desperately.*

*He unwrapped the umbilical cord from the baby's neck—*

*Don't let my baby die.*
*Darkness.*
*He cut the cord. Tied it off.*
*Don't let my baby die.*
*Darkness.*
*She caught a glimpse of her stomach—so much blood.*
*Don't let my baby—*
*Darkness.*
*The baby wasn't breathing.*
*Don't—*
*Darkness.*
*Kamal shoved the bulb syringe into the baby's mouth, frantically suctioning his airway. Nothing.*
*No cry. No breath. Just silence.*
*He flipped the baby upside down, cradling his tiny body in his hands, and slapped his feet. Hard. Rubbed his tiny chest. Come on.*
*He didn't believe in God anymore, but he prayed anyway.*
*Please don't let my baby die.*
*Breathe.*
*Breathe.*
*Goddammit, please just breathe.*
*Nothing.*
*Ara was unconscious.*
*Kamal was alone.*
*Please.*
*Please.*
*And then—*
*The tiniest gasp.*
*A sharp little inhale.*
*And then a wail.*

*Raw, newborn, perfect.*

*"He's going to be okay," Kamal cried. "I think—he's going to be okay."*

*He didn't know who he was talking to. He just needed to say it out loud.*

*Quickly, he swaddled his son and set him down beside the bloody towels. He had no time to celebrate. Ara was barely breathing.*

*He turned back to her, hands shaking as he grabbed the sutures. His son was safe—but she was dying.*

*The IV wasn't enough. He had to work fast. He stitched her uterus. Then her abdominal wall. The bed was soaked in blood.*

*And now—he had to wait.*

*Kamal brushed damp curls from her forehead and pressed his lips against her skin.*

*"I didn't let the baby die."*

*He washed his son in the basin, gently scrubbing the vernix from his peach-pink skin. He should be happy. This was supposed to be the best day of his life.*

*But when he looked into the dark, vacant eyes of his newborn child, he wished he had saved her first.*

*He loved this baby.*

*But he loved her more.*

*"Please don't leave me."*

*Ara woke two hours later.*

*Her body was weak, her vision foggy. But she nursed him. And he latched instantly. His tiny mouth suckled without hesitation.*

*She held him in silent awe.*

*His dark eyes wandered up to her blurry face.*
*He reached for her hand.*
*His tiny fingers wrapped around hers.*
*He had nearly killed her coming into this world.*
*And still, she had never known such instant, absolute love.*
"You're going to break my heart someday, aren't you?"
*She pressed a soft kiss against his wrinkled forehead.*
"Your name is Isah."

### Isah's First Letter

I'm sitting here writing this next to what I assume is my mother's grave. The charred bodies of my father and uncle are beside me. My little brother Kosha must have buried her before he took off. There's no sign of him anywhere, which means he's alive—or was. I've never met the kid, but he must be a gritty little son of a bitch to walk away from a drone strike. I bet he's scared shitless right now.

There's a four-foot-long indentation in the dirt where he slept. He must be seven or eight years old by now. I looked for him, but he's long gone.

I'm going to find Wali soon, see if he knows anything. He's the guy who tended to my father's sheep. If I'm lucky, Kosha's with him.

I can't stop thinking about everything that led up to this moment. The fights with my parents. The moment I ran away to join Ishmael's men. The truth I didn't understand back then—the reason my father tried to keep me away from Nader. Maybe it was for the best that I left anyway. I was a mess of a kid, pulled in every direction, my own emotions ripping me apart.

By the time I joined the fight, our forces were already thin. Years of war with the government, the Kurds, and now the Americans had left us desperate. Ishmael's men went door to door, demanding each family send one son to join the cause. If I hadn't snuck away, my father would have volunteered himself instead.

I'm not proud of the shit I've done, but my father was a good man. I couldn't let him do the things I've done.

At first, I believed in the cause. I know what you're thinking—this guy is a fucking moron—and you're right. I was an idiot. But things have changed. My eyes are wide fucking open now.

I just do what they tell me because there's no other option.

I don't like killing people. But there's no path of redemption for remorseful terrorists. You can't just say, *Hey, I'm sorry I convinced that kid to strap on a suicide vest and blow up a marketplace.* There's no coming back from that shit.

Sorry doesn't mean shit when you're a terrorist.

I'm not asking for forgiveness. I just want people to know that if I had a take-back, I'd use it. That I wish I hadn't done all the fucked-up things I did.

Yesterday was a bloodbath.

We were in the Spera corridor, had the high ground, and somehow still got ambushed. Before the shooting started, some of the fellas were passing around a picture of a girl from a porno mag. Somebody had ripped it off a dead Marine. There were drops of blood on the corner of the page where the guy got shot.

    She was blond. White. Huge tits.

    Her pussy was shaved smooth.

    I don't even know how to explain it, but it made her look more naked than other women I'd seen—spiritually naked or something. Her blue eyes stared directly at the camera, her lips parted in a smile that didn't quite reach them.

    She was spreading herself open with two fingers, offering it up like a goddamn buffet.

    It had been so long since we'd seen a pussy—let alone a white one. The fellas couldn't help themselves. They took turns jerking off to it.

    When my turn came, I couldn't do it.

    Believe me, I fucking tried—but I couldn't get it up.

    It wasn't because I don't like women—I fucking love them—but something about the way she was looking at the camera got to me. She was smiling, but she looked lonely. Lost.

    I saw myself in her.

    And the fucked-up part? If she were here, we would have called her a whore and stoned her to death. But that didn't stop us from jizzing all over our boots like she was the last woman on earth.

    I sat there, my limp dick in my hand, just staring at her.

    I didn't want to fuck her. Or kill her. Or degrade her.

    I just wanted to hug her.

Tell her I understood that weird, empty feeling inside of her.

Tell her I wanted her to understand me too.

Crazy, right? This world makes you crazy.

And then the bullets started flying.

Two minutes ago, these guys were jerking off and laughing. Now they were stuffing their guts back into their stomachs and crying for their mothers.

Everyone's a tough guy until they catch a 5.56mm round to the chest.

I wasn't even hit, and I already wanted to go home.

I shouldn't have left in the first place. If I had it to do over again, I would have let my father take my place. That's how scared I was. That's how big of a piece of shit I actually am.

If my father had been there, he would have known what to do.

But he wasn't.

The day before I ran away, Nader and my father got into it. Nader had been trying to recruit me for a while. My father said he was filling my head with ideas, but it wasn't Nader's fault. I would have run away no matter what.

Back then, I thought I was doing God's will.

What a fucking joke.

What kind of God makes you kill the innocent?

Then again, *who's innocent?*

They are. The people we kill.

We kill anyone who doesn't see the world the way we do.

But here's what I've figured out: There is no love without freedom. And if God is love, then there is no God without the choice to love Him.

I sat there in that firefight, curled up behind a rock, pissing myself.

Literally. Pissing my pants.

Thinking about all the people I've killed.

Thinking—this is how they felt. Right before I pulled the trigger and put them down.

Machine gun fire chipped away at the boulder. Shards of stone and bullet casings flew everywhere.

I hugged my knees to my chest and tried to imagine being in love with the blue-eyed girl from the photo.

Could we ever be happy together?

No. Not in this life.

Maybe in the next one. If that's even a thing.

I don't believe in reincarnation, but if I came back, what would I be?

What kind of animal would a terrorist and a pornstar be reincarnated as?

I'm not lucky enough to come back as a dove or anything beautiful. But maybe, if I play my cards right from here on out, I could be a goat or something.

Would I still think she was pretty if she came back as a goat too?

I bet she'd be the sexiest fucking goat in the whole damn world. With udders so big they'd drag the ground.

I bet we could be happy as goats.

By the time the fighting stopped, most of us were dead. Those of us who made it out scattered. Nader must have thought he'd be safe here.
    What a fucking idiot.
    Nobody is safe from a Reaper drone.
    They see everything.
    My mom and dad never saw it coming.
    Goddammit, they didn't even have anything to do with this shit.
    They just wanted to live in peace. Raise their youngest son.
    Fuck you, Nader.
    Why couldn't you just stay away and give them that much?
    They deserved it.
    I convinced my CO that Nader deserved a proper burial. He let me put together this search party under the guise of recovering his body. But I'm never going back.
    I purposely picked the greenest recruits I could find for this mission.
    The oldest is seventeen.
    They barely know how to clean their rifles.
    When this is over, I'll put a bullet in each one of them and make for the border.
    I don't know if I'll ever find a pornstar to marry. Or be happy. Or live some normal, meaningless fucking life.
    But I'll try.
    I swear to God, I'll try.

## Isah's Second Letter

 I just finished talking to Wali, and it's as bad as I thought.
 Once we got through the pleasantries and condolences, he told me he saw Kosha on the high ridge two days ago. He hollered at him, but Kosha just ran. Wali didn't understand why—he seemed pretty gutted about it. I told him I knew exactly where Kosha was going.
 He wasn't running *from* anything.
 He's after revenge.
 He's heading for The Land of The Silverbirds.
 Goddammit, Kosha.
 I have to go after him.
 The kid has no idea what he's walking into. If I don't catch him before he reaches that military base, he's dead. He's got a two-day head start, but I know these mountains better than he does. If he's lost, I'll find him. If not, then we're both fucked.
 I've never met him, but he's still my brother.
 Dammit, Kosha. What the fuck are you

thinking?
Fuck.
I don't want to die.
But if I can save him before they get me—maybe my life won't feel like such a colossal fucking waste.
My mother died with a broken heart. Kosha was all she had left. I can't undo what I've done, but I can save him. Maybe, in some small way, that'll give back a part of her heart I helped break. Maybe it'll be enough to earn me something better than hell.
Maybe I'll come back as a goat.
That's something, isn't it?
I don't even know who I'm writing this to. There's nowhere left to send it.
Maybe I'm writing it to myself. Maybe to my mother. Maybe I just hope somebody finds it after I'm gone, and knows—knows that despite all the shit I've done, I had a family.
And I loved them.
And they loved me.
Maybe that's enough.
Maybe they'll understand that I'm not just a murdering bastard.
I mean, I *am* a murdering bastard.
But I'm also a son. A brother.
I know that's not worth much. But I'm sorry.
I swear to God, I thought I was fighting for Him.
I don't anymore. I haven't for a long time.
Now, I'm just fighting because there's nothing else left.

Just delaying the inevitable. Trying to live long enough to rewrite my own history, to make up some grand reason why I did all this.

That's how it works, isn't it? Whoever wins the war writes the books.

But the dead don't get a say.

So many people are gone.

For what?

To justify our own insecurities? To protect us from ourselves?

I remember walking down a street in Shakar Dara a few months back after a bad firefight.

We'd rigged the city with IEDs. Somebody fucked up the calculations—underestimated the C4. The result? A street overflowing with meat and blood.

Even in my boots, I couldn't take two steps without slipping. By the time I reached my regiment, I was soaked in it—American blood, flesh, bone.

When the others saw me, they laughed their fucking asses off.

I was picking pieces of Americans out of my hair for days.

If you watched western news, you'd think their soldiers were all heroes, saviors of the free world.

But they're no better than us.

Their president sits in the White House, getting rich off our blood.

It's all the same—billion-dollar corporations manipulating the desperate for their own gain.

Everyone pretends they don't know what the fuck is going on.

It's about power.

We want power over our country.

The Americans want power over our government, over our land, over our resources.

And the people stuck in between?

They just want power over their own fucking lives.

Once, I shot a schoolgirl in the street just to earn the respect of the man next to me.

People will do anything to escape the shithole life they were born into.

In America, we're portrayed like Arabic blackface.

And we live that portrayal because we have nothing else left.

So fuck everyone else.

We kill and we die—

And what do we get for it?

We break our mother's heart.

We break their mother's heart.

We take husbands from wives.

We kill innocents—people who just want to live, and love, and be loved.

I can't see God in any of this.

Ours or theirs.

When you think about it, the story of Samson is essentially just a story about an ancient suicide bomber.

This isn't what I signed up for.

This isn't what they promised me.

So I'll leave this here.

Right here, on my mother's grave.

If you find it—
Please.
Remember me.
Remember that I never wanted to do the things I did.
I know it doesn't mean much. Because I still did them.
But God knows—I'm sorry.
I was young. And blind. And needed someone to blame.
I wanted to be strong.
To have somebody assign value to my life.
To know that I existed.
If I could take it back, I would.
But I can't.
So I keep going.
Until my number's up.
I know it doesn't make any sense.
But I'm too scared to kill myself.
Because if God is real, then I know I'm fucked.
I can already feel Hell's rotten fingers stretching toward me.
I know I keep apologizing—
Saying the same shit over and over again.
It won't change anything.
My fate is my fate.
I just have to find Kosha before I go.
Tell him I'm sorry.
And if he forgives me—
Then maybe that's enough.

## Isah and Kosha

Isah sits on the hood of his truck, staring at the road. He's circled the wailing woman's house more times than he can count. He knows Kosha was in that ditch last night.
*Why did I stop?*
*Why didn't I go after him?*
By now, Kosha has probably made it to the Air Force base. Or he's dead.
Nader's coal-black corpse lays in the truck bed. He could take it back to camp and follow orders. Or he could still go after his brother, even if it's too late. Or he could make a break for the northern border.
There are so many refugees these days, anyone can lie about who they are.
He wanted to start a new life with his brother. That's gone now.
*I should just go back to camp and act like nothing happened.*
But something happened. He left his confession on his mother's grave. It's out of him and in the world now.
None of it matters.
Kosha is gone.

His men lean against the truck, smoking. "What do you think, boss?" one of them asks.

Isah stares at the road. "If he's not dead yet, he will be soon."

"So what do you wanna do?"

At this point, there's only one thing left to do.

Before they can react, Isah pulls his pistol from the back of his waistband and puts a bullet in each of their chests. Once they're down, he fires two more into each for good measure.

In the grand scheme of things, what's a few more dead kids?

He walks to the truck, opens the bed, and dumps Nader's charred body onto the ground. The corpse splits apart. He barely notices. Kicking a detached leg aside, he climbs into the driver's seat, starts the engine, and pulls away.

There is no warning before the missile strikes.

The blast obliterates the truck, twisting metal and rubber into an unrecognizable wreck. A crater yawns where Isah was. What isn't vaporized is burning. Thick black smoke rises into the sky.

This is how the silverbirds hunt—first, nothing. Then they're there. Then everything is gone.

## Kosha: Part XI

Kosha stares at the horizon. A posse of Humvees rumbles over the wasteland, their M2s rattling in the divots.
    He clutches the arrow in his hand. He looks down at the AK-47 lying next to him. Empty. Useless.
    No time to think about that now.
    He doesn't know what he's going to do—just that he isn't scared. He can't be.
    Maybe he's not strong enough to kill a silverbird, but he can kill these guys. They aren't made of metal. They're just meat and blood. Like a squirrel. Like a leopard. Like his family. Like everyone else who's gone.
    He notches the arrow, draws it back.
    The Humvees skid into a circle around him. Soldiers pour out, screaming.
    "Drop the bow!"
    "I said drop it!"
    "Drop it! Drop it! Drop it!"
    They aren't silverbirds. They have faces. He can see the fear in their eyes—except for one guy wearing sunglasses.
    "Drop it or we will shoot!"

A sergeant jumps out of the nearest Humvee. "Goddammit, don't shoot! He's just a kid."

An interpreter follows him, kneels down. "Come on, kid," he says in Pashto. "Just drop the bow."

Deep in the valley, Wali is tending to the sheep. He is at peace because he is just himself, not trying to be anything more.

I should have stayed back there and helped him take care of Dad's flock.

Kosha is still trying to become the man he wants to be instead of accepting the man he is.

He points the arrow at the Sergeant's heart.

The clack of gun hammers cocking echoes around him.

"Don't shoot!" orders the Sergeant. "Everybody just stay calm."

Kosha's nose itches.

The interpreter extends his hand. "Come on, kid. Just give me the bow."

They're scared to kill him. He isn't scared anymore. He is, but he can't be.

The biggest tears he's ever felt press against the back of his eyes. He fights them, but it doesn't matter if he cries anymore.

"You killed them."

The interpreter hesitates, then turns to the Sergeant. "He says... you killed them?"

"Killed who?"

The interpreter asks Kosha.

"All of them!" Kosha screams.

The Sergeant looks lost. "I don't know what he's talking about."

Kosha looks up. The best sky he's seen in weeks—blue, endless. No silverbirds in sight.

But skies are worthless if you don't have anyone to share them with.

His nose still itches, but he ignores it. His arm is out of breath from holding the bowstring. His heart is out of breath from carrying so many ghosts. He misses his family. Even Uncle Nader. Even Isah. He misses people he never knew.

His legs can catch their breath all they want now.

His memories can fade.

He can cuss all he wants now.

He wishes he could kiss his mother one last time. He just wants to make his father proud.

Nobody comes back from the land of the silverbirds.

Poyas never run.

The Sergeant pleads, "Come on, kid. Help me out. Just give me the bow, and we can all go home."

The interpreter translates.

Home is something Americans take for granted.

Home is gone.

Kosha's lips tremble. He grips the bow tighter.

"Fuck you."

## Blood

Blood.
In the end, it's all we have.
Bloodlines.
Bloodlust.
Blood loss.
Spilled blood.
Blood on our hands.
Blood in the dirt.
Blood seeping from an arrow wound in the upper right thigh of a U.S. Marine Sergeant.
Blood gushing from the countless bullet holes in a child's body.
The blood of thousands and thousands of bombing victims.
Blood from when the Twin Towers came crashing down.
Bloodshot eyes of the soldier who wakes in the middle of the night, cold sweat and tears streaming down his face.
It's all just an endless stream of blood, flowing from one source to another.
Seventy-one percent of the world might be covered in water—
But we're drowning in blood.

But there is good blood as well.

Blood, sweat, and tears raising new towers from the rubble.

Blood pumping through the heart of a marathon runner as he crosses the finish line on the one-year anniversary of the attack.

Blood pulsing through the veins of two men standing forehead to forehead on the dance floor, kissing without fear of the repercussions of true love.

There is blood spared.

There is mercy.

There are times when you don't shoot a child, even though he has an arrow pointed straight at you.

Or when you put down your bow and go home, even though you have no home left to go home to.

Printed in Great Britain
by Amazon